"Colleen Coble's latest has it all: characters to root for, a sinister villain, and a story that just won't stop."

—Siri Mitchell, author of *State of Lies*, on *Two Reasons to Run*

"Colleen Coble's superpower is transporting her readers into beautiful settings in vivid detail. *Two Reasons to Run* is no exception. Add to that the suspense that keeps you wanting to know more and characters that pull at your heart. These are the ingredients of a fun read!"

—Terri Blackstock, bestselling author of *If I Run, If I'm Found,* and *If I Live*

"This is a romantic suspense novel that will be a surprise when the last page reveals all of the secrets."

—*Parkersburg News and Sentinel* on *One Little Lie*

"There are just enough threads left dangling at the end of this well-crafted romantic suspense to leave fans hungrily awaiting the next installment."

—*Publishers Weekly* on *One Little Lie*

"Colleen Coble once again proves she is at the pinnacle of Christian romantic suspense. Filled with characters you'll come to love, faith lost and found, and scenes that will have you holding your breath, Jane Hardy's story deftly follows the complex and tangled web that can be woven by one little lie."

—Lisa Wingate, #1 *New York Times* bestselling author of *Before We Were Yours,* on *One Little Lie*

"Colleen Coble always raises the notch on romantic suspense, and *One Little Lie* is my favorite yet! The story took me on a wild and wonderful ride."

—DiAnn Mills, bestselling author

"Coble's latest, *One Little Lie*, is a powerful read . . . one of her absolute best. I stayed up way too late finishing this book because I literally couldn't go to sleep without knowing what happened. This is a must read! Highly recommend!"

—Robin Caroll, bestselling author of the Darkwater Inn series

"I always look forward to Colleen Coble's new releases. *One Little Lie* is One Phenomenal Read. I don't know how she does it, but she just keeps getting better. Be sure to have plenty of time to flip the pages in this one because you won't want to put it down. I devoured it! Thank you, Colleen, for more hours of edge-of-the-seat entertainment. I'm already looking forward to the next one!"

—Lynette Eason, award-winning and bestselling author of the Blue Justice series

"In *One Little Lie* the repercussions of one lie skid through the town of Pelican Harbor, creating ripples of chaos and suspense. Who will survive the questions? *One Little Lie* is the latest page-turner from Colleen Coble. Set on the Gulf Coast of Alabama, Jane Hardy is the new police chief who is fighting to clear her father. Reid Dixon has secrets of his own as he follows Jane around town for a documentary. Together they must face their secrets and decide when a secret becomes a lie. And when does it become too much to forgive?"

—Cara Putman, bestselling and award-winning author

"Coble wows with this suspense-filled inspirational . . . With startling twists and endearing characters, Coble's engrossing story explores the tragedy, betrayal, and redemption of faithful people all searching to reclaim their sense of identity."

—*Publishers Weekly* on *Strands of Truth*

"Just when I think Colleen Coble's stories can't get any better, she proves me wrong. In *Strands of Truth*, I couldn't turn the pages fast enough. The characterization of Ridge and Harper and their relationship pulled me immediately into the story. Fast-paced, with so many unexpected twists and turns, I read this book in one sitting. Coble has pushed the bar higher than I'd imagined. This book is one not to be missed. Highly recommend!"

—Robin Caroll, bestselling author of the Darkwater Inn series

"Free-dive into a romantic suspense that will leave you breathless and craving for more."

—DiAnn Mills, bestselling author, on *Strands of Truth*

"Colleen Coble's latest book, *Strands of Truth*, grips you on page one with a heart-pounding opening and doesn't let go until the last satisfying word. I love her skill in pulling the reader in with believable, likable characters, interesting locations, and a mystery just waiting to be untangled. Highly recommended."

—Carrie Stuart Parks, bestselling and award-winning author of *Relative Silence*

"It's in her blood! Colleen Coble once again shows her suspense prowess with a thriller as intricate and beautiful as a strand of

DNA. *Strands of Truth* dives into an unusual profession involving mollusks and shell beds that weaves a unique, silky thread throughout the story. So fascinating I couldn't stop reading!"

—Ronie Kendig, bestselling author
of the Tox Files series

"Once again, Colleen Coble delivers an intriguing, suspenseful tale in *Strands of Truth*. The mystery and tension mount toward an explosive and satisfying finish. Well done."

—Creston Mapes, bestselling author

"*Secrets at Cedar Cabin* is filled with twists and turns that will keep readers turning the pages as they plunge into the horrific world of sex trafficking where they come face-to-face with evil. Colleen Coble delivers a fast-paced story with a strong, lovable ensemble cast and a sweet, heaping helping of romance."

—Kelly Irvin, author of *Tell Her No Lies*

"Coble . . . weaves a suspense-filled romance set during the Revolutionary War. Coble's fine historical novel introduces a strong heroine—both in faith and character—that will appeal deeply to readers."

—*Publishers Weekly* on *Freedom's Light*

"This follow-up to *The View from Rainshadow Bay* features delightful characters and an evocative, atmospheric setting. Ideal for fans of romantic suspense and authors Dani Pettrey, Dee Henderson, and Brandilyn Collins."

—*Library Journal* on *The House at Saltwater Point*

"Set on Washington State's Olympic Peninsula, this first volume of Coble's new suspense series is a tensely plotted and harrowing tale of murder, corporate greed, and family secrets. Devotees of Dani Pettrey, Brenda Novak, and Allison Brennan will find a new favorite here."

—*Library Journal* on *The View from Rainshadow Bay*

"Coble (*Twilight at Blueberry Barrens*) keeps the tension tight and the action moving in this gripping tale, the first in her Lavender Tides series set in the Pacific Northwest."

—*Publishers Weekly* on *The View from Rainshadow Bay*

"Filled with the suspense for which Coble is known, the novel is rich in detail with a healthy dose of romance, allowing readers to bask in the beauty of Washington State's lavender fields, lush forests, and jagged coastline."

—*BookPage* on *The View from Rainshadow Bay*

"Prepare to stay up all night with Colleen Coble. Coble's beautiful, emotional prose coupled with her keen sense of pacing, escalating danger, and very real characters place her firmly at the top of the suspense genre. I could not put this book down."

—Allison Brennan, *New York Times* bestselling author of *Shattered*, on *The View from Rainshadow Bay*

"Colleen is a master storyteller."

—Karen Kingsbury, #1 *New York Times* bestselling author

PROWL

ALSO BY COLLEEN COBLE

Sanctuary Novels

Ambush

Prowl

Conspiracy (available
July 2026)

**Tupelo Grove Novels
(coauthored with Rick Acker)**

What We Hide

Where Secrets Lie

When Justice Comes
(available March 2026)

Annie Pederson Novels

Edge of Dusk

Dark of Night

Break of Day

Pelican Harbor Novels

One Little Lie

Two Reasons to Run

Three Missing Days

Lavender Tides Novels

The View from Rainshadow Bay

*Leaving Lavender
Tides* (novella)

The House at Saltwater Point

Secrets at Cedar Cabin

Rock Harbor Novels

Without a Trace

Beyond a Doubt

Into the Deep

Cry in the Night

Haven of Swans (formerly
titled *Abomination*)

*Silent Night: A Rock
Harbor Christmas Novella*
(e-book only)

Beneath Copper Falls

Sunset Cove Novels

The Inn at Ocean's Edge

Mermaid Moon

Twilight at Blueberry Barrens

Hope Beach Novels

Tidewater Inn

Rosemary Cottage

Seagrass Pier

*All Is Bright: A Hope
Beach Christmas Novella*
(e-book only)

Under Texas Stars Novels

Blue Moon Promise
Safe in His Arms
Bluebonnet Bride
(novella, e-book only)

The Aloha Reef Novels

Distant Echoes
Black Sands
Dangerous Depths
Midnight Sea
Holy Night: An Aloha Reef Christmas Novella
(e-book only)

The Mercy Falls Series

The Lightkeeper's Daughter
The Lightkeeper's Bride
The Lightkeeper's Ball

Journey of the Heart Series

A Heart's Disguise
A Heart's Obsession
A Heart's Danger
A Heart's Betrayal
A Heart's Promise
A Heart's Home

Lonestar Novels

Lonestar Sanctuary
Lonestar Secrets
Lonestar Homecoming
Lonestar Angel
All Is Calm: A Lonestar Christmas Novella
(e-book only)

Stand-Alone Novels

I Think I Was Murdered
(coauthored with Rick Acker)
Fragile Designs
A Stranger's Game
Strands of Truth
Freedom's Light
Alaska Twilight
Fire Dancer
Where Shadows Meet
(formerly titled *Anathema*)
Butterfly Palace
Because You're Mine

PROWL

A Sanctuary Novel

COLLEEN COBLE

THOMAS NELSON
Since 1798

Prowl

Copyright © 2025 by Colleen Coble

Published in Nashville, Tennessee, by Thomas Nelson. Thomas Nelson is a registered trademark of HarperCollins Christian Publishing, Inc.

Thomas Nelson titles may be purchased in bulk for educational, business, fundraising, or sales promotional use. For information, please email SpecialMarkets@ ThomasNelson.com.

Scripture quotations are taken from the Holy Bible, New International Version®, NIV®. Copyright © 1973, 1978, 1984, 2011 by Biblica, Inc.® Used by permission of Zondervan. All rights reserved worldwide. www.zondervan.com. The "NIV" and "New International Version" are trademarks registered in the United States Patent and Trademark Office by Biblica, Inc.®

Publisher's Note: This novel is a work of fiction. Names, characters, places, and incidents are either products of the author's imagination or used fictitiously. All characters are fictional, and any similarity to people living or dead is purely coincidental.

Any internet addresses (websites, blogs, etc.) in this book are offered as a resource. They are not intended in any way to be or imply an endorsement by Thomas Nelson, nor does Thomas Nelson vouch for the content of these sites for the life of this book.

Library of Congress Cataloging-in-Publication Data

Names: Coble, Colleen author
Title: Prowl / Colleen Coble.
Description: Nashville : Thomas Nelson, 2025. | Series: Sanctuary novels ; 2 | Summary: "Prowl, the second book in USA TODAY bestselling author Colleen Coble's Sanctuary series (following Ambush), delivers exactly what her fans want: the ideal blend of suspense that keeps you on the edge of your seat with just the right amount of romance. Perfect for fans of Laura Dave, Allison Brennan, or Dani Pettrey"-- Provided by publisher.
Identifiers: LCCN 2025017283 (print) | LCCN 2025017284 (ebook) | ISBN 9780840714374 trade paperback | ISBN 9780840714497 hardcover | ISBN 9780840714480 | ISBN 9780840714381 epub
Subjects: LCGFT: Fiction | Romance fiction | Detective and mystery fiction | Christian fiction | Novels
Classification: LCC PS3553.O2285 P76 2025 (print) | LCC PS3553.O2285 (ebook) | DDC 813/.54--dc23/eng/20250626
LC record available at https://lccn.loc.gov/2025017283
LC ebook record available at https://lccn.loc.gov/2025017284

Printed in the United States of America

25 26 27 28 29 LBC 5 4 3 2 1

CHAPTER 1

THE SUN PEEKED OVER the eastern horizon in a perfect Alabama sunrise as Ivy Cook lugged the pails of raw meat out of the Gator utility vehicle and walked toward the hyena enclosure. She shivered a little in the February chill. She'd arrived at work early to do what she'd been paid to do under cover of darkness.

She paused when she saw the hyenas head for the fence. The leader, Clara, always gave her the creeps with her laughing mouth and evil eyes. A hyena pack was weird, too, with a dominant female that didn't let any of the others eat until she was full. The males all ate last even when Ivy tried to toss food their way. They watched Clara for permission.

Ivy had heard her boss, Blake Lawson, mention he was giving them to a nearby zoo. If the owner and head zookeeper didn't trust the hyenas, she shouldn't either. And she didn't. She opened the outer gate and locked it behind her, then approached the inner one.

A sound came from her right, and she spun that way. Nothing there. She was losing it. Rubbing the gooseflesh from her arms, she reached into the pail and began to toss food over the fence. Clara ate piece after piece while her clan watched avidly.

"Let your clan eat," Ivy said. Clara's returning stare held animosity, and Ivy stared her down. "You can't get out of here too soon for me."

She had worked here for two weeks, but it felt like two years with the stink of the animals and the hard work involved. But if she had any hope of paying off her gambling debt, she needed the extra cash, and this job had seemed an easy way to earn a little. She'd been wrong. Now that she was here, Ivy wasn't enjoying the work or the animals. The smell got to her, and so did the fear of them.

The sooner she got the information she'd been hired to extract from Paradise Alden, the sooner she could leave.

The first chance Ivy got she'd look for a job that didn't involve getting so icky. She wiped blood from her hands onto the grass and shuddered. She stood and whirled at a soft scraping noise. Still nothing there. Why was she so jumpy this morning?

She retraced her steps and locked the gate behind her, then moved on to the tiger enclosure. Her gut tightened at the sight of the tiger staring at her. Some of the keepers were able to touch the ones born and raised here, but Raj was new and was kept separated from the rest. He was not one of the animals they could trust, but Ivy didn't trust anything with teeth and claws.

"Hi, Raj," she said in a calm voice. She unlocked the gate and stepped into the outer perimeter area. She moved toward the inner gate and caught her breath. It was open.

Barely breathing, she backed away toward the exit behind her.

The huge cat moved to the open gate and pushed through. His golden eyes followed her, and he crouched with his tail lashing the air. She didn't dare take her eyes off him, but she would have to in order to get through the outer gate.

She edged back two steps, then three, reaching her hand

behind her to find the gate. Her blood thundered in her ears and her breath rasped in her throat. She had no chance against those teeth, those claws.

Tears blurred her vision as her fingers touched the gate. Maybe she could escape. This might not be the end.

She was so intent on escape she barely took note of the sting at the back of her neck. The gate resisted her attempts, and her vision blurred even more. Her legs didn't seem to want to work either. The tiger took another step closer, and she knew she wasn't going to make it.

———

The smell of big cat in the treatment room made wildlife vet Paradise Alden's mouth go dry. The black jaguar lay limp and seemingly unconscious for her to treat the abscessed tooth, but she couldn't assume Midnight wouldn't react. The fingers on her right hand started to stray to the ugly ridge of scar tissue on her other arm, from an attack when a panther came through a door left open to the habitat, but she took hold of her fear and moved toward the animal instead.

Her new vet tech, Warren Gibson, moved to the side. "Respiration and heart rate are good. Should be an easy extraction, and we can let her wake up."

She could only hope.

Her pulse accelerated as she ran her fingers over the jaguar's smooth fur. She was a beautiful specimen. Her arrival yesterday to The Sanctuary Wildlife Preserve had caused a lot of excitement mixed with worry when her mouth problem surfaced. And it was up to Paradise to make sure she made the move to her new home easily. The poor thing had been in a ten-by-ten cage her whole life until the owner died, and his kids had to get rid of the beautiful black cat.

Paradise steeled herself and plunged into the task. Thankfully Warren was right, and fifteen minutes later, the female jaguar was back in her crate sleeping off the anesthetic.

"Nice job, Doc." Warren's red hair stood up like a rooster's comb, and his easy grin vanished when his gaze lingered on her scars. "It took a lot of courage to jump in there after all you've been through."

"Piece of cake thanks to your skill with anesthesia." She glanced at the clock on the wall. Her first day as the vet in Nova Cambridge would start in half an hour. She would be working mornings at the clinic before returning to the park. Midnight had been an emergency she'd squeezed in this morning, but the quick procedure had made her late.

She grabbed her bag and raced for her green Kia Soul. Though she glanced around the compound as she drove off, she didn't catch sight of anyone, not even Blake, whom she'd hoped would see her off on her new adventure. A morning kiss for good luck would have come in handy.

The outskirts of Nova Cambridge came into view around the corner, and she accelerated. It wouldn't do to arrive late and find customers waiting in their vehicles or at the door.

She braked at the sight of the new blue-and-white sign hanging from a post outside the veterinary business. Pawsome Pets—Paradise Alden, DVM. Paradise was buying the business from Jenna with quarterly payments, but she still wasn't sure how she felt about the new venture she'd been talked into. Caring for domesticated animals hadn't been on her radar, not when her heart belonged to the wild ones since her teen years.

She parked in the lot and hurried to unlock the front door.

Luckily no one was outside to notice her late arrival. She stepped into the waiting room and stopped short at the scent of sweet cake instead of cleaning solution. Congratulations banners and balloons fluttered from the ceiling and reception desk.

Blake Lawson and his mother, Jenna Anderson, shouted, "Surprise!" Jenna's boys, Isaac and Levi, bolted toward her with shrieks of excitement. Five-year-old Isaac already had cupcake frosting around his mouth, and he planted sticky hands on her jeans. "Are you surprised, Paradise?"

"I sure am." She scooped him up, and he wrapped his arms and legs around her like a monkey. She turned a wide smile toward Blake and Jenna. "I wondered where everyone was when I left." Paradise should have realized something was up when they weren't outside to wish her well on her first day. Especially when this whole vet thing was their idea.

Blake's thick dark brown hair was still damp, and his blue eyes were tender. "We couldn't let this monumental day go uncelebrated, babe. Brownies and cupcakes are on the table over there." He gestured to a decorated card table piled high with treats. "We're taking you to Jesse's tonight to celebrate."

"That sounds wonderful." She stepped into the circle of his arms and inhaled the scent of his eucalyptus and cypress soap. His lips found hers, and her breathing quickened. His steady presence was her world ever since she'd found her way back to him. He'd broken her heart when she was sixteen, but she'd forgiven him.

He pulled away reluctantly. "*You're* wonderful. And you'll do great with this. It will expand your horizons."

She leaned against his broad chest. "I think coming here did all that." It was hard to remember her former quiet, lonely life. Blake and his family had burst the bubble she'd pulled around herself since the murder of her parents, and while it hadn't always been easy to reveal the soft parts of her heart, doing so had changed her for the better.

The door opened, and her new receptionist entered. Honey Hopkins was Evan's wife, and though Paradise had hesitated to interview her because her husband worked at The Sanctuary as a predator keeper, she'd soon been won over by the perky blonde's customer service skills.

"Good morning," Honey sang out. "Are we ready for the influx of patients? Everyone in town is excited to meet you, Paradise. You're a little bit famous after all the hoopla at The Sanctuary."

Hoopla? Was that how people felt about the trauma they'd all lived through? Paradise managed to smile. "I'm as ready as I'll ever be. Who's our first patient?"

"A wiener dog named Chloe. She's as fat as a potbellied pig but very sweet." Honey glanced out the window. "Here she comes now with her owner. Let the games begin."

Paradise pinned on a smile and waved goodbye to Blake and the family as they headed toward the back exit. They paused long enough for the boys to grab another cupcake, and she wished she had time for a sweet treat to help her face this new adventure.

CHAPTER 2

THE GATOR WAS MISSING from the lot, so Blake walked across the compound to make rounds. His sweatshirt warmed him against the mid-February chill, and the fresh scent of the morning air added to his sense of well-being. They'd mostly finished cleanup after the tropical storm two weeks ago, thanks to the hard work of the community and the park's employees.

He still smiled at Paradise's surprise this morning. Her amber eyes had filled with moisture at the family's excitement for her, and he prayed her first day would be a good one. He glanced at his watch. Just after ten and the first visitors would be here soon.

He found the Gator outside the tiger enclosure, but he didn't see anyone around. He lifted the lid on the predator food and frowned. The raw meat had barely been touched. Where was Ivy?

He shaded his hand as a familiar truck pulled into the lot. Clark got out and approached him. It always struck Blake how alike Clark and Kent Reynolds were. They were twins and it showed. Being around his best friend's brother helped Blake release some of the pain and guilt he felt over Kent's death. Clark had hated him for a while after Kent's death in Afghanistan, but he'd stepped up to help Paradise save Blake during the tropical storm and flood a couple of weeks back, and all those hard feelings had been washed away.

Blake slapped him on the shoulder when Clark stopped in front of him. "You're just the man I wanted to see. That main perimeter fence by the tigers looks like it could let go. I'm not sure even you can fix it, but I wanted you to take a look before I spent the money to replace it."

Clark gave a cocky grin. "I can weld anything but a broken heart and the crack of dawn."

Blake grinned at the familiar line. "I believe it."

Clark's appearance had changed since he'd released his anger and grief. His broad shoulders were squared instead of hunched with defeat, and his shaggy brown hair stayed neatly trimmed.

Clark shuffled and looked down at his feet. "I had an idea. Feel free to say no. What would you think if I moved my trailer into that empty lot out by the cottages? It could be my salary for working around here."

"That's not enough of a salary, but I'd be thrilled to have you work for the park. I can cough up some actual dollars too."

"Not necessary. I would still have time to do the occasional odd job for gas and groceries. I like being here. It's given me purpose, and you're not so bad to be around."

That was saying a lot coming from taciturn Clark. Blake squeezed his shoulder. "You're a good man, Clark, and I'm honored to call you friend."

The man's brown eyes glistened. "I'll move the trailer over tonight. Thanks, buddy."

He started for the fence perimeter, but Blake called him back. "Did you see Ivy's car when you came in? I'm not sure she fed the animals."

"I saw her car but not her."

"Thanks, I'll try to find her."

He'd had his doubts about the new hire, Ivy Cook, when she showed up for work. Mom was a soft touch, and the girl was the granddaughter of a friend from church. Doing a favor wasn't always the best idea, but so far Ivy had done a good job. If the predators hadn't been fed yet, it would set his day back by hours. He might have to call all hands on deck to feed them before he took out his first busload of visitors.

The hyenas barely gave him a glance, and even Clara slept through his call. The Birmingham Zoo was picking them up this afternoon, and he'd be glad to have them gone. He'd never been able to look at them the same since they'd tried to kill him during the tropical storm.

He moved to the tigers and found all of them hungry. He fed the ones who would be in the pool performing for visitors later before moving on to the last enclosure. Raj was new and a little hostile. He banged on the metal fencing around the enclosure.

"Raj, meat."

The big white cat licked his chops and settled onto his haunches. He turned his huge head and stared at something in the corner inside the inner enclosure. Blake followed the direction of Raj's gaze and froze. What appeared to be a pile of clothing was something much more terrifying.

Ivy Cook lay curled in a fetal position, and she wasn't moving. His stomach plummeted at the sight of way too much blood.

He started to open the gate to the outer enclosure and stopped. The inner gate wasn't latched, and it swung a bit in the breeze. There would be nothing to stop Raj from coming through the inner enclosure to the outer one.

Had Raj been in the outer perimeter when Ivy came to feed

him? Blake spotted drag marks from the outside gate into the inner area, and the likely scenario played out in his head in sickening detail.

He whipped out his phone and called Evan Hopkins to bring him a tranquilizer gun. "And call 911." He grabbed the bucket of meat and took off running to the building beside the enclosure. Time seemed to slow as his feet slapped against the grass and hard dirt on the path to the shelter. His fingers fumbled with the lock at the door, and it seemed an eternity before he stepped into the dim interior that held the strong odor of cat urine. He made sure the door to the habitat area was locked, then went through the security door.

Please let her be alive. He threw down some raw meat before he opened the door to the habitat. *Please, God, let him smell the food and come.*

He could barely breathe while he waited for the big white cat to amble into the interior and go to the food. When the last of the tiger's lashing tail was through the door, Blake pressed the button to shut the cat inside away from the habitat area, then raced back outside to run across the habitat to Ivy. Evan sped toward the enclosure with the tranquilizer gun.

Blake reached the gate at the same time as Evan. "I coaxed Raj into the building with food, so we won't need the gun after all." He hurried with Evan through both gates and headed toward Ivy, who hadn't moved.

When he dropped to his knees and touched her, his gut made a sickening twist. He pressed his finger to her neck to make sure.

"She's dead."

Paradise's first day had been more fun than she'd imagined. With only five patients, she only had to work two hours, but the owners of the three dogs and two cats had made her feel like an integral part of the community. Two of the families had been former classmates when she'd lived here, so it felt as though she'd slipped back into the flow of life in Nova Cambridge. Her longtime friend Abby Dillard—now McClellan—had been here with her beautiful golden.

This quiet town was only fifteen minutes from Foley and the shopping malls, and only half an hour from the busyness of the Gulf Shore beaches, but it was another world along these quaint streets. How had she ever left this place?

Paradise mopped the exam room and grimaced at the stinging scent of antiseptic before heading back to the park. Honey had offered to do the cleaning, but Paradise needed an opportunity to get to know her spaces. There was something about the detail of cleaning that made the place seem familiar—and hers.

Her phone sounded with a message, but she ignored it until she was finished and in her car. Once she was behind the wheel, she dug out her phone and tensed. In her inbox were results from the DNA test she'd run to try to find the brother she hadn't known she had. It was already nearly eleven, and she had a full afternoon at the park. The results would have to wait until she had a chance to log in to her computer and take a look.

She buckled in and drove out Beach Road toward the Weeks Bay Bridge. She braked to avoid a fox that darted out of the ditch and across the road. An ambulance, its lights flashing and sirens blaring, came up fast behind her, and she pulled over to let it pass. Right behind it, two sheriff's department cars zoomed past as well. They disappeared over the bridge, and her gut clenched. Could they be going to The Sanctuary?

She stomped on the accelerator and headed in that direction. The emergency vehicles weren't in sight when she crossed the bridge and turned onto Bay Road. Maybe they'd turned off on Beach Road. A few houses were out that way on Bon Secour Bay.

But she caught the shriek of the sirens as she neared the turn-off to the preserve, and her pulse skipped. Her fears for the boys were ever present ever since Isaac had gone into the tiger enclosure. The boys were adventurous and no amount of diligence kept fear from raising its head. She punched the button on her dash to call Blake, and her mouth was dry as she waited for him to pick up.

When the call went to his voice mail, her agitation increased and so did her speed. She took the turn nearly on two wheels and prayed for Blake's family as she raced to see what had happened. Maybe a visitor had been injured. None of the scenarios were good.

She followed the flashing lights of the two sheriff's cars through the parking lot and out toward the employee area near the predator enclosures. The fact that the emergency vehicles were directed to private areas wasn't a good sign. She parked in her usual spot and jumped out. Blake stood talking to their archenemy, Detective Creed Greene. It figured that they'd have to deal with him.

She steeled herself for his familiar leer—he was like most of the other men she'd met with one thing on their minds. At least Blake had shown her how a real man acted.

She rushed to his side and touched his arm. He drew her against his side with his left arm as he spoke with Creed. She heard *tiger enclosure* and *checked for pulse*, but she heard no name mentioned. She examined the faces around her and spotted Jenna and her boys heading their way. The tenseness in Paradise's throat released, and she nearly sagged against Blake.

Jenna reached them, and she waved an employee over. "Evan, would you take the boys to see the capybaras?"

Irritation creased his forehead, but he nodded. "Sure thing, Boss."

"Hazel had babies," Isaac told him. "I get to hold one now. They're old enough, right, Mama?"

"They are." Jenna waited until they were out of earshot. "Do we know how Raj managed to get to Ivy?"

"Not yet," Blake said. "I found her in the inside enclosure. There would have been no reason for her to go in there, and I think maybe Raj dragged her to his lair."

Paradise shuddered at the graphic image that sprang to life with his words. How had this happened? Blake was meticulous about safety precautions at The Sanctuary, but human error was always a concern. She didn't know Ivy well since she'd just started, but she'd seemed pleasant and was hardworking. The young woman had wanted to chat about personal things, and Paradise suspected she was lonely.

The deputy took his detective position to the nth degree, and she knew he'd be pointing blame before he left. That was his modus operandi. Accuse first and pivot later. Wasn't a detective supposed to examine the evidence before he came to a conclusion? Creed Greene made snap decisions first and tried to find details to support his belief. It was all backward.

"Is the tiger secured?" Greene asked.

Blake's fingers tightened around Paradise's waist. "I coaxed him into the shelter so I could get to Ivy. I left him locked in there."

Creed turned toward the walkway to the predators' area. "I'd like to see the scene and the body now that the paramedics are done making sure there was no sign of life. Forensics should be here soon as well."

Blake's arm slid away from Paradise, and he turned toward the walk. "I'll take you."

She hugged herself in spite of the warm sun touching her arms. They'd all hoped their troubles were over, but they weren't that lucky.

CHAPTER 3

WHY DID GREENE HAVE to be so unpleasant? Blake couldn't figure out why the man walked around with a chip on his shoulder the size of their rhino. Not everyone was a criminal like the detective assumed.

Blake stopped at the enclosure and opened the gate with his key. The stench of a big cat mixed with blood blew toward him on the wind. "I came in to see if Raj had been fed. I could tell Ivy hadn't gotten to all the animals." Her body was still in the corner of the field where he'd found her, and he averted his gaze.

Greene stepped into the outer perimeter. "Was that a usual occurrence?"

"She's only worked for us a couple of weeks, but she was very reliable. Showed up on time, was pleasant." *Was.* A sad word he didn't like to say. The three letters wrapped up a world of lost opportunities and a life cut too short.

Greene's eyes narrowed. "Did you know her outside of work?"

"Never met her until she was hired. Ivy's grandmother was a friend of Mom's."

Greene nodded and turned to survey the space. "Walk me through your actions."

Blake bit back a groan and showed the detective every step he took until he finally led him to where Raj still roamed on the other side of the shelter door. The tiger chuffed, then roared, and Greene flinched before he stepped back. "It wasn't until I had Raj secured that I was able to check Ivy's status. She had no pulse."

"You touched the body?"

"Of course. Any paramedic would do the same. If there was any hope of saving her, I would take it."

"Uh-huh." Despite the agreeable word, Greene's raised brow conveyed his skepticism. Several vehicles pulled into the lot, and he gestured. "Forensic techs are here. I want to take a look first." He didn't wait for Blake to take him to Ivy's body but moved past him. "Stay here. I don't want any interference in my investigation."

What did the guy think Blake would do? Pick her up, move things around? Greene needed to get a clue. Blake thrust his hands in the pockets of his jeans and hung back to catch two people in light blue uniforms approaching from the forensic van. He lifted a hand in greeting as Nora Craft and a man he didn't recognize approached. "Glad you're here, Nora."

She poked her glasses up on her nose and glanced toward the enclosure. A frown creased her forehead, and Blake pressed his lips together to avoid agreeing with her obvious disdain. "I think he'll be done shortly."

"Once he establishes his dominance like a cat marking his territory," she muttered.

Blake had always liked the forensic tech. She was in her thirties with brown hair and brown eyes and had a no-nonsense manner. She'd circumvented working with Greene several times and cared more about getting to the truth than following the detective's orders.

Greene turned as if he'd sensed her discontent and moved toward them. "The body is all yours, Craft. I saw no sign of any foul play, but the autopsy will tell us for sure." He didn't wait for a reply and brushed past them. "I'm going to talk to Jenna to find out what she knows about the victim."

Blake fell into step behind him. "I don't think she knows much."

"We'll see. I won't need your help with this."

Blake swallowed back the retort hovering on his lips and reversed direction toward the capybara enclosure. It was easy to find the boys—all he had to do was follow the sound of giggles. Those guys loved capybaras, and there was nothing cuter than the pups.

He grinned when he heard Isaac regurgitating everything he knew about capybaras to Paradise—which was extensive even though he was only five. His brothers were on the grass inside the capybara enclosure beside Paradise, and they all held pups. Another two babies snuggled closer to their mom, who looked on.

"They're the largest rodent in the world," Isaac said.

She listened intently as if she'd never heard any of this. "Is that anything like the Rodents of Unusual Size mentioned in *The Princess Bride*?"

Isaac petted the little pup on his lap. "I think those are bigger. People used to think they were water pigs, but I don't think they look like pigs, do you?"

"Only a little bit."

"Not at *all*," Levi put in. The pup he held squirreled under his arm. "They look more like beavers. Or guinea pigs, only cuter." He petted the back end of the pup he held, which was all he could reach with the capybara trying to wiggle under his arm.

Paradise examined the pup she held. "You've taken good care of them."

"I want to be a capybara keeper when I grow up," Isaac announced.

"You'd be very good at it."

Blake stepped out of the tupelo tree's shadow. "There you guys are. Is there room for me?"

Paradise patted the spot beside her. "I'd even share the pups with you."

"You can't have my pup," Isaac said. "His name is Dale."

"Like the famous chipmunk?"

His little brother nodded. "And Levi's is Chip. They're best friends like we are."

"That's pretty perfect." Though he was itching to talk to Paradise alone, he hid his impatience. The boys needed calm and assurance after the trauma of what had happened. He picked up the closest pup and settled it on his lap. "What's this one called?"

Isaac eyed the pup. "That's Gaston. Paradise has Newt and the other one is Pug."

"Excellent names."

Tension radiated through Paradise's form, and she kept glancing at her phone. What was up? He set the pup back on the grass. "I think we've probably handled them enough today. They need to go see their mama, and Mom has some lessons waiting for you."

Levi set his pup down. "Is it painting? Mom said we could paint this afternoon."

Isaac nodded. "She did." After moving the pup off his lap, he jumped up and both boys ran off toward the house.

Blake leaned back on his hands. "What's wrong? Well, other than Greene is an idiot and he'll be pinning Ivy's death on me before he's done."

The capybara on her lap hopped off and went to join its siblings. Paradise reached for her phone. "I got DNA results back but haven't had a chance to see if there's a match."

He scooted closer as she called up her mail program. A frown crouched between her eyes. "The email is there, but earlier there was an attachment with the results. I know I saw it."

"Let's check your computer. Maybe your phone ate it." He got up and held out his hand to help her to her feet. "It has to be there somewhere."

⁓

Paradise settled on the sofa beside Blake with her MacBook and called up the DNA website on her browser, but it showed no results, just like on her phone. "Blake, it's not there, but there's an email telling me the results are in."

"Maybe it went out in error?"

"Maybe." She went back and reread the email, which clearly stated the results were available. "I think I'll call them." She punched in the digits for customer service and explained the situation to the friendly man on the other end.

"This is quite strange," he said. "Our system shows the results were received, but when I try to call them up, the document is missing. Yet I can see where we had something last night when the email went out. I suggest waiting another day and seeing if it shows up. Maybe we have a glitch on our end."

"I'll do that." She ended the call and updated Blake. "He seemed puzzled too." She snuggled against Blake's side and inhaled the scent of his eucalyptus soap and spicy cologne. "How are you doing? Finding Ivy had to be hard."

He tensed. "It's hard to get that image out of my head. And

you know Greene will try to make this our fault somehow. Lacey and Owen are behind bars, facing charges for Danielle Mason's murder, but it's clear Greene isn't convinced we had nothing to do with it."

"He makes up his mind and tries to find evidence to support his viewpoint. That's not the way investigations should work."

"And we were just recovering from the media storm after the Mason woman's body was found here. This new incident will ramp up the social media nightmare again."

"I'll work on new posts. What is our official stance when asked?" She watched the wheels turn in his head. What did someone say about this kind of awful discovery? It would be better to say nothing, but they likely didn't have that luxury.

"Maybe we should put out a statement about it. I'll ask Hez to help me craft something."

"Good idea."

Chairs scraped across the kitchen floor, and moments later his little brothers burst into the room waving painted pictures. Isaac had painted a sloth, and Levi showed them a picture of a giraffe. What must it be like to grow up in such a close family—and on a wildlife refuge like this with all those wonderful animals in their backyard? The boys had no idea how blessed they were, but they'd all look back on these magical days with nostalgia.

"I love your pictures," she told the boys.

Isaac thrust his in her face and Levi presented his big brother with his giraffe. "You each can have one," Levi said. "Want me to stick it on the wall so you can see it in the night? Aren't you getting tired of sleeping on the sofa?"

Blake took the picture before his brother could go in search of a pushpin. "It's worth it to have Paradise here, don't you think?"

"I thought she was going to move to town."

"I'm in no hurry for her to do that."

Paradise lifted the seven-year-old to her lap. "Are you getting tired of me, Levi?"

He gave a vehement shake of his head. "I don't *ever* want you to leave, but have you seen Blake get up in the mornings?" He slid off her lap and bent over like an old man and put his hand on his back. "He's like this and he kind of hobbles to the bathroom."

"Hey, buddy, it's not that bad. I'm just a little stiff."

"It looks like a *lot* stiff," Levi said.

Isaac turned back toward the kitchen. "Mommy said we could have a brownie since dinner won't be for a while. I didn't get one."

"I didn't either." Levi followed his brother.

"Don't listen to a word they said." Blake wrapped one of her tawny curls around his finger. "You don't have to go anywhere. I can move back upstairs now that you're not in danger any longer. I've just been too lazy to haul my things."

"The new paint is going on tomorrow in the apartment above the vet clinic. I can move over the weekend. It's time for me to let the boys return to normal life."

He made a face but didn't object. "How'd your first morning go?"

"I'm still learning where to find everything. Honey was wonderfully encouraging, and the pet owners all wanted to chat. They didn't look at me like I had four eyes or anything. One of them was a former schoolteacher from fourth grade." The woman's kind manner had been a balm in the middle of a frantic day of learning. "I thought about asking her what she remembered from when I was little. I think I need to find people who knew my parents over twenty years ago. Mom surely has some good friends who still live here. Someone might remember more than my cousin did."

His breath whispered across her cheek as he leaned in closer. "That's a great idea. We could go to the library and look at old yearbooks."

She couldn't think with him so enticingly close. Before she could lean in for a kiss, the boys burst back into the room. They each had a brownie in one hand and a second brownie on a plate in the other. "We brought you a snack too," Isaac said. "But Mommy said we could only have one because we're going to Jesse's for dinner in an hour."

She accepted the still-warm and chocolaty brownie. Maybe having her own space wouldn't be so terrible. She loved the boys dearly, but she and Blake would have a little more privacy, and that wouldn't be a bad thing at all.

CHAPTER 4

SERGEANT ROD MCSHEA STOOD hands on hips in the back parking lot of the preserve, waiting for Blake to pull the safari truck into its space. Blake squinted in the bright sunshine as he exited the vehicle for the final time of the afternoon. The day was warm for February, and his forehead beaded with perspiration. "Hey, Rod, are you looking for me?"

"Sure am." Rod gestured for Blake to follow him to a shady spot under an oak tree. The wind lifted his light brown hair.

Bison grazed on the other side of the fence, and Blake moved a few feet away from their pungent odor. "What's up?"

"Something interesting turned up in the search at Ivy Cook's house. We found a chain of emails on her computer from someone who agreed to pay her for information about Paradise. The anonymous email account isn't traceable by our computer forensic lab, so we don't know who sent her here or why."

Blake absorbed the unsettling news. "Did you tell Paradise?" She was Rod's cousin, but that didn't gain her any points when it came to interrogations.

"Not yet. I don't want to worry her unnecessarily if I don't have to. She's been through enough trauma. If further investigation turns up anything, I'll question her more, but at the moment, I don't think scaring her would serve any purpose. In her interview after the discovery of Cook's body, she said she didn't know her."

If Rod didn't want to worry his cousin, there must be something to be concerned about. "She didn't. Even Mom had never met her before the interview. We only know her grandmother. Did the emails sound threatening, like the other person wanted to harm Paradise?"

Rod shrugged. "Nothing overt, but it's odd. Keep an eye on her."

"I will." Blake barely noticed Rod walk back to his car and drive off. Hadn't Paradise been through enough? Why would anyone want to target her? He didn't agree with Rod. Paradise insisted on knowing when danger might present itself, and she would want to know about this.

He walked along the stone path toward the clinic building where he could usually find Paradise this time of day. He stepped inside and saw her in the office doing her shoulder exercises. He paused for a moment and watched her. Her tawny hair was in a neat bun today, pulled back from her tanned face, and the sunlight brought out the reddish tints. He liked the way he could see the planes and angles of her delicate bone structure and long, slim neck. What a blessing that she was back in his life. He never wanted to take that for granted.

She looked up and her face lit with affection. "Have you been standing there long?"

"Long enough to know I'm a lucky guy." He crossed the small

space in three steps and leaned down to brush his lips across hers. She tasted of chocolate and peanuts. "Yum, any chocolate-covered peanuts left for me? I didn't get lunch."

She gave a throaty chuckle and pulled open a drawer in her desk. "I wouldn't share these with just anyone, you know."

"I'll bet the boys could coax them out of you." He popped one in his mouth and crunched down on the nut.

"Okay, guilty as charged. They both just left." She studied him for a long moment. "What are you doing here? Shouldn't you be starting dinner rounds?"

He perched on the edge of her desk and told her what her cousin had said. Her smile faltered as he talked, and he hated the fear that crept into her amber eyes. "Rod isn't necessarily worried yet, but he didn't like it. I'm not sure about you moving into your new apartment now. It would be safer to stay here."

She took her attention from her computer. "I'll be fine, Blake. I know how to take care of myself, and you installed that security system. The sheriff substation isn't far, and with people around in town, the danger might be less than in an isolated place like The Sanctuary." Her smile finally returned. "Besides, I was think-ing the other night about how nice it will be to have some alone time with you. I don't think I'm willing to give up the thought of snuggling on the sofa and watching a good chick flick."

He faked a groan. "And here I thought you agreed we'd only watch all the spy shows. I'd even settle for animal documentaries."

The truth was, he'd watch every chick flick ever filmed if he got to have her tucked up against his side with the plumeria scent from her hair curling around him. The light in her eyes and the teasing smile on her lips were almost enough to make him forget the danger of her living alone. Almost.

An outside iron staircase accessed Paradise's apartment above her veterinary office from a little-used alley. She hid a smile at the distaste on Blake's face when he saw the narrow strip of gravel with weeds poking through. He'd already voiced his opinion about it being too easy for an intruder to come up those stairs without being noticed.

She opened the passenger door of his truck and climbed out. "I know what you're thinking, but I'm not worried. That new dead bolt would keep Dozer out. I'll be fine."

He smiled at the mention of their only rhino. "Dozer would make short work of that lock." He checked the camera above the door. "Everything looks in order."

She unlocked the door and stepped into the living room with Blake on her heels. The space held the odor of fresh paint and the new vinyl plank flooring. Light bounced off the light gray walls and pooled on the pale wood-toned floors. "I love it! All this sunlight streaming in makes me happy."

She'd found nice used furniture at a store in Foley, and the light gray leather complemented the space and color scheme. An inexpensive rug she'd bought online anchored the space under the furniture. She wandered through the kitchen and two bedrooms. "It's all ready. After I move in, I want the boys to have a sleepover tonight."

"They'll be happy to christen the new bunk beds."

"Well, they aren't new, just new to me."

"I'm impressed. You managed to get everything you need on a shoestring budget, and it all looks great. I'll start hauling your things up now. If you're *sure* this is what you want to do."

"I'm sure."

While he clanged down the staircase, she checked out the refrigerator. Empty. She'd have to grab food before the boys came. They'd want yogurt and string cheese. Pepperoni too. The kitchen supplies she'd found at a thrift store occupied the upper cabinets. The new creamy paint she'd rolled on the cabinets hid the dented and chipped wood. They looked almost new. She could see herself cooking in here.

Blake came through the door with a tub of belongings in his arms. Everything she owned was in three tubs, including the items belonging to her mother that Evan had found in his attic. "You can put everything in my bedroom. I can come help grab the last two."

"They're smaller than this one. I can make one trip." He dropped a kiss on her head as he maneuvered around her and went to the bedroom.

A call came through on her phone, and she glanced at the screen. Unknown. She almost didn't answer it, but it could be someone calling with an animal emergency, so she didn't want to ignore it. "Dr. Alden."

Music played into her ear, and she recognized it as "The Music of the Night" from *The Phantom of the Opera*. A chill shuddered down her back, and she licked her lips. "Hello? Is anyone there?" There was a strange discordant sound before the call ended.

"Who was it?" Blake asked behind her. "You went pale. Is everything all right?"

"I—I think it was a prank call." She told him about the music playing.

He reached for her phone and called up the number, then

punched it into his phone. "Nothing comes up about the number." His frown deepened. "I don't like it, Paradise. I don't think
you should stay here tonight. We wouldn't want the boys in the
line of sight of some nut either."

Trepidation replaced her earlier euphoria, but she strove to
hide her fear from Blake. "I'm sure it was kids playing a prank.
I'll put my things away while you bring up the rest. I'm going
to run to the grocery store while you go get my boys. I'll get the
beds made, and we'll have a pizza party tonight. I'm not going to
let something so silly derail the fun I have planned for tonight."

"I'll sleep on the sofa then." His firm tone allowed for no
dissent.

She managed not to show her relief despite her earlier projec-
tion of confidence. *Bravado, mere bravado.* The call had already
drained her anticipation and left dread in its wake. Those sweet
boys would restore her equilibrium.

She lifted her chin and marched to the bedroom where she
unpacked her clothing and put her things in the dresser and the
closet. The bottom drawer held sheets, and she yanked it open
to pull out a set for her king-size bed. A paper rustled inside the
folded material of the top sheet, and she dug around until she
could pull it out.

You must know that I am made of death, from head to foot,
and it is a corpse who loves you and adores you and will never,
never leave you!

The ominous line from *The Phantom of the Opera* made her
shudder. Her pulse kicked, and the paper dropped from her
nerveless fingers. This could not be a coincidence. Who would
do this—and why?

She forced herself to pick up the paper, but she kept her gaze from the highlighted words and placed the paper face down on her dresser.

She didn't dare show this to Blake. He'd insist she come back to stay at The Sanctuary, and she wasn't willing to let fear rule her.

Was this a warning for her to stop looking for her brother? The emphasis on the past made her think it was either that or her investigation into who had killed her parents. But she wouldn't let this go—she couldn't. She'd lived too many years in a fog where she remembered nothing, and she wasn't willing to go back there. Better to face the demons in the daylight than to worry about them lurching out of the shadows in the night.

CHAPTER 5

BLAKE WATCHED PARADISE'S EARLIER ebullience evaporate, and her efforts to interact with the boys over pizza felt forced and artificial. Her amber eyes held more worry than she wanted to admit. They played Uno after eating, and she brought a bowl of buttered popcorn into the living room.

He started *Moana*. "We're about to watch this for the twenty-two thousandth time."

"You're exaggerating." Levi liked to use new words.

"Prove it," Blake said. "I'm sure it's only a slight exaggeration."

Levi threw a pillow at him. "I don't want to count that high."

Paradise set the big bowl down on the coffee table and handed each boy a smaller one. "Where did you say your mom was tonight?"

Blake sent her a questioning glance. He'd already told her Mom was out on a date with Frank Ellis, a local developer she'd dated in high school eons ago. He was a widower, and they'd rekindled their romance at their high school reunion a few weeks ago. "She and Frank were going to a new end-of-the-world film." He'd withheld that detail.

One of her eyebrows winged up. "Your mom's idea or Frank's?"

"Definitely Mom's. She loves apocalyptic films. Dystopian ones too. This one is right up her alley with an EMP bomb that takes out the grid."

The glint in those gorgeous eyes of hers told him he'd gotten through whatever worry she'd been battling. "Want to take me to one?"

"You like them too?"

"No, but I wanted to see how far you'd be willing to go to make me happy." She leaned down and kissed him.

He took her hand and pulled her onto his lap. "If you give me another buttery kiss, I'd even take you to a chick flick. Or a zombie movie. You like zombies, don't you?" She'd once told him she liked zombie films because she knew monsters existed in real people and they felt true to her.

"I watched every episode of *The Walking Dead*. Twice, in fact." She leaned in for another kiss.

He took his time with the kiss so she knew he was serious, and when he let her go, her cheeks were pink and she was fully with him with no hint of worry in those amber eyes. Luckily the boys were engrossed with the movie.

He toyed with a stray curl. "Something's been bugging you ever since I got back with the boys. Are you sure you want them to have a sleepover?"

Her smile faded, and she looked away. "I'm sure. Um, do you remember how much I liked *The Phantom of the Opera*?"

"How could I forget? I'm sure we watched it a thousand times plus one."

"You're on a roll with the hyperbole. It wasn't that many."

"Close." He studied her shuttered expression. "That so-called prank call bothered you more than you were letting on, didn't it?"

"I was trying to remember if anyone else in my class liked it. I mean, Abby knew I was obsessed, but I'm not sure if anyone else did."

"You never shared personal details with friends much, so I doubt if you told anyone about it. And I wasn't about to admit I'd watched it with my girlfriend nearly every night. That was back when we were into *Die Hard* and action movies. Do you suspect someone you know was the caller?"

She shrugged. "I hadn't thought about it in a long time, and when I heard 'The Music of the Night,' it brought back a lot of memories, that's all."

She didn't fool him—that wasn't all—but if there was one thing he knew about this woman he loved with everything in him, it was that she'd tell him when she was good and ready.

She escaped from his lap and moved off toward the kitchen. "I made strawberry lemonade for the boys. I'll get it." She called back over her shoulder, "I left my phone on the dresser in my bedroom. Could you grab it for me?"

"Sure." Blake ruffled Isaac's hair as he moved toward the bedroom. Her personal space was already neat and put together. She'd even set out a picture of all of them mugging it up in front of their one and only sloth. He smiled and touched her smiling lips in the picture on her dresser. With every day he was more and more thankful she was back in his life.

He walked around the bedroom but didn't see her phone. Her scent lingered in the room. He started toward the door to tell her he couldn't find it when he heard music playing. He followed the sound to her closet and slid open the door. He spotted the phone on the floor of the empty space. It was lit up, and it only took him a few seconds to recognize a tune from *The Phantom of the Opera*: "Angel of Music." He scooped up the phone and stared at the name on the screen. *Phantom.* Hadn't it read *Unknown* before?

Frowning, he carried the phone back to the living room. The boys were drinking their lemonade, and he found her humming in the kitchen. She was cutting cheese squares and placing them beside pepperoni and crackers on a plate. "I found your phone. You missed another phone call."

She eyed his frown and took the phone. She tensed when she touched the missed call list. "I—I have no idea who that is."

"Somehow he made 'Angel of Music' play as it rang. He's got some skills. I don't like it."

Turning away, she dropped the phone on the coffee table. "Thanks for finding it."

~

"I want you to stay with us at The Sanctuary."

Paradise fisted her hands at her sides. "You're smothering me, Blake. I've done fine running my own life for the past fifteen years." He paled at her pointed reminder of how he hadn't been there for her, but she stood her ground. No one was going to run her off this place she'd claimed as her own. "If I ever expect to be part of the community again, this is where I make my stand."

His nostrils flared, and a frown settled on his brow. "You forget what we've just been through, and it doesn't all seem to be over. Doesn't this feel as ominous to you as it does to me?"

She lifted her chin. "I think it's a prank." She wasn't about to tell him about the note in her bedroom. He'd throw her over his shoulder and carry her down to the truck. Someone wanted to scare her away, and she refused to give in to the fear shuddering down her spine.

"What could be the reason and who would do it? What would be the point?"

"Who knows why anyone pulls harmless pranks? I'm right in the middle of downtown Nova Cambridge. I don't think I'm in danger here."

The lines on his face smoothed. "I don't want to risk you in any way. I realize I can be overly protective, but I'm working on it." He sighed. "You're really not worried?"

Instead of telling a blatant lie, she shrugged. "We risk our lives every day just getting in a car. I don't want to live in fear. I understand your concern about the boys though, and I share that. If you want to take them home tonight, I understand."

He smiled, but worry still lurked behind his direct gaze. "I'm camping out on the sofa. The boys can be a handful by themselves, and I'll be here to help out. I'm worried about leaving you here alone."

She was worried, too, but Blake had installed a security system with cameras. With pepper spray in her bedside drawer, she'd be prepared. *Wait, the security cameras.* She could check those later and see who had entered her building to leave the note. Once she made sure Blake was asleep.

Her phone sounded, and she tensed until she realized it was the DNA center she'd contacted about the missing results. She turned her back to Blake while she answered it. "Paradise Alden."

"Hi, Ms. Alden. This is Chad calling back about your DNA results."

His tentative tone made her straighten. "Hi, Chad. Did you find the report?"

"I'm sorry to say that it seems to be completely gone. I called the lab, and they find no record your samples were ever received."

"But I got an email when the lab got them. And I received

that other email saying the results were available. So that makes no sense."

"I agree. And after extensive digging, I have no answers for you other than there was some kind of glitch. Could you please repeat the test and send it in? We'll refund your money and run the new tests for free."

She had no choice if she wanted to know more about her missing brother. "I'll pick up another test."

"I've already had one sent out, and it should be in your mailbox tomorrow. It's marked high priority, so we should have a quick turnaround with special care given to the final results. I'm sorry this happened, Ms. Alden, and we want to make it right."

"I appreciate that." They exchanged platitudes and goodbyes before she hung up and turned back to Blake. "You probably gathered the DNA results are still missing."

Did someone want to block her efforts to find her brother? And would that same person be trying to scare her into leaving?

CHAPTER 6

IF BLAKE HAD SLEPT on a harder sofa, he couldn't remember when. He flipped over on his other side and tried to ease the ache in his back. The used sofa held the scent of spearmint, and his feet hung over the end. The boys had finally settled down in the bunk beds around nine, and when he'd checked his phone, it was nearly midnight. His mind wouldn't shut off long enough for him to fall asleep though.

The squeak of a floorboard alerted him, and he raised his head to stare in the direction of the hallway. A faint glow came from under the closed office door. After rising, he unplugged the lamp and took it with him as he moved noiselessly down the hall. Next time he'd make sure he had his gun with him.

He eyed the door, then tightened his grip around the lamp's base. He couldn't guarantee it would be a good weapon, but the heft of it gave him hope. The door stood open two inches, and he spotted movement. He peered through the crack and saw Paradise sitting at the computer. Her mane of light brown hair curled down the back of her pink pajamas, and she hunched forward as she stared at the computer screen. A handful of chocolate-covered peanuts lay beside the keyboard.

He noiselessly eased the door open more. His gaze went to the video streaming on the screen. It appeared to be from the security camera focused on the outside iron staircase on this building. The time stamp in the corner was 12:26 a.m. yesterday morning, almost twenty-four hours ago.

He shuffled his feet to alert her he was there. "What are you doing, babe?"

She whirled and her hand went to her throat, but she didn't meet his gaze. "You startled me." She scrambled to her feet. "I should go back to bed."

The darting gaze that wouldn't meet his, the hurried movements, and her nervous habit of twisting a lock of hair were all obvious tells. "You're hiding something. What's wrong?"

"Nothing." She darted a glance at the screen and froze.

And then he saw why her eyes had widened. A shadowy figure in a dark hoodie crept up the steps, pausing halfway up to furtively glance around. The person went on up to the door at the top where he or she fiddled with the lock, opened the door, and vanished inside. Whoever it was hadn't paused much longer than it would take to insert the key and twist it.

He gestured to the computer. "You weren't surprised. You knew someone had been in the apartment." She started to brush past him, and he caught her arm. "Don't shut me out, Paradise. Talk to me."

Indecision sparked in her eyes, and she edged far enough away that he released her arm. "Someone left a note."

He inhaled sharply. "You knew someone had been inside and stayed here anyway?"

"I thought it might have been when the work was being done. That didn't feel too scary."

He gestured to the computer screen. "Someone has a key, and I find that very scary."

She chewed her lip and nodded. "It was a surprise. I wouldn't have kept the boys if I'd suspected someone had access to the apartment now. I truly thought someone had come in while work was being done."

"You would have stayed here by yourself without telling me about the note?"

Her eyes flashed, and her chin came up. "This place is *mine*, Blake. I've faced down bullies in the past, and I will do it again. I won't let anyone drive me from here. I know how to take care of myself."

She was such a little slip of a thing, but her courage was as great as that of any man he'd served with in the Marines. Even though he wanted to protect her from any more hard knocks, she was wise enough to know she had to stand up for herself. "I get it, I do. Was this guy the only surprise? Did you see anyone else?"

"No one was on the staircase except this guy. The camera picked up people walking past, but that's all. Roger Dillard wandered past on his way to Chet's BBQ, and Evan stopped by to say hello to Honey. I didn't recognize anyone else."

"But grit isn't enough to face down some guy lurking in the shadows with an unknown agenda. We need a plan, a strategy to flush him out into the light and keep you safe."

Her defiant expression ebbed at his lack of anger. "Like what?"

"First of all, you need better security here. I'll change the locks and the dead bolt too. Add more cameras. Hidden ones he can't see, so if he breaks in here again, we can identify him. And either a gun or bear spray—maybe both. Have you ever used a pistol?"

"I have bear spray." She gave him an impish grin. "I'm really good with a tranquilizer gun, and I have one hidden in my bedroom. It's not loaded, of course. Not with the boys here. But when they're gone, I'll load it and have it ready."

"A second one might come in handy. I'll dig out another one. What about a real gun with bullets?"

"I'll stick with a dart gun."

He didn't argue with her. Not everyone was as comfortable as he was with firepower. And the tranquilizer gun would be a good deterrent. "I'll install motion-detector security lights along the exterior stairs as well. You might want blinds to block out the light, but if someone tries to come up here, he'll think he's onstage. I'll have an alert set up on your phone as well. That way you'll have a few minutes of warning if someone tries to come up that way."

It wasn't as perfect as having her where he could protect her, but Paradise had never been a wilting wallflower. Her spirit was one of the many things he loved about her, and he wouldn't strip that away even if he could.

———

The park was busy today, despite the news of Ivy's death. Hez had helped them craft a statement she'd put on their socials, and it seemed to have worked. Paradise counted twenty-eight youngsters mixed in with the adults in the treetop structure overlooking the giraffe enclosure. This guided tour was all about the tall, gentle creatures so beloved by everyone.

She fanned her face before gesturing for the children to come to the front of the group. Kids had a natural enthusiasm that made talking about the animals more fun. "Who's ready to feed the giraffes?"

All the hands shot up, and one little boy about Levi's age waved his hand wildly. "Me, me!" She gave him a frond and passed more out to the rest of the children as well as to the adults who asked. The air held the scents of the marsh in the distance and newly mown grass from the fields on the left side of the enclosure.

"What's the first thing you noticed about the giraffes as they came this way?" she asked the children.

A little girl raised her hand. "Their back legs are shorter."

"I know it looks that way, but they're about the same length. How many vertebrae do you think are in that long neck? A human has seven."

"At least twenty," a boy said to her left.

"You think so? They actually have the same number we do, but each one can be over ten inches long. Isn't that crazy? Why do you think they all have horns?"

"They are all males?" a boy asked in an uncertain voice.

"That's a good guess. Those are called ossicones, and all giraffes have them. They are covered with hair, and males use them to spar. So we have giraffes of both genders." She let the visitors feed the giraffes, who took turns snatching the treats with their long tongues. These animals were some of her favorites in the park—always gentle, with intelligence in their eyes. She didn't have to worry about one charging at her out of nowhere or a painful bite that took the strength out of her muscles. She absently rubbed her aching shoulder, then finished up with her talk and waved goodbye to the guests.

She loved this job so much. Working with the animals and

being surrounded by Blake's loving family had allowed light and joy to begin the healing process in her soul.

She glanced at her watch, then headed down the steps from the high platform. She'd scheduled neuter and spay surgeries this afternoon, so she'd flipped her park and clinic schedules. She needed to grab something from the grocery to have on hand for lunch since she didn't think there was much in the fridge in her apartment. The boys had swept through the fridge like small locusts last night.

She found Blake waiting at her Kia with a small cooler bag. He held it up with a smile. "Yogurt, a couple of mozzarella cheese sticks, and an apple to stick in your fridge."

She wanted to kiss him, but the people getting out of the car next to hers were staring. "You are too much. Did you just read my mind? I was trying to decide if the boys had left even a pepperoni or two."

"They didn't, but I dropped them off at Mom's and raided our fridge for something for lunch. Not much there either, but I'll run to the grocery after work."

The carful of people had wandered off, so she leaned against his muscular chest and gave him a lingering kiss. He tasted of spearmint, and his hair smelled like hay from feeding the animals this morning. She pulled back reluctantly. "You are wonderful."

He winked. "I've got you fooled."

"Not a bit." She opened her car door and was hit with a stench. She wrinkled her nose involuntarily. Manure was in a pile on the driver's seat. Cat scat. She reached out for Blake, who hadn't spotted it. "Blake."

"What is it?" He stepped closer and froze. "Was your car locked?"

"No. I didn't think about it this morning." She stared at the pile of excrement. "I would like to believe it's a simple prank, but—"

"But with the events that happened at your apartment, that doesn't seem likely," he finished for her.

"Exactly."

"We'd better call it in. We haven't even reported the break-in at your place."

"For all the good it will do if Greene is the responding detective."

"I'll call Jane directly instead. It would be reasonable since Pelican Harbor PD oversees Nova Cambridge, and I can report the intruder we saw on the camera first and then mention this act of vandalism. That way she'd have jurisdiction over both incidents since they're related." He pulled out his phone.

She stared at the seat damage. This was going to take way too long, and she had patients waiting for surgery. She put her hand on Blake's arm and listened as he left a message for Jane to call him back. "I really need to get to work. Can this wait until after lunch?"

He nodded. "It may take a while for her to get back to me. We can't clean up the mess yet though. You can take my truck, and I'll have someone bring me to town after I'm done here."

She took the keys he dug out of his pocket. "I thought we would get a chance to work at building The Sanctuary and start my new practice without distractions. I can't even think about what needs to be done."

His blue eyes softened. "I know, babe, but God's got this. We'll get through it."

She'd seen God's hand recently for the first time in her life, but it was still hard to trust like Blake did. Right now, all she could do was hang on to his certainty.

CHAPTER 7

POLICE CHIEF JANE DIXON was a petite thirtysomething woman with light brown hair and angular features. She reminded Blake of a younger Reese Witherspoon.

Her nose wrinkled when she saw the mess in Paradise's car. "Nasty business. Have you checked the cameras in the area?"

With the door open, the stench wafted out their way. "The one that usually surveys the parking lot malfunctioned two days ago, and I had to order a new one. It arrived today, but that doesn't help what happened here this morning."

"What time did Paradise arrive for work?"

"Around seven."

Jane glanced around. "Where is she, by the way?"

"I had her take my truck. She had patients coming in at eleven, and I told her I'd handle it. She can come by the office if you need to speak with her personally."

"I'll need to hear if she has any idea who might have done this." Jane put her pen away and fixed her penetrating hazel gaze on him. "This happened in the county, but you called me. More problems with Greene?"

"I knew he'd dismiss it like he has everything else. And there was an earlier incident, one more serious, that falls under your jurisdiction. I had you come here first so I could clean up the mess and deliver the car to Paradise."

"More serious? What happened?"

"Someone broke into her apartment over the vet office." He told her about the phone calls with *The Phantom of the Opera* music and the note with the quotation. "So we checked the camera under the eaves looking onto the exterior stairs and found a person breaking in. He or she wore a dark hoodie, and we couldn't make out any facial features, unfortunately."

A worry line settled on Jane's brow. "I don't like the sound of that. Is she staying there tonight?"

"I'm going to change the locks and install some other cameras."

Jane's expression didn't clear. "You and I both know someone determined to get in won't let a lock stop them."

"She's armed." He didn't mention it was only with a tranquilizer gun.

"That's good at least. But I still don't like it."

"Me neither, but she's stubborn."

"I tend to be that way myself." Jane's lips slid into a half smile.

Sirens blared behind him, and he turned to see four police vehicles, lights flashing, barreling toward the parking lot. His gut clenched so hard he fought a wave of nausea. This was bad, very bad. What was happening?

The first car whipped into a parking spot beside Blake. Greene. A forensic van parked nearby and two more vehicles, orange dust billowing from under their wheels, parked as well.

"Steady," Jane said under her breath. "Show no emotion, Blake. The autopsy report came back early this morning."

He swallowed back the questions and stood waiting for someone to tell him what this was all about. The driver's door on the first car flew open, and Creed Greene exited. His frown was directed at Blake, and he approached with quick steps.

When he saw Jane, his stern expression faltered for two seconds before he grunted her way. "What are you doing here, Chief Dixon? This is our jurisdiction."

"I'm here about a breaking-and-entering incident in town." Her even tone seemed to take the heat in Greene's manner down a degree or two.

"I see." Creed's green eyes were accusatory, but he said nothing at first as the other officers and forensic techs exited their vehicles and fanned out toward the park. "Where do you keep the tranquilizer?"

Blake folded his arms over his chest. "What's going on?"

"Answer the question," Greene snapped.

Blake started to refuse to answer, but he caught a faint shake of Jane's head. Raising the level of antagonism probably wasn't a wise move. "In the medical facility. It's locked in a safe with the other medicines."

"I'll need to see it."

"Do you have a warrant or something? Why are the forensic techs back?"

Jane shifted on her feet and took a step toward Greene. "I suggest you tell Mr. Lawson what's going on, Detective Greene."

Greene's nostrils flared, and he shot her a glare. "This is my investigation, Chief Dixon."

"But there are other investigations running that may be related to ones under *my* oversight. Don't make me call the sheriff about your behavior. It's hostile and uncalled for."

Greene's expression stayed belligerent, but he swung his attention back to Blake. "Ivy Cook's autopsy came back. She was murdered, and we're here to collect more evidence."

Murdered? Blake gave a slight shake to his head. "Raj attacked her."

"Nice try, Lawson. *Someone* tried to cover their tracks with the big cat."

"How do you know it was murder?"

"The drug screen found Telazol in her bloodstream."

Telazol was the tranquilizer loaded into dart guns to subdue large wild animals. Like tigers. "Someone shot her with it? Was a dart found or the wound where it entered?" When Greene pressed his lips together and didn't answer, Blake turned to Jane with bewilderment. "I don't understand."

"The dart wasn't found, not yet. But there was a puncture wound on her neck where the dart went in. We're going to need your cooperation." She nodded toward Greene and his team. "Please show the detective where you store your drugs and the equipment. I'd suggest you move all visitors away from the area and any surrounding spots where a shooter might have a line of sight into the tiger enclosure. How far does the dart shoot from one of the guns?"

"Let me ask the questions, Dixon," Greene snarled.

She leveled her gaze back his way. "Then ask them yourself but in a civilized manner. Mr. Lawson is not under arrest."

"Maybe not yet, but he clearly had access to the murder weapon."

"As did a significant number of his employees. Do your job, Detective."

Greene turned an arrogant sneer toward Blake. "From how far away can an animal be sedated?"

"Depends on which tool we use. A pistol will handle distances under a hundred feet. The rifle can be used as far away as two hundred feet. We've also got a blowgun for short distances with smaller animals."

"Show me," Greene ordered.

Blake caught the sympathy in Jane's eyes as he turned to show Greene and his entourage the equipment.

———

The mewing was the first sign of disturbance. Paradise heard it in the recesses of her brain as she comforted the Benson family over the loss of their dog. Willow had been struck by a car, and though Paradise tried her best, she'd been unable to save her. She held the sobbing daughter against her chest while Mr. Benson comforted his wife.

It was after five and her assistant had already left. The mewing intensified as she showed the bereaved family out the front door. A box with holes poked in the lid sat to the right of the door.

"Kittens!" The ten-year-old Benson girl sank to her knees beside the box and lifted the lid.

Paradise counted four tiny furballs loudly protesting the indignity of being cooped up. "What do we have here?" Her knees scraped the pavement as she knelt and lifted one of the kittens out of the box. "I think they're about six weeks old."

They would have been better off to have been allowed to stay with their mother another four to six weeks, but their coats were shiny and their eyes were bright. She placed the gray kitten back in the box.

The family left with the little girl looking back longingly. Paradise picked up the box when they were gone. "What am I going to do with you?" The kittens didn't answer—they simply sat and mewed pathetically. This was a question she'd have to answer for herself. They were very cute though. One gray, one black-and-white, one mostly white except for a black spot on its face, and one all black. Quite the menagerie.

She made a stop inside and grabbed a bag of Evanger's Rabbit & Quail canned food for kittens. Her other supplies would need to be found at a pet store or a big-box store. She ticked them off mentally—litter and a box for it, a scoop for waste, bowls for food and water, and cat toys.

Whoa, hold on there. She couldn't keep four kittens. Maybe two. They were littermates after all, and she didn't want them to be lonely. All she'd have to do was find one other family to take the other two. Or two families to take two kittens each, though the thought of giving them all away didn't appeal to her. She imagined nights spent shining a laser light for them to leap after and cat toys strewn around her living room. The boys would love them too.

She exited the clinic and started for the steps to her apartment before pausing. What if someone was up there? Blake hadn't come by to change the locks or install cameras. She frowned at her watch. He'd promised to come by around four thirty. A shower and a change out of hairy, smelly clothes sounded much more appealing than hanging out in her office waiting for Blake.

She turned decisively toward the stairs and headed that way. Halfway to the landing, she spotted her green Kia coming her way. She waved at Blake as he parked in the alley, then went on toward the door. The bolt of relief she felt at seeing him startled her. For all her determination to stand on her own two feet, she wasn't as self-sufficient and independent as she'd always thought. Or maybe that was something that came with love.

The smile that curved her lips fell away when she turned to watch him come up the steps. His mouth was set in a grim line, and fatigue pulled at his lids. She took a step down toward him. "What's wrong?"

He gestured toward the door. "Let's go inside. I need coffee."

She unlocked the door and carried the box of kittens inside to set it on the floor. The furballs were all sleeping, and the black one cocked open one blue eye before going back to sleep. Poor Blake. The last thing he needed was another problem.

She washed her hands to make coffee. "I'll make a whole pot. I could use some too."

He shut the door behind him and locked it before he dropped onto a stool at the counter. "Kittens?"

She turned on the grinder and raised her voice over the noise. "Left on my doorstep at the clinic."

"There's nothing cuter than a kitten. The boys will want them."

"I think I might keep two of them." She filled the carafe and poured the water into the pot, then turned it on before joining him at the counter. "Tell me."

"Raj didn't kill Ivy Cook. Someone shot a tranq dart into her and made it appear like a mauling." He went on to lay out what he'd learned about the murder.

Paradise rubbed the gooseflesh on her arms at the thought of being shot with a dart and left in the tiger enclosure. "What was the actual cause of death?"

"The ruling is that Raj delivered the killing blow, but she would have died anyway from an overdose of the sedative. That's why they're calling it murder. Even if Raj hadn't been there, she'd still be gone. At least there probably won't be an outcry to put down our tiger. Greene's coming over to question you."

"Of course he is. He loves throwing his weight around. None

of the employees will feel safe around Raj since he, well, you know."

"I've already made inquiries to a zoo. I hate to lose him, but with the boys living on the premises, Mom would be a nervous wreck. Me too."

"Isaac especially likes the tigers." She shuddered at the memory of the five-year-old's visit to the tiger enclosure. They could have lost him that night.

"Social media is already full of the news. This won't make the job of rebuilding any easier." He ran his hand through his hair and the thick dark brown strands stood on end. "You sure you want to stick around, Simba? None of this will be easy. I thought we'd start by talking to Ivy's grandmother. We can go after church on Sunday."

She loved his nickname for her because of her lion's mane of hair. She stood and wrapped her arms around him. He buried his face in her neck, and she held him tight. "You're stuck with me," she whispered.

"Good. I kind of like you even if you do smell like dog poop and kitty litter." He kissed her on the nose.

CHAPTER 8

THE KITTENS EXPLORED THE apartment while Paradise answered questions from Greene and his partner. The room smelled of garlic and tomato sauce from the untouched pizza she'd ordered before the officers showed up. Square jaw tight and shoulders tense, Blake sat close beside her on the sofa. A tiny black furball leaped at her bare feet, and she scooped up the fluffy kitten for even more moral support.

Though Blake had brought in kitchen chairs for the two officers, they ignored them and continued to stand, most likely as an intimidation tactic. She lifted her chin and stared at Greene. There had been far more intimidating characters to come at her than him. He was like a banty rooster, all feathers and no substance, and she refused to look away from his accusing eyes.

"Why would Ms. Cook have a file containing your life's history?" Creed demanded.

The kitten kneaded her lap, then curled into a ball to sleep. Paradise tipped up her chin to meet his glare. "I have no idea. I had the briefest encounters with her. My primary job is caring for the animals' medical needs, and as far as I recall, I might have said hello to her a total of three times in passing. I never met her before she started working at the park, and her name wasn't familiar—in other words, her surname wasn't one I recognized."

"Did you feel threatened by her? Was she blackmailing you about something?"

Blake tensed beside her, and she put her hand on his forearm. "Detective Greene, listen to yourself. Do you realize how ludicrous your questions sound?" She ignored the flush making its way up his neck and his tight mouth. "I've had enough of your accusations over the past few months. I'm done answering questions."

"I can take you down to the station."

She set the kitten on Blake's lap and stood. "Fine. Let's do that. I'd love for Rod to see how you treat a victim." Her cousin Rod McShea was the sergeant in charge over at the Bon Secour sheriff substation. "It's about time you let go of your vendetta and focused on finding out who is behind the attacks on The Sanctuary—and on me personally. I'm not going to tolerate your behavior any longer. I'm this close"—she held her thumb and forefinger an inch apart—"to filing a complaint with Internal Affairs. I'm not kidding."

He took a step back at her belligerence. "You have no grounds."

"I think I do," she shot back. "Sexual harassment for starters." His partner startled and gave Creed a questioning stare. "This vendetta started when I turned down your overtures." She gestured at his left hand where a gold ring glinted. "Don't make me go to your wife and let her know what a sleazeball you are."

The angry color fled his cheeks, leaving his green eyes to stare out at her from a pasty face. "You'd better not do that. I don't take kindly to threats."

"I'm not making threats—I'm making promises of what I'll

do if you don't stop this." She took a step toward him. "*Find* the person behind all this. That's your job—not wasting time by accusing the victims."

Her lungs heaved in and out, and she couldn't remember ever being so angry or fed up. Deep down she knew she and Blake would have to solve this. The police would be no use. Rod might want to help, but he was short-staffed and harried with other cases.

Greene's partner headed for the door without a word. Greene's fists clenched and he turned and stomped after him. The kittens dashed under the sofa to hide when the door slammed.

Still holding the black kitten, Blake stood and reached for her hand. "Wow, you were amazing. I wanted to do the same but you stopped me, and after you took care of it, I could see why. Only you could point to the sexual harassment." The kitten struggled, and he put it down where it pounced on one of its littermates. "Has he made any more advances since that day you arrived in town and he pulled you over?"

She didn't want to answer, but anger pushed the words out anyway. "He leers all the time and made another pass when he came to pick up the blasting materials we found the day we were taking care of the hippo."

His lips flattened, and a dangerous glint sparked in his blue eyes. "I see. Why didn't you tell me?"

"I love you, Blake, but I can handle my own battles. I'm no damsel in distress, wringing my hands while a train barrels down on me." She managed a smile at his somber expression. "Most bullies turn tail and run when you hit back at them, and Greene is no exception. I meant what I said too. I'll file a complaint if this continues."

"He's not the type to back off, Paradise. His kind gets meaner and sneakier. If he can't wear you down, he'll go at you another way. I think he's out for revenge."

"And I'll be ready," she countered. For all her bravado, she couldn't forget the hatred in Greene's eyes as he stalked away. Maybe she'd better be prepared with more than a dart gun. "Would you teach me to shoot a gun?"

He pulled her into his arms. "I'll teach you. I might sleep easier at the thought of you here alone if I know you're well armed."

That made two of them.

"I'll go get one right now while you shower."

This sleek little SIG P365 would fit nicely in Paradise's small hands and would go a long way toward allaying his fears. Blake left the gun shop with it and walked down Magnolia Street toward Pawsome Pets. He felt better knowing she had something more than the tranquilizer gun. The smoky aroma of barbecue enveloped him as he walked past the newly opened Chet's BBQ. He could grab some for dinner with the family and take Paradise home with him.

Pawsome Pets' Closed sign was in the door window, and he tucked the gun into the back of his jeans before climbing the steps at the back of the building. As he ascended he checked the camera to make sure it was in place, then called the video up on his app to make sure it was working. His own face stared back at him from his phone, and he swiped through the videos from the past twenty-four hours. Only a curious raccoon had triggered it in the night.

Paradise opened the door before he could ring the bell. She'd showered, and a sleek bun tamed her light brown mane. "You were gone so long I was about to call you. I wanted to see what you thought about taking the kittens to show the boys."

He stepped into the apartment, careful not to trample the kittens milling around her feet. The gray one leaped onto his jeans, then dashed away. "You realize they'll want to keep them. All of them. Mom will kill me."

Her smile widened. "Big tough guy like you can handle your mother." She stood on her toes and kissed him. "I'll help you out and tell them I have to keep at least two."

Her fresh plumeria scent filled his head, and he pulled her closer. "I appreciate that," he murmured against her lips. He released her. "See if this fits." He reached behind his back and tugged out the SIG. The little black gun lay in his palm as he extended his hand. "It's a SIG Sauer 365."

She gasped. "Blake, it's so cute! Almost too cute to cause much damage." In a flash she had the gun in her hand. "It fits my hand so well."

"It's lightweight, so you'll have a good aim. The magazine has seventeen rounds, and I think you'll like the trigger. Firm but responsive. We need to go back to the gun shop and fill out the paperwork. I have ammo bagged for you behind the counter too. It won't take up much room in your purse or bedside table and it will be easy to grab."

"I'll need to learn to shoot it."

He nodded. "The Dillard Ranch has a shooting range that butts up to the back side of The Sanctuary, and I'll give you your first lesson there. I have permission to use it anytime. We can grab barbecue for dinner and take the kittens with us on the way out of Nova Cambridge."

"Sounds like you've got the evening all planned out. I miss the boys and your mom. I haven't spent any real time with them in three days."

"I had strict orders to bring you home with me tonight." He scooped up the fluffy black kitten rolling around on his shoes. "You have a box for these little furballs?"

"I have a crate." She went to get it, and the kittens leaped after her. She corralled them into the crate and fastened the door. "How about you grab the food while I go to the gun shop and fill out the paperwork? It will get us home faster if we divide and conquer."

"Deal. I'll take the kittens and meet you at my truck. It's parked in the lot by the gun store."

She opened the door and went down the stairs. He grabbed the crate and locked the door before following the aroma of barbecue to Chet's. They had an exterior window so people could take their food and eat at the picnic tables under the large overhang, and he set the crate on the ground and got into line to place his order.

When the woman in front of him turned, he recognized Mary Steerforth's profile. She and her husband, Allen, had owned The Sanctuary property before Hank and Mom bought it at auction. "Mary, good to see you."

She turned with a smile that made people forget the scars on her face from a tiger mauling. "Young Blake, you're a handsome sight for sore eyes. How's your sweet mama and those little brothers?"

"They're all good. You're a little far from home." She lived off Fort Morgan Road, and he guessed it would have taken her forty-five minutes to get here in traffic this time of day.

"Allen's nephew, Dean, got hired here, and I wanted to encourage him." She limped closer and lowered her voice. "He's been a challenge, that one, but he seems to be making a new start. I wish it had happened before Allen passed. We raised the boy off and on after his dad died, but he left with friends six years ago and hasn't called or contacted us. I heard a couple of months ago he was back in town, and I wanted to reconnect with him. For Allen's sake." Her eyes filled with tears. "And my own. He's the only family I have. He's already driving me a little crazy though. He keeps talking about a will Allen left, leaving him everything. There was no will, and I don't believe Allen would ever do that anyway. Back then, Dean would have spent it all on drugs."

Blake squeezed her hand. "I'll pray it works out."

Over her shoulder he spotted a young man taking orders at the window. He looked to be about twenty-five with curly brown hair and brown eyes. The smile he flashed at Mary was engaging and hopeful, which was a good sign.

Two more customers were ahead of Mary. "Did Allen ever hear there might be oil or gas deposits under The Sanctuary?" A woman had trespassed with equipment that suggested she was looking for gas deposits, and Blake still wondered if that had anything to do with the events that kept slamming them. He'd gone so far as to order some tests, but they weren't back yet.

"There was some talk about it," Mary said. "Allen planned to get it checked, but he was killed before he could order it."

She persisted in her belief that her husband's wreck was no accident, and she refused to believe he'd willingly taken drugs. Blake wasn't sure she was wrong.

CHAPTER 9

FOUR KITTENS PROWLED THE length of the living room, much to the delight of two little boys. Jenna had shot Paradise a *help me* look when the boys asked to keep them, and Blake had quickly jumped in with a claim that Paradise wasn't looking for a home for them.

It wasn't exactly how Paradise felt, but she didn't want to cause a ruckus in the peaceful evening that unfolded in front of her. New gun in hand, she left the boys in charge of the kittens and followed Blake outside to his Gator. The short ride to the shooting range at the Dillard Ranch blew back her hair and lifted her spirits.

He drove through a gate and parked the UTV. "This is it."

The range backed up to a huge mound of dirt that served to contain any stray bullets. The place was deserted, though she heard one of their lions roar in the distance. The area was clean of debris, and she didn't even see any shell casings. Targets at various heights were situated on the far side by the berm. Several trees had targets as well, and the bark was missing in places where someone had missed. Paradise suspected she'd add her own dings to the terrain.

A tremor moved in her belly, and she pressed her palm there. "I'm not sure I'm ready for this. I'm not afraid of the gun, but I don't think I could aim it at a person."

He turned from rummaging in the storage compartment. "You're smart, Paradise. I think you'll know when someone is trying to kill you. Your lesson today will mostly be about gun safety." He held out ear protection. "These amplify noises like voices while muffling the gunshots. I think you'll like them. Let me grab the safety glasses too." He reached back into the box.

She drew a breath and put on the ear protection and slipped on the glasses. He was right—this was self-protection. So many crazy things were happening right now, and she had to be prepared.

"I really like this little SIG. It's got a manual safety." He showed her. "You operate it with your thumb." He demonstrated, then had her try. "Good job."

His biceps flexed as he moved, and her gaze lingered on the muscles of his chest beneath his tee. He was handsome, tanned, strong—and hers. How was she so blessed to have won the love of a man like Blake? The amazing bit was that his character was even more compelling than his good looks. He loved fiercely and forever, and she didn't ever want to take that for granted.

He grew still and a smile lifted his lips. "You didn't hear a word I said, did you?" He set the SIG onto a metal table and stepped closer.

"Sure I did."

"What did I say about loading and unloading the ammo?"

She cast back for some snippet of his instruction and came up blank when his eucalyptus scent wafted her way. The smile vanished, and his blue eyes grew intense as he gazed into her face. Her mouth dried at his smoldering expression. He stepped closer, and her lids fluttered shut as she tipped her head up. His lips came down on hers, and she sank into his embrace.

His passion matched hers until he stepped back with regret on his face. "I don't remember anything I was going to tell you."

"I don't remember anything you said," she admitted. Her fingertips touched her lips. "And it's all your fault."

He barked out a laugh. "What's a man to do when you look at him with those amber eyes that say 'kiss me'?"

"My eyes don't talk," she said primly.

"They telegraph every single thought in your beautiful head." He raked his fingers through the long strands of her ponytail and took it out of its band so her hair was spread out on her shoulders. "I don't think I want to shoot. I'd rather sit in the Gator and kiss you." He nuzzled his face in her hair. "You smell like sunshine, and I can't think when you're around."

She wrapped her arms around his waist. "You are way too distracting. You know your mom will ask how the lesson went."

"We'll tell her it went great," he murmured against her neck. His lips trailed along her shoulder and back to her neck.

A delicious cascade of goose bumps shivered down her back and arms, and her knees went weak. His lips found hers again, and she didn't even remember where she was until he sighed and stepped back.

"You're right, and we need to make sure you're equipped to deal with an attacker. I can't be with you every second, and you need to be able to protect yourself." He reached for the gun again. "The nice thing about this gun is you can load it and unload it with the safety on. We don't need you accidentally shooting yourself."

She pushed away her regret and gathered her scattered thoughts. "Or someone else."

"That too." He nodded.

She paid attention as he took her through all the safety precautions and practiced flipping the safety on and off so she
recognized the click it made. He had her load and unload the
magazine in the gun before he let her shoot it. The trigger had
just the right amount of pull, and she was instantly in love with
the little gun when she hit the target every time.

She loved it almost as much as she loved Blake. Almost.

Paradise's car smelled fresh thanks to Blake's thoughtfulness in
cleaning out the dung left on her seat. He'd detailed the car completely, and it felt like a new vehicle. With Blake's good-night
kiss still on her lips, she got in and started her Kia. The gold-and-
orange sunset had come and gone, leaving darkness to shroud the
tupelo and oak trees.

Though the drive to Nova Cambridge was short, she hated to
leave with the two kittens still in her care. Jenna had caved to
the boys' pleas the minute Blake had taken Paradise out to the
shooting range, which had surprised no one. Kittens were hard
for anyone to resist, least of all an animal lover like Jenna. Paradise smiled, remembering how the boys had carted the furballs
off to sleep with them. Levi had claimed the black-and-white
female, dubbing her Selah, while Isaac wanted the gray one, also
a female, and named her Bailey.

She started the car and drove away. The silence after the welcome chaos at Jenna's house felt oppressive, so as soon as she
crossed over the bridge, she flipped on the sound system. The
strains of "The Phantom of the Opera" blared from her speakers.
Her pulse went into overdrive, and she slammed on her brakes
as a reflex.

Pulse pounding and chest heaving, she pulled to the side of the road and fumbled with the controls. Instead of the radio being set to a radio station, she found a USB drive streaming the movie soundtrack into her speakers. She threw open her door to leap out.

Scents blew in her face: dew, grass, and wildflowers, and she heard a boat puttering past the bridge. An owl hooted from the woods on her right, and the wind fluttered the leaves. Normal sounds that should have soothed her but didn't. She peered through the window into the back illuminated by the interior lights. No one was lurking inside the car, just kittens sleeping in their carrier. Just to be sure, she checked the trunk and found it empty as well.

Someone had done this while it was parked at The Sanctuary.

The tightness in her chest eased, so she got back in the car and locked the doors behind her. Glancing in her rearview mirror, she realized she was closer to her apartment than to The Sanctuary. The boys would be in bed now, and if she returned, she'd disrupt the whole household. There was no physical danger to her. It was a prank designed to scare her, and to her shame, it had succeeded.

She hadn't turned off the music and she listened to the familiar tune as the Phantom crooned about being inside her mind. That was what this faceless person wanted—to get inside her mind and confuse her. Why? What threat did she pose to anyone? Her reasons for being here were strong enough that no one was going to scare her away. If anything, she was more determined to find out who had killed her parents.

Her phone lit up with a message, and she picked it up. Her DNA results were in. Before they could disappear, she clicked on the link and went to the site and downloaded the document. She stared at the folder she'd saved. The subtle fear campaign had started when she began to search for her brother. Why would someone be so determined to keep her from talking to her brother?

She changed the media input back to her Christian music station and put the car in Drive. When she got home, she'd call Blake and tell him about the incident. Maybe something would show up on the cameras in the parking lot. The kittens had awoken and were meowing in their crate. She moved her foot from the brake to the accelerator and heard a rustle—a rattle.

She froze. There was no mistaking the sound of a rattler. The noise reverberated in the enclosed space, and she wasn't sure where it was coming from. The kittens were going crazy, too, scratching at the carrier and yowling. Could the snake get to them? Did she dare move?

Aware any noise could rile the snake, she silenced her phone before texting Blake. *There's a rattler in my car. What should I do?*

Don't move. I'm on my way.

There was a slithering sound, and she pinpointed the location. The snake had been under her feet and was moving beneath her seat to the back. The kittens were in danger. Blake would be here in five minutes, but she couldn't wait.

She threw open her door and catapulted from her seat in one seamless movement. Her bad shoulder hit the pavement, and pain flared white-hot down her arm. She groaned and sat up, holding herself and rocking back and forth until the agony eased a bit.

Though all she wanted to do was not move until Blake arrived, she forced herself to her feet and took a step toward the open car door. The triangular head of an eastern diamondback rattler turned her way, and she paused before beginning to inch away. Maybe the snake would leave her car of its own volition.

When she was three feet from the car, the snake slithered down the side and disappeared under the vehicle, but she didn't dare approach without knowing where it was. She went down on one knee and tried to see where the rattler had gone, but it was too dark.

Tires on the road growled from the bridge, and she needed to get out of the middle of the pavement. She moved to the other side in time to see Blake's truck fast approaching. Relief left her lightheaded.

CHAPTER 10

BLAKE GRIPPED THE STEERING wheel of his truck so hard his hands ached, and he exhaled a sigh of relief when he spotted Paradise along the side of the road opposite where her car was parked. Visions of her nearly dead from a bite had haunted him on the short drive here. Especially after a worrisome phone call from Savannah.

He parked behind her Kia and leaped out to rush to take her in his arms. "Are you all right? Did the snake bite you?" The scent of her hair was a balm to his fear.

She rubbed her arm. "I got out when it moved under my seat. My shoulder took the brunt of it when I hit the pavement. I'll soak it in the bath tonight." A shudder ran through her. "It was next to my leg until it tried to get to the kittens. I knew I had to do something, so I moved fast. When I left the door open, it escaped and disappeared under my car. I'm not sure where it went."

"I'll look." He guided her back across the road to his truck. A deer flicked its white tail and bounced away. "You can wait inside."

"I need to make sure the kittens aren't hurt. It could have bitten them and I didn't know."

From her determined tone he knew better than to try to dissuade her. He leaned inside his truck and grabbed a flashlight from the dash compartment. The beam of light pushed back the night, and he saw movement in the grass near the back passenger wheel. "There it is."

The snake raised its head and flicked its tongue in the light before it disappeared into the tall grass. The vegetation rippled as it headed away. It was large—easily six feet long and probably eight pounds. Paradise wasted no time rushing to seize the carrier from the back seat. She opened the door and reached inside to stroke the kittens. The car engine was still running.

He joined her. "Are they okay?"

"They're purring, so I think they're fine." She pulled her arm out of the carrier and shut the door.

"How crazy it got in. It was a big one too."

"I think someone placed it in my car. That someone left me another present." She sat on the driver's seat and reached inside before opening her palm to reveal a USB drive. "It was in my sound system playing 'The Phantom of the Opera.'"

The USB was a generic white like a million others. "I doubt we can trace where it was bought. Those are everywhere."

She nodded. "And I probably shouldn't have touched it. We could have had it checked for fingerprints."

"We'll do it anyway." He grabbed it by the cord and carried it back to his truck, where he fished a plastic bag out from under the seat and placed the drive inside.

She followed him. "Let's give it to Nora."

Nora had been sympathetic to the way Creed Greene tried to sabotage every piece of evidence they gave him to investigate. If not for her, Blake would be in jail for a murder he had nothing to do with.

"Yeah, that's what I had in mind. I don't like this at all."

"I was going to text you once I got home and have you check the cameras to see who might have put the drive in my car. That was before the snake made its appearance."

"You were lucky that rattler didn't bite you, babe. They don't have to rattle to bite."

"I got out once to check the car and the trunk to make sure no one had hidden inside. Maybe the snake was sleeping and my rustling around woke it. Though they're nocturnal, so it could have just been hiding."

He embraced her again, relishing the way she nestled against him with such trust. He kissed the top of her head and stepped back. "I'll follow you home."

"You don't need to do that. It's only three miles."

"A lot can happen in three miles."

She smiled. "I'm not made of glass."

"You're much more precious." He pulled her back for a thorough kiss that stole his breath and made his heart pound. "It should be illegal to love someone as much as I love you," he whispered when he released her.

"Should I call the cops to take us both away?" she teased.

"Greene would be only too happy to lock me in one cell and you in another."

The reminder wiped the smile off her face. "We have to report this."

"It's closer to Nova Cambridge than the park. I'll tell Jane." He escorted her to the Kia. "Let's get you home where your pulse rate can come down."

"I don't think that will happen with you around." She blew him a kiss and closed her door.

His smile faded as he walked back to his truck and followed

the taillights of her car toward town. Nothing would have saved her tonight if that rattler had struck when she got in the car. It all would have happened too fast. How could he keep her safe?

She's mine.

The whisper in his heart was a reminder she belonged to God, not Blake. He'd thought he was getting better at not feeling so responsible for those he loved. The way he'd failed his best friend resurfaced often, and he wasn't sure he would ever get past it. About the time he thought he could let go of his guilt, it came roaring back.

Just like tonight. He would have thought of a dozen ways to take the blame if something had happened to Paradise during those short miles to town. How did he let go of his need to control things like this? He had no power over life and death, success and failure, good times and bad. No matter how many times he reminded himself of the fact, he found himself in the same old loop. God had a lot of work to do in him.

―――――

By the time they were done reporting the snake and music incident to Officer Jackson Brown from Pelican Harbor PD, fatigue made Paradise's brain feel like it was stuffed with cotton. She was so tired she could barely think, but she had to see the DNA report she'd downloaded.

The kittens clambered over her bare feet where she sat on the sofa, and Blake winced beside her when one of them pounced on his leg and left claw marks. "You're a menace," he told the black one.

She caught the weary note in his voice. "You should go home and get some rest."

"Too much on my mind to sleep. I didn't get a chance to tell you, but Hez took a bad blow to the head during a break-in at the Justice Chamber and has a concussion. He had a seizure, but the doctor thinks he'll be fine. He won't be able to drive for a while though."

"Oh no!" She liked Hez and Savannah. They already felt like her family.

Blake's shoulder brushed hers, and his breath stirred her hair. "Besides, this is finally the big reveal to find your brother. I don't want to sleep through it."

With his arm around her and his warmth pushing away the chill of the late-February night, she was tempted to close her laptop and forget this for now. Kissing Blake would let her forget the trauma of the evening, but she'd been waiting and praying for these results, so she settled for a lingering kiss. "Manage your expectations. There won't be a list of relatives with addresses and phone numbers." If only it were that easy. "I want to see if it's still on the server. I downloaded it from my phone in case it disappeared again."

She logged in to her account and went to the Results tab. Even though she'd taken precautions, she hadn't expected the results to be gone. But the file was empty.

She sat back and exhaled. "Blake, what is going on? Someone has to be deleting the results. There's no other explanation." Fatigue made tears rush to her eyes. She rubbed her lids and swallowed down the lump in her throat. "I saved it in an encrypted file in the cloud."

With his arm around her, he pulled her close to his side. "You're right. Check to see if the file is there."

She called up her iCloud folder and sorted it by date. There it was, right at the top. "It's here." Her hands trembled as her fingers hovered over the track pad. What if her brother's name was really in this document? Was she ready for her life to change so drastically?

"You want me to look first? Someone is very determined to keep these results from you."

She exhaled and pressed her lips together. "I have to know."

"You don't always have to do everything yourself, babe. I'm here to help."

A flash of irritation surprised her. She'd done life on her own for so many years, it felt *wrong* to let someone else carry a burden. If she handled things, she was always in control and had no one to blame but herself if something went wrong. Blake was a caring guy and just wanted to help, but he didn't seem to understand that she wanted to stand on her own two feet.

She swallowed back the anger before it could take control of her tone. "That's okay. I have to face this anyway. Besides, I want to know, even if it's bad."

Could her brother know she was looking for him? Maybe he didn't want to be found. She hadn't thought of that before. He could be the one involved in erasing the first results and the efforts to scare her off.

There was only one way to find out. She opened the file, and the results filled her screen. Her gaze landed on the table listing Immediate Family. One name only was listed, a male. Drew Bartley. She'd been looking for Andrew Bartley, but he'd used the abbreviated name. There were matches in the Close Family column as well, and she spotted her cousin Molly's name. Lily's and Rod's names were there too.

She took a deep breath and moved the cursor to the link for a secure message. "I'm going to message him now." But nothing happened when she clicked the link. She punched the button again. "It's not working to message him."

"Probably because the results were erased. It's no longer connected to the database. Try copying the file to your Results tab on the database and see if it will link up."

There was a plus sign for adding documents in her personal file on the database, so she clicked it and added the document. It appeared in her files, and she clicked the message button again. This time a secure message box popped up. Her pulse stuttered in her chest and she paused.

Blake moved close enough that she caught his eucalyptus scent. "What's wrong?"

"What if I'm putting him in danger by contacting him? Someone doesn't want us to talk."

"You could wait and talk to the guy who called from the DNA company. Maybe with the weird circumstances we could get him to tell us where he's living so we could approach him personally. Someone is monitoring the database."

The thought made her delete the file she'd just uploaded. "Good point. We don't want whoever is doing these things to know I have those results. I'll try calling in the morning."

"We could ask Jane or one of the detectives to do it. They might get more action."

Patience wasn't in her personality, but she wouldn't be able to live with herself if something happened to Drew. She closed her laptop. "You're right." She smiled into his weary blue eyes. "It's nearly midnight. I'll walk you to the door and lock up."

"Let me text Jane first and ask her to talk to the genealogy company." He patted the sofa. "I think I'll bunk right here. After what happened tonight, I don't think you should be alone."

That flash of irritation reared its head again and she jumped up. "You're smothering me again, Blake. I want you to go home and get some rest. I'll be fine. I've got a tranq gun and the real one. There's a dead bolt on the door."

He rose slowly with his lips pressed together. She caught the flash of hurt on his face and nearly backed down, but this was a disagreement that needed to be addressed. They both had to figure out the parameters of their relationship or it wouldn't work.

CHAPTER 11

"I WANTED TO COME sooner to offer condolences," Blake said as he parked on the street in front of the modest mid-seventies brick home in Foley where Ivy's grandmother lived. The landscaping was meticulous, and Karen Cook seemed especially fond of azaleas and rhododendrons. "Mom said she called Karen once she was notified of Ivy's death, and Karen wouldn't talk to her. She thought we'd skirted safety procedures. I'm hoping she'll talk to us when we show up on her doorstep. Especially now that we know Ivy was murdered."

Paradise studied the property. "No vehicles in the driveway. Maybe she's not home."

"Only one way to find out." Blake opened his door and got out, and Paradise did the same. He took her hand as they walked to the door. "You sure you want to handle asking the questions?"

"She has probably heard by now that Ivy was being paid to find out info about me. I think Karen is more likely to tell me than someone else since I was the one being targeted."

She might be right, but Blake didn't have to like it. He pressed the doorbell and heard it peal from inside. The breeze rustled the hanging basket of ferns on the porch as they waited. The door opened and Mrs. Cook's welcoming smile vanished.

Her lips flattened and she said nothing, so Blake hurried to fill the silence. "We're sorry to bother you in your grief, Mrs. Cook, but we really need your help. I assume you know by now Ivy was shot with a tranquilizer gun? Some strange things are happening at the park, and we'd like to talk to you."

She regarded them through narrowed eyes for a long moment before she stepped out of the way to allow them to enter. Karen was in her late fifties. She normally wore her blonde hair in a sleek bob and usually was well dressed. Today her hair was flat on one side, and the yoga pants and tee she wore had food stains on them like she'd worn them for days. Maybe she had. Blake had looked for her at church today, but she hadn't shown up.

The curtains and blinds were all closed, and it took a moment for Blake's vision to adjust to the darkened space. She led them past the dining area and kitchen to a family room at the back of the house. The television was off, and the house echoed with silence. An orange cat scuttled off to hide when it saw them. A flickering candle pushed the scent of vanilla into the room.

"Have a seat."

He and Paradise settled on the beige sofa. The hardwood floors were dusty, and so were the tabletops. Grief had hit the poor woman hard.

Paradise glanced at Blake and leaned forward. "Mrs. Cook, I'm Paradise Alden."

The woman's hazel eyes flickered. "The vet."

"That's right. I'm so sorry for your loss."

"I still can't believe it. Why would anyone want to kill her?" Her voice trembled. "You have no idea what it's like to know my Ivy was murdered."

"My parents were murdered when I was nine, so I know how hard that kind of thing is to take. Even all these years later, I'm not over it," Paradise said.

Karen's interlaced fingers tightened. "I'm sorry I spoke to you like that. I'm not myself."

"I understand, truly." Paradise fidgeted on the sofa. "Did Ivy ever mention my name? My cousin is Rod McShea, and he's the sergeant in charge of the Bon Secour substation. He mentioned they'd found emails from someone who was paying Ivy to feed them information about me. Did she ever mention those emails to you?"

Karen bit her lip and looked down as the orange cat made a reappearance. She picked up the large feline and petted it for several long seconds. "She mentioned it just before she died. We had a fight because she asked me for money. Again. She had gambling debts she needed to pay, and, well, there was no way I was giving my money to con artists and criminals. She promised she'd repay it as soon as she was paid for finding out information on you. I never would have helped her get a job there if I'd known she was going to spy on anyone."

"I'm sure that's true," Paradise said in a soothing voice. "Did she give you any clues to the identity of who hired her or why?"

"I asked her, and she said it was someone from your past who wanted to see what you were up to since you'd come back to town."

"My past. I was a teenager when I moved away from here. I'm nobody important, so this makes no sense."

The cat jumped down from Karen's lap, and she brushed hair from her black yoga pants. "I'm a big fan of lists. Maybe you should make a list of everyone you know from when you were a teenager. It might help."

They'd still never gotten a lead on who killed Paradise's parents.

At first they'd thought it was the former sheriff, Gerald Davis, since his shoe size fit with the impressions found at the scene of the murders, but his DNA wasn't a match. Their investigation had gone nowhere since then, and Paradise abandoned it to focus on getting the veterinary business on solid footing.

But what if the murderer was behind the break-ins and sabotage events? He might be trying to drive Paradise away before she remembered his face. She hadn't mentioned having more nightmares or snippets of memory of that night, but they'd been concentrating on other things.

There were still plenty of people around who lived here at the time of the murders. He glanced at Paradise's set face and knew she would not be run off.

Someone I know hates me enough to stalk me.

While Paradise worked, the thought kept reverberating through her head. When her workday was over, she rushed to Jenna's house and went through the empty house to Blake's office. In one of the bookshelves lining his wall she found the yearbook from her sophomore year. She carried it out to the living room where she settled on the sofa with the kittens leaping on her legs and burrowing into her lap.

Sweet little nuisances. She launched the Notes app on her phone, but the back door opened before she could start going through the yearbook. Jenna's voice called from the kitchen.

"I'm in here," Paradise said.

Small bare feet slapped on the wood floors as the boys ran to her. Two warm little bodies swarmed into her lap, each one grabbing up a kitten as they snuggled close.

Levi patted her cheeks with both of his hands. "I missed you, Simba."

The boys had quickly taken to calling her by Blake's nickname for her, and she didn't correct him. "I missed you too."

The seven-year-old had been gaining muscle and bulk in the past few weeks, and his weight was heavy on her leg. She didn't mind though. Before they knew it, the boys would be too grown up to want to snuggle on her lap. Five-year-old Isaac still held on to his skinny little-boy frame.

Jenna appeared in the doorway. "I've got hummus and carrot sticks for you guys. If you eat all of it, you can have a brownie."

The black bean brownies were tasty enough for the boys but healthy enough for their mom to allow as treats. The boys scattered, taking the kittens with them to the kitchen, and Jenna joined Paradise in the living room. She nodded at the yearbook. "Blake will be here any minute, and the two of us will help you make a list. He told me what Karen said. It's disconcerting."

"It's hard to wrap my head around someone watching me, keeping tabs on where I am and what I'm doing. A cornered animal is a dangerous one."

Jenna winced. "Finding out Owen Shaw and Lacey Armstrong were behind what was going on here really shook my belief in people. I never would have believed they could do what they did—Owen especially."

The former vet had fooled everyone. Paradise opened the yearbook and paused when she heard Blake come in the door and speak to his brothers before heading to join her. The afternoon wind and sun had roughened his skin and tousled his dark hair. She was tempted to skip the research and kiss him instead, but the stray thought made her realize she was reluctant to find out more about her adversary. It was unnerving to be so hated.

She patted the seat cushion beside her. "Let's go through the yearbook and list people who still live here."

He dropped down to her right. "You realize it could be a shopkeeper or one of your parents' friends and not a student."

"But this is a place to start and it might remind us of other people or circumstances we've forgotten." She tried to ignore how much she wanted to lean against him and forget all this. "Start at the beginning." She held out the yearbook.

He took it and flipped it open. The first few pages were pictures of clubs and activity groups. "Hey, didn't your mother sometimes help at the pottery club at Tupelo Grove University? And she taught in the Art Department, so maybe something happened at the college."

"Yes, she did. The older girls were always sweet to me and sometimes braided my hair. I don't think I would have remembered it if you hadn't mentioned it though." She jotted down *Pottery Club*. "We should get a yearbook from back then and see if we can find out other parents who helped out."

"One from TGU would be helpful." Jenna frowned and leaned forward in the armchair. "Your mom had a blowup with a woman she worked with at TGU. It wasn't even about the pottery class but something else." She rubbed her forehead. "I wish I could remember."

"Do you know the woman's name?" Paradise asked.

"No, but the yearbook might refresh my memory."

"Hez's girlfriend, Savannah, could get us the yearbooks." Blake pulled out his phone and typed out a message to Savannah.

They went back to flipping pages, and by the time they were done, Paradise had a list of twenty names, including her cousins who were still around. "I think I should talk to Lily again and ask about Mom's friends. I remember she and my dad used to play cards with another couple down the block, but I can't remember their names." She vaguely recalled a woman with fiery-red hair. Wasn't her husband a police officer? She rubbed her forehead and wished her memories from back then were sharper. Another image dropped into her head. "She created pottery with Mom. We could check pottery shops."

Blake's phone sounded. "Savannah has the yearbooks and said we could come get them anytime."

"How about right now?"

"I've got a roast in the slow cooker, but it won't be ready for another hour," Jenna said. "And it will keep if you're late. In fact, take her out somewhere, Blake. It's been a stressful few days. A seafood dinner on the water sounds like a great idea."

Paradise's pulse kicked at the way Blake smiled. She couldn't think of anything she'd rather do than watch the sunset glimmer on the water and forget for a few minutes that someone wanted her dead.

CHAPTER 12

SAVANNAH WEBSTER POPPED THE trunk lid of her car parked in her driveway under a giant live oak tree draped with lacy moss. "I wasn't sure how many years you needed, so I grabbed all of them from when your mom worked at TGU, Paradise."

Blake grabbed the handles of the cloth bag. "That was a great idea. It might help us know who to talk to about her mom. She likely had friends among the faculty."

The wind blew Savannah's shoulder-length auburn hair around her head, and she batted it out of her face. "I just thought of someone who might be able to help you. Don Phillips was head of HR for forty years. He's retired now, but I'm sure he would remember your mom." She pulled out her phone. "I'm texting you his number and address, and I'll let him know to expect to hear from you."

"Thanks so much," Paradise said. "This is the best lead I've had."

"I'm happy to help." Savannah shut the trunk and walked with them to Blake's truck. "Let me know if there's any other way I can help."

"We sure will." Blake opened the passenger door for Paradise, then set the bag of yearbooks on her lap before going around to the driver's side. "What years do we have there?"

Paradise had them out on her lap. "We have 1989 through 2005, which was when my parents were murdered."

Blake inhaled the scent of old paper permeating the truck as she leafed through the first book.

"Are you sure we should be spending time doing this?" Paradise asked. "It's a distraction from getting the park on its feet and finding out who's trying to shut you down."

"Now that we know someone from your past is targeting you, we have to, babe. You're more important than anything else." He put the truck in Drive and headed toward Pelican Harbor for dinner. "Are you sure you're ready for the truth? Is that what this is all about?"

She closed the book and set it back on the stack. "I'm afraid, Blake. Afraid the nightmares will come back, afraid I'll find out I caused their deaths in some way."

He reached over and took her hand. She held tight with cold fingers. "You were nine. It's not possible it was your fault."

"I'd like to believe that, but the nightmare always leaves me feeling guilty." Her long lashes swooped down and masked the pain in her amber eyes. "What if I don't like what I find out?"

"Let's bring the truth out of the shadows. Things hidden are always scarier. We'll do this together."

"You already have so much on your plate." She ticked them off on her fingers. "Greene is trying to pin Ivy's murder on you, someone is sabotaging the park, and receipts are suffering from the backlash of those things. My parents' murder was a long time ago. I want to find the truth—it's why I came back. But securing the park's future is more important for the boys."

"I'll take care of the boys even if we must sell the park. That's not an issue. So we have a lot of arrows aimed at our heads. The question I keep coming back to is that maybe they're related, Paradise. What if your arrival here triggered all of it, and the attack on the park is really an attack on you? Someone wants you gone. I think we have to find that person in the shadows."

Her chin came up and she nodded. "I'd thought of that, but it seemed too ludicrous to believe."

"So we go to the root of the problem—the person who paid Ivy Cook to spy on you. Once we find that out, a lot more pieces might fall into place."

Pelican Harbor's city limits sign was just ahead. "Moreau's Seafood sound good?"

"It sounds perfect. I can already smell the grilled oysters."

Her stomach rumbled, and his own answered. "Was that my stomach or yours?"

"I didn't hear a thing."

He chuckled and pulled into the restaurant's lot on Bon Secour Bay. The scent of fish and seawater greeted them when they got out, and a bold gull swooped down, almost landing in Paradise's hair. Blake shooed it away and took her hand. Light jazz music wafted from the low-slung building. Inside he asked for a table out on the deck. If they were going to have a romantic dinner, they might as well do it up right.

The server led them to a table at the end of the deck that overlooked the water and several pelicans watching for fish. The moonlight glimmered on the waves gently washing against the shore. Gulls hopped along the boards looking for scraps, and he pushed one away with his foot. "Maybe this wasn't a good idea after all."

She took his hand. "Mine, mine," she chanted, imitating the

gulls in *Finding Nemo*. "I can learn a lot from them." She laced her fingers with his. "The odds seem overwhelming to me, but I can face anything as long as we're together."

He squeezed her fingers. "Even Bertha couldn't drag me from your side. You're stuck with me."

She smiled at the reference to their hippo. "We found out who was behind the attacks last time. We can do it again." She released his hand and scooted her chair back. "I think I'll wash my hands. They smell like old yearbook. I'll be right back."

He watched her enter the restaurant and head for the restroom. What a lucky man he was.

———

Paradise washed her hands in the restaurant bathroom and stared at herself in the mirror. Dark circles lurked under her eyes, and her hair was a windblown mess. With no comb, she'd have to make do, so she smoothed it with her fingers. She pinched some color into her cheeks and went to grab a couple of squares of toilet paper from the stall to wipe the mascara smears from under her eyes.

As she was bending over, the metal stall door slammed behind her and she whirled. She pushed on the door, but it didn't budge. "Hey, it's occupied."

"You shouldn't be here." The low, guttural voice sounded like a man's. "If you want to live, you need to leave and never come back."

Her hand fell back to her side and she backed away from the door. If only she had her phone or some kind of weapon. She stooped to look at the person's shoes. Her tormentor wore jeans and sneakers, about a nine or a ten, so it could be a man or woman.

She straightened and shoved at the door. "This is my home. I grew up here."

"And you'll die here if you don't listen and quit poking around. Go back to where you came from and forget about this place. 'No one ever sees the Angel; but he is heard by those who are meant to hear him.'"

Paradise gasped when she recognized the line from *The Phantom of the Opera*. The gap between the door and the frame opened half an inch, and steps went quickly away.

Paradise pushed open the stall door, but she was too late to see more than a glimpse of blue as the door to the bathroom closed. She rushed out of the stall and threw open the exit into the hall.

No one was there.

She stepped into the restaurant and looked around for that shade of blue she'd glimpsed. It was not quite royal and not quite navy, but no one wore that unique shade. Maybe she hadn't seen it clearly enough.

Shaking now that it was over, she headed back to the deck. The night breeze cooled her overheated cheeks when she stepped outside.

Blake's welcoming smile vanished. "What's wrong?"

Her legs felt wobbly and rubbery beneath her, and she sank onto the chair. "There was a welcome committee of one in the bathroom." She told him about being trapped in the stall and the warning that had been issued. "I checked the restaurant but didn't see the color of top they wore."

"Call Jane. I'm going to see if there's anyone matching that description in the parking lot." He leaped to his feet and rushed for the side of the restaurant.

Paradise called Jane and left a message on her voice mail. By the time Blake returned, she was beginning to feel less vulnerable and shaky.

He dropped into his chair and took her hand. "No one was out there. Clearly this is someone who knew you from when you were a teenager. This has to be connected to the murders."

She took comfort from his warm fingers. The shivers didn't seem to want to leave her. "There's one other thing it could be related to."

He searched her face and realization dawned in his eyes. "The search for your brother. Everything ramped up with that. As soon as you sent off that DNA, things started happening."

"But it makes no sense. When I find him he can tell me whether or not he's interested in meeting me. Where's the danger in that?"

"We don't know what we don't know. I think you're onto something though. Someone doesn't want him found. It might not even be Andrew who is trying to discourage your search."

A thought found its way to her tongue. "What if Andrew is dead and someone doesn't want me to know? What if whoever killed my parents killed him too?" She rubbed her head. "That's crazy, isn't it?"

"But he was adopted. Your mom got letters from his adoptive parents." A frown settled between his blue eyes. "I think the priority should be on finding Andrew. That feels right. We can work on your parents' murders once he's found."

She nodded, relieved he was tracking with her. "Our romantic evening got derailed."

His thumb made lazy circles in her palm. "I have you all to myself, so I wouldn't say it's completely derailed. And we're about to have grilled oysters, so that's a plus. I'll take you home and we can make a plan of action."

"You always do that."

"What?"

She smiled. "You always know what to say to give me hope."

"God has plenty of hope to pass around."

A quote from *The Two Towers* by Tolkien came to mind. "'You can only come to morning through the shadows.'"

He grinned. "Exactly."

The server came with their drinks, and Paradise forced away her worries. Blake was right—there was always hope. And she was determined not to stop until she found out the truth.

CHAPTER 13

A FULL TRUCK OF visitors always made for a fun day. Blake was able to put aside his worries about the murder on park property as well as the "surprise" left in Paradise's car. Her stressful day was likely to blame for her irritation with him last night.

A large homeschooling group occupied most of the seats, and he drove into the fenced Serengeti preserve. Animals roamed the acreage freely. One boy chattered about having seen a rhino sleeping under a tree this morning, and he exchanged an amused glance with the kid's mom. "Are you learning about rhinos in school?"

The boy nodded. "Did you know their horn is made of keratin and not bone? It's like hair and fingernails."

"You're right," Blake agreed.

"I didn't get a good look at the one this morning. I was too scared it would see me and charge." The boy pointed. "Zebras!"

All the kids squealed when several ostriches ran alongside the truck. The giraffes and zebras moseyed over as well, and he parked to hand out fronds to feed the giraffes. The tall animals lumbered over to stick their heads in the windowless openings of the safari truck, and one of the girls squealed when a giraffe licked her with its long tongue. The chatter rose to deafening proportions as kids vied for the best spots to interact with the animals.

It was part of a normal day's work, and he loved seeing the kids' excitement at simple things like animal dung. He parked and moved the large steps into place for his guests to disembark. Most of the moms stuffed tips into the coffee can by the door as they exited, and he thanked them. He high-fived several of the boys as they finally got off the vehicle. The group moved toward the parking lot to their vehicles.

His phone dinged with a message from his mom. *Can you get here ASAP? Dozer is missing!*

He bit back a gasp. He'd thought the boy was playacting. He shot a text saying he was on his way and started driving for the Serengeti exit. The rhino enclosure wasn't far. Maybe he should walk and look for Dozer along the way. The boy said he had been sleeping under a tree. Blake should have asked more questions.

Dozer was normally a calm rhino and enjoyed rubs and attention. This was the first time he'd escaped. Blake shot Evan a text and asked him to find out how the rhino got out of his enclosure and to repair any damage. Blake grabbed a tranq rifle and a rope from the truck, then headed for the open field behind the tree line.

His mother came around a curve in the inside walkway and spotted him. "Thank goodness you're here. I had our employees close the park and start evacuating visitors. I told them not to mention the reason."

"Good. The last thing we need is more grist for the rumor mill to impact our bottom line. I'll find him first, and then we can form a perimeter with park vehicles to guide him back to the enclosure." He spotted Evan in the distance and waved him over. "Any sign of him?"

Evan shook his head. "Not yet. There's a break in the electric fence, so I called and asked Clark to fix it pronto."

"Great, now let's find Dozer."

Evan nodded. "I'll take the west quadrant." He grabbed a catch pole and headed for the park's vehicle lot.

Blake turned back toward the tree line. A stiff breeze from an approaching storm moaned through the eaves of the building and rustled the leaves of the trees. As he headed toward the field, he saw Clark talking with Mason Taylor, a fourteen-year-old volunteer, near the lemur enclosure. The boy sat in his wheelchair with a drone on his lap, and he petted Clark's German shepherds as he and Clark talked. The boy was always so enthusiastic about the animals, and everyone loved having him around.

From the right Paradise exited her car and approached the two. She still wore her pale green clinic uniform, and Blake doubted she knew about the rhino escape. She reached Mason and Clark and stood talking to them. Blake's smile faltered when he saw movement just past the trees in the field.

Dozer snorted and swung his head toward Clark and Paradise when she laughed. The rhino charged a few feet and stopped at the tree line.

"Don't move!" he shouted as he ran that way. The wind snatched his words away, and they still smiled and talked.

Blake cupped his hands. "Don't move! Escaped rhino!"

Paradise turned her head toward him, and her eyes went wide. Blake held up his hands as he neared. "Stay relaxed with no sudden moves. Clark, get in your truck and try to herd the rhino toward the enclosure. He's unusually agitated, so move slowly. Paradise, you stay with Mason."

Mason glanced over. "Let me help, Blake. Dozer likes me. I take him snacks and scratch his backside every day."

"I can't let you put yourself in harm's way. If you stay with Paradise, it might protect her." The boy would probably see through Blake's ploy to keep him safe, but Blake didn't wait to argue.

Dozer circled again and charged at a tree. Rhinos had very poor eyesight, and being in the open field had disoriented the big fellow.

Thunder rumbled in the distance, and the first few drops of cold rain fell. Clark backed toward his truck and got in. The vehicle rolled slowly toward the rhino, and Blake waved his arms to distract Dozer. "Hey, big guy. Want a back rub?" The massive animal snorted again before starting to trot toward Blake. There was no charging, so he must have recognized Blake's friendly voice.

Evan arrived in one of the big safari trucks and parked along the path toward the rhino enclosure to direct Dozer the right way. Blake texted him to stay in the vehicle.

Blake's pulse rose as he neared the animal. "Hey, Dozer. I'll bet you're ready for dinner. Want to come with me?" He reached out and rubbed the animal's shoulder. "Let's go home." He slipped the rope around the animal's massive neck, and Dozer let him lead him toward the gate.

This could have ended badly. Blake breathed a sigh of relief when he got Dozer inside the enclosure safe and sound.

Blake exited the medical building with Paradise and stood listening. Night had cloaked the park with shadows that grudgingly moved away from the security lights. In the dark the sounds of the animals had always made him feel one with the park residents: The screeches of the monkeys, the high-pitched yips of the fennec foxes, the shuffling splashes of the rhino and water buffalo in the pond, and the chirping of the otters all combined to give the park a sense of harmony.

But those soothing, homey sounds tonight were a reminder that everything was not as it seemed. His sense of peace was gone, and he wasn't sure how to regain it.

Paradise took his hand. "Are you okay?"

"I don't know how to fight this, babe. Every time I think we're over the sabotage, something else goes wrong. Even though Dozer got out on his own, the park evacuation is sure to cause chatter in the community. There's no way to get our feet under us again with these constant problems. And the snake and USB drive left in your car worry me even more."

Everything depended on him, and right now the burden seemed more than he could carry. Yet he had to shoulder it and move on. Somehow. This place was home for all of them, and he loved the animals in their charge. So did Mom and the boys. He didn't see them ever being truly happy if the park failed. And who was trying to frighten Paradise?

She stepped close and slipped her arms around his waist to lean against his chest. Her fragrance blended with the scent of newly mown grass in the field to their left. Her wordless comfort soothed him more than anything else could right now. They were together and she'd forgiven him, which was more than he'd ever hoped for. Dreams did come true, and God still performed miracles. That's what he was asking for now—another miracle.

She lifted her head. "Hey, I just thought about Mason and his drones. I think he takes pictures with them. What if he happened to pick up whoever left the stuff in my car? We should ask to look at his footage."

"That's a great idea." He kissed her. "He and his dad live in a trailer on the next road over. You game to go see him with me?"

"I left food out for the kittens, so they're fine. And my growling stomach will be fine as long as you feed me when we're done."

"We can run into town and get po'boys."

"Deal."

He relished the passion and tenderness in the kiss she gave him before stepping away. "We can go together in my truck, then stop by to grab your car on the way to town." He opened the truck door for her and she slid in.

It was a short drive to Mason and his father's trailer. It was a fifth wheel that had the truck end resting on cinder blocks, but the area around it was neat and clean. The shrubs were kept trimmed, and the wind fluttered the curtains in the windows, which were open to the night air. When they got out and approached the home, he heard someone playing a banjo. The sound floated out the screens. Was Mason or his father the musician?

"I've only met his dad once," Blake said in a low voice. "He came with Mason to ask if the boy could volunteer. Nice guy. He's a mechanic at the Chrysler dealership in town. His wife died in the accident that left Mason in the chair. He's staying here to save money to pay off a nice piece of land down near Pelican Harbor. The accident was his wife's fault—she'd been drinking."

"How terribly sad." Paradise squeezed his fingers as they went up the handicap ramp to the door. "He's clearly taking good care of Mason." She pressed the doorbell and the music stopped.

"Coming!" Mason called. "Dad, we've got visitors." The boy's voice was high with excitement.

Maybe they didn't get many visitors out here. The door opened and Blake smiled at Randy Taylor, an older version of his handsome, dark-haired son. Mason hadn't grown into the muscular, broad shoulders his dad possessed, but Blake saw the beginnings of the same physique in the boy.

Uncertainty flickered across Randy's face. "Blake, come in. Is everything okay? Mason told me about Dozer's escape."

Blake let Paradise slip through the door first before following her into a small but pristine living room that smelled of fresh popcorn. A banjo leaned against the navy sofa. "Dozer is safe and sound back in his habitat. Your son was so brave—he offered to go rub the rhino's back and soothe him. I appreciated the offer, but I couldn't let him do it." He smiled at Mason. "But there's something else I hope Mason can help us with."

"Me?" Mason gave a little bounce in his chair. "What can I do?"

"Paradise thought about how you love flying your drones. Do you fly over the park a lot?"

"Like all the time. The animals are different when I watch from the air. They're never scared, and I can see them loving life as they roam around."

"Do you take video or pictures?"

Mason nodded. "I have lots of both. That's okay, isn't it?"

"It's more than okay. Someone is trying to terrorize Paradise, and I thought your drone might have picked up who might be responsible. It might even show who shot Ivy with that tranquilizer dart. Could we look at what you've got?"

"I have lots of SD cards with pictures and video. You can take them to look at, but you'll give them back, right?"

"We'll make sure you get them all back." Blake nodded. "You started volunteering two weeks ago. Did you shoot video right away?"

"Yeah." Mason's gray eyes were anxious. "You're sure I'm not in trouble?"

"No trouble, just a lot of thanks."

"I'll get his stash." Randy returned a few moments later with a plastic storage container full of SD cards. "This will take you a while to get through."

Blake glanced at Paradise, who was smiling. Neither of them minded staying up late in each other's company to check out this lead.

CHAPTER 14

THE VIDEO BEGAN TO play on the laptop in Paradise's living room, and she nestled against Blake on the sofa to watch it. The black kitten on her lap she'd named Merlin, and the mostly white one sleeping on her foot was Luna. "The view from the drone is incredible. I think I'll use some of this footage for social media. He got some great shots of the white tigers in the water with the trainers."

The video showed a white tiger leaping for a balloon as it played with Evan, and Paradise couldn't stop the shiver that traveled down her spine. That would never be her "playing" with a big cat. She pointed out Mason in his wheelchair with the controller in his hands. The boy's enthralled expression made her smile.

Blake poked a finger at the screen. "Look there. Is that someone with binoculars?"

She squinted at the figure crouched behind a water trough outside a shelter in the African safari enclosure. "There's something in his hand, though I can't quite tell what it is. Or even if the person is male or female." A hoodie covered the man or woman's head and hung down over jeans. "I think it might be binoculars. They appear to be focused on the big cat habitats."

The video blanked out for a few seconds before changing as the drone moved from the white tigers to the pond where the otters lived. She spotted Mason in his chair again near a park bench along the stone sidewalk. The picture grew closer and sharper as the camera angle zoomed down to show the otters frolicking on the grass by the water. "Fast-forward," Paradise said. "See if you can find that guy who was watching the big cats."

Blake nodded and the speed of the video picked up. The camera angle changed again to higher above the park and panned back toward the shelter's roof in the safari area again. Zebras strolled after a bus that lumbered through the double gates, and two giraffes hurried toward the leaves waving outside the open windows of the vehicle. Paradise watched tourists feed the animals before the drone lifted higher in the sky and moved closer to the shed and water trough where they'd seen the figure.

"He's gone," Blake said. "But he left the binoculars behind."

She spotted them on the lip of the trough. "This was recorded the morning of Ivy's death. We should see if they're still there. Maybe they have fingerprints or DNA evidence on them."

"I doubt they're still there, but we can check. A curious zebra probably carried them off by now." Blake ejected the card from the portable device attached to the laptop. "See if you can find a video closer to the time she died. Maybe late the night before."

Paradise flipped through the container of SD cards, each one carefully printed by date and time. "Here's one. It's 10:00 p.m. on February 14, the night before her death."

He took it from her and put it in the laptop, then hit Play. The video was surprisingly clear. "Looks like Mason used a night-vision camera."

The recorded scenes showed Raj walking through the enclosure to the steps leading up to the zip line platform. The big tiger urinated on the stairs before padding over to plop down beside a tree and pond. The drone hovered over the big cat for a few seconds before panning over toward the barn where the tiger took shelter in bad weather.

Paradise studied the lock on the inner gate and touched it on the screen. "Look, Blake, is that gate standing ajar? I don't think it's locked."

He froze the video in place, then zoomed in. "You're right. It's standing open about two inches. Either someone forgot to lock it or left it unlatched on purpose. Is there a video just before this one?"

Paradise checked and handed him one. "This was taken at eight p.m." Her pulse accelerated and her breath quickened. Were they about to find out who had murdered Ivy? The elusive answers had to be out there.

The video flickered by quickly as Blake fast-forwarded through scenes of animals sleeping or roaming about. He stopped once when a figure leaped from the barn, but it was just a tiger wandering over to get a drink at the pond. Paradise glanced at the time: 9:44 with only another fifteen minutes of footage left.

A figure on a bicycle came into view from the left side of the screen. That same hoodie covered the person's head. The hands on the bike's handlebars appeared male. Strong fingers squeezed the brakes, and then the guy dismounted, lowered the kickstand, and walked with purposeful steps to the first lock.

He inserted a key and was inside the first enclosure, then went to the next and unlocked it as well. He left it standing ajar and hurriedly turned back when a female tiger rose and padded toward him to investigate. As he slipped through the outer gate and locked it, he looked up to the sky, and the drone captured his face.

Paradise often saw that face in her nightmares, and at first her mind refused to believe it. She gasped at the same time as Blake when Mr. Adams's features came into sharp focus. The foster dad who'd tried to molest her had been handsome once, but though the years had slackened his jaw and softened his neck, she'd never forget that face.

Lloyd Adams should not be in town. As far as Blake knew, the family had left under a cloud of shame and scandal over his treatment of Paradise. "The last I heard, they moved to Birmingham." Blake had followed them for a while, and it had upset him that Adams had gotten a good job as if it didn't matter that he'd nearly ruined Paradise's life.

Paradise's amber eyes flashed, and she rose to pace her small living room with the black kitten in her arms. "And for him to be *here*, he has to have some plan. Why would he sabotage the gate? It doesn't seem like it can only be about me. I'm not a predator keeper but a vet. It would have been a fluke for me to have gone into that pen. So what is going on?"

"Maybe he hired Ivy. Karen Cook said it was someone from your past who was curious what you were up to." Had Adams wanted to eliminate the possibility of Ivy telling anyone he'd hired her? But what could make murder a viable option to silence her about such a small thing? It wasn't against the law to gather information about someone.

Blake kept his thoughts to himself. The worry line between Paradise's brows told him she didn't need more on her plate.

Adams being around was a danger Blake didn't like, but he couldn't change the situation.

He struggled to control his desire to protect her. She'd made it clear she wanted—and needed—to stand and face the dangers on her own. Failing her was his biggest fear, but it was his problem, not hers. She didn't need to deal with that as well as the real danger Adams presented.

Just how dangerous was the man? If Hez hadn't just been conked on the head, Blake would've talked to him about it.

Paradise held Merlin to her chest, and the black furball began to purr loudly enough for Blake to hear. Paradise settled back on the sofa beside him. The tight line of her back softened and she sighed. "I wish we could let Jane know about this. Calling Greene won't do much good, but we have to give him the evidence. Maybe he'll arrest Adams."

"We can tell Jane about him first. I'll make a copy of this video and email it to her before we tell Greene. He'll whisk these SD cards away and we might never see them again. Mason won't be happy to have them tied up in evidence."

"We could make copies for him, put them all on a big hard drive maybe. I have one here. Let me find it." She rose and went down the hall.

If only Greene was someone they could trust to really pursue this lead to find the truth. He would likely toss the videos in a box and never look at them again.

Paradise returned with a hard drive. "It's empty. Let's download all of the SD cards onto it, and we can give it to Mason while he's waiting for his original SD cards to make their way back to him."

One by one Blake downloaded the box of SD cards onto the drive before uploading them onto his computer and the cloud.

"We'll watch all of them eventually." He ejected the last one and dropped it into the box. "I'd better call Greene." Her scent enticed him, and he leaned in to brush his lips across hers. "I needed a little fortification first."

"It might not be enough. Let's try one more time." She caressed his cheek with her hand and leaned in for a more tender kiss. "I'll admit that seeing Adams's face again after all these years scares me. I'm glad we've got lots of locks on this place."

The fact she admitted it made his gut twist. She never liked to show fear. "It disturbs me more than a little. I wish you'd come home with me tonight. The boys would be overjoyed."

She hesitated before shaking her head. "I'm not fifteen anymore. And I'm armed now—not just with a gun and a tranq pistol but with knowledge and confidence. He won't push me around. And he may not even be in town. He could have come to town, killed Ivy, then headed out for parts unknown."

Overconfidence could be fatal. "Or he could still be here. He's six-two and two hundred pounds, babe. If he comes around, don't let him come close."

Her gaze went far away. "I wonder if his wife is still with him."

"I heard she left him after his behavior came out."

They didn't have kids. To the community, they presented the image of a model couple who cared about hurting kids. Until the man showed his true character—a monster hiding behind a pious mask.

She touched his chin. "Your face is getting red. You can't fix everything evil in the world, Blake. All that weight doesn't rest on your shoulders."

He forced a smile. "I have to remind myself of that a lot. I know I'm not God, but I hate injustice. I want to fix things, but I'm more apt to make them worse the way I did with your situation."

"It was the system. In a perfect world I wouldn't have had to take the punishment for his aberrations. I should have had the weight of law on my side, but CPS wanted to hide it all under the rug. They didn't want me to talk about it, and when I refused to shut up, they wanted me out of town. It wasn't your fault."

He smiled. "That's a big change—you blamed me when you came back to town."

She cupped his face in her palm. "I'm sorry about that now. I was hurt and angry, still looking for someone to blame. You helped me see we can't change other people or prevent bad things from happening, but we can choose how we react and shoulder the blame that's pointing our way. It's easier to play the victim, and that's what I did for years. I held my anger and pain like a shield when it was really a prison. I'm glad God set me free from that."

She released his face, then reached for his phone and handed it to him. "It's already eight. If you delay calling Greene any longer, we'll be too tired to work tomorrow by the time he's done with us."

Blake grimaced and took the phone from her. "I know his number by heart, and that's a sad commentary on how life has been lately. I want to send the video to Jane first in case Greene comes in here throwing his weight around." He opened an email and attached the link to the online video before sending it to Jane. "I'll call Greene. Wish me luck."

"He can only yell. His words or actions won't break us or change anything." Her gaze softened. "Why does he hate you so much?"

"I think maybe he's jealous." He wrapped one of her curls around his finger. "If you looked at him the way you look at me, I'd be jealous."

"He's married and shouldn't be hitting on other women. I wonder if his wife knows."

The way her expression hardened alarmed him. "Don't make any calls to her. The last thing we need is for him to become deranged and come gunning for you. I can handle him."

He dialed Greene's number. "Pray for me."

"Always," she said softly.

CHAPTER 15

WE'RE MISSING SOMETHING. PARADISE punched her pillow and glanced at the clock: 2:00 a.m. The pain in her shoulder hadn't been conducive to sleep either. She'd soaked it in the bath and iced it, but it still throbbed.

Greene had been every bit as difficult as they'd feared, and it was after eleven when Blake left and she crawled into bed. Watching all that film data had felt a little creepy, and she was jumpy. She should have let Blake sleep on the sofa. He'd offered, but she thought she'd be fine.

The kittens curled by her feet, and she rolled onto her side and closed her eyes to practice deep breathing. Six would come way too soon. A memory slammed into her before she could drift off to sleep.

It was dark, so dark. Paradise crouched in the closet with her Rosyshine CuddleBrite puppy clutched to her chest. She could barely hear through her heart pounding in her ears.

She wished Mama was still with her reading Paradise's favorite story, Where the Wild Things Are, *but the door opened, didn't it? She clutched her stuffie and burrowed in the back of the closet where she could smell the vanilla sachet her mom had put in last week.*

She rocked back and forth and whisper-sang the little ditty her mother had taught her. "No monsters under my bed, not with angels watching my head. No monsters under my bed, not with angels watching my head."

The song failed to drive away the terror that encased her like ice. She swallowed hard and tried to make sense of what had just happened. Mama whispered for her to hide, and Paradise had done just that. She slipped out the side of the bed farthest from the door and slid under the bed.

She saw her mother's bare feet hit the carpet and saw a baseball bat leaning in the corner lift away before Mama's toes turned to face the door.

Paradise slid out on the floor on the other side and crawled into the back of the closet. She closed her eyes and covered her ears when Mama screamed, but the sound of a smack of the ball bat penetrated anyway.

Paradise covered her head with her hands and stifled the scream trying to bubble up from inside.

And waited for the man to find her. But he never came.

Paradise struggled to remember the man's face as he'd come through her bedroom door but failed.

She sat up and wiped away the tears streaming down her cheeks. It was the most detail of that terrible night she'd remembered so far. The man's face eluded her, but she knew he'd been slim and strong. Not big and bulky like Sheriff Davis. And her mother had picked up the baseball bat. He must have taken it from her and used it on her and Paradise's father.

But nothing had been her fault, so why did she feel such a sense of guilt? She'd been nine and no match for a grown man.

There would be no sleep now. Paradise got out of bed and went to the kitchen for some cheese and crackers. Maybe a bit of food would calm down the way her heart threatened to beat right out of her chest.

She so desperately wanted to remember, to bring the murderer to justice. This small memory was an encouragement, but it wasn't enough. She had to remember that face.

Blake had bought cubes of cheddar and her favorite crackers, so she prepared a plate and ate on the sofa without tasting the food. The kittens, delighted she was up, played around her feet. Did all of this even connect, or was everything happening separately? She didn't see any threads of the current events connecting to the murders, but the danger had ramped up when she'd tried to find her brother.

Chad from the DNA center hadn't returned her call yet from the other morning, and she made a note on her phone to try calling again when the place opened. He'd been so responsive before, and it was odd he hadn't called her back, but maybe he was out of the office. Someone else might be able to help, though, if she couldn't get him. She wanted to figure this out.

She hugged herself and wished she could talk to Blake, but he should be sleeping. She opened the Photos app on her phone and scrolled through all the pictures she'd taken since she came to The Sanctuary. Every picture was a precious reminder that no matter how events changed minute by minute, her life here held fresh and new adventures. Jenna had sent her a shot she'd taken of Paradise staring up at Blake and him looking down at her. The love on both their faces brought a lump to her throat.

She sighed and put the phone down to carry the plate back to the kitchen. Merlin put one black paw on her foot, and she paused to extricate it so she didn't step on him. A creak came from the outside entry steps. Without stopping to think, she raced for her bedroom and snatched up the SIG Sauer in her bedside drawer, then stood in her bedroom a moment to gather her courage. She slipped to the door and peered back into the living room. The door was closed, and she heard nothing more until a message pinged on her phone.

She kept her gun up and ready as she went to get her phone on the coffee table. It was a message from Blake. *Are you up? I saw the lights on. I'm outside on the steps.*

Her limbs loosened. Blake was here. Why wasn't he home in bed? She rushed to the door and threw it open before launching herself into his arms. "You scared me. I heard your feet on the steps."

His strong arms sheltered her, and he held her close before glancing around and leading her back into the apartment. "I was trying to sleep in my truck. I didn't like leaving you alone now that we know Adams is around."

Ever the protector. She both loved that he was eager to protect her and hated that she needed protection when she wanted to stand on her own. He'd never thought she could hold her own against Adams, and maybe she was fooling herself that she was sure she could.

⁓

By 3:00 p.m. Blake was feeling the effects of very little sleep last night. He'd spent 2:30 to 5:00 a.m. on Paradise's too-short sofa, and he didn't think he'd closed his eyes. But at least she was safe.

This morning he'd also found the binoculars left behind by the intruder and had asked an employee to run them to Jane. Maybe they would provide some kind of information.

He parked the safari vehicle in the utility truck lot and chatted with his passengers as they disembarked and left tips in the coffee tin. Several had been generous, and his small stash of cash for an engagement ring was growing. Still not enough, but he had to start somewhere.

Most of his salary he redirected back into the business. The fear in his mom's eyes had been increasing, and he wanted to do what he could to lessen her worry about the future. What would any of them do if they lost The Sanctuary? A couple of donations had come in this past week, but it still wasn't enough to overcome the bad publicity Ivy's death had brought to the park.

He gathered the tips from the can and stuffed the cash in his pocket. His phone dinged with a message, and his pulse blipped when he read what his cousin Hez had sent over.

Interesting soil test report. Need to talk ASAP. Come by the hospital when you get a minute.

Blake had had a slim hope the test would reveal another source of income for Mom and the park. Could it be happening? He texted back that he would come as soon as he could, then jogged past the amphitheater to listen in on Paradise's informative talk on lemurs. He stopped behind the bleachers and watched her interact with the lemurs.

A group of children from a local elementary school pressed close to the three-foot-high fence. The lemurs were always popular, and Blake had loved them since he first saw one at age three. Paradise had brought in the new babies, and he itched to hold one himself.

Paradise caught a glimpse of him and smiled. "Here's our resident lemur expert, Mr. Blake Lawson. Come join us, Blake."

Caught. He smiled and strode past the bleachers and into the amphitheater with her and the two primate keepers. He faced the audience. "Anyone know how old these babies are?"

A boy in the front row shot up his hand. "Over two months? They aren't on their mom's back right now."

"Very good. Mom mostly carries them around on her back until they turn two months old and start exploring. And they're also starting to snatch bites of fruit like the older lemurs. Where are lemurs found in the wild?" He suspected they all knew that, and many hands waved in the air with shouts of "Madagascar!" Thanks to the movie, most people knew that one. "They're very endangered, and we're lucky they breed well in captivity. What exactly are lemurs?"

"They're primates," a girl in the back called out.

"They're more than just primates—they're a type of prosimian, which means they came before monkeys and apes. They're super smart and live in troops. We call a group of lemurs a conspiracy." He pointed out a lemur grooming another one. "Lemurs are the only primates to have special tools for grooming each other. They use an elongated nail on the second toe, called a grooming claw, and finely spaced teeth, referred to as a toothcomb, for grooming." He paused to let the audience watch the activity. "Do you know what the word *lemur* means?"

The kids looked at one another and said nothing. One of the moms seemed to start to raise her hand, then put it back down.

"It means 'spirits of the night.'" The phrase made him think of *The Phantom of the Opera.* Could there be any connection? He turned the lecture back over to Paradise and settled on the ground for the young lemurs to come over and interact with him.

A dominant female was in charge of each troop, and the babies waited for permission from Mama to approach. It didn't take long because Mom Loki adored him. He let the lemurs scamper around his lap and climb up his head, much to the delight of the kids.

Paradise ended the lecture, and he glanced at the time. He needed to go see Hez, so he dusted off his shorts before approaching Paradise. "Do you have time to come with me to see Hez in the hospital? He says there's something interesting about the soil tests that just came back."

"I'm done for the day."

He took her hand and they strolled toward his truck. "You don't even look tired."

She squeezed his fingers. "I probably got more sleep than you did."

"Hez wants to talk to me about the rare earth report. Trust him to be taking care of us even while injured. Thanks for coming with me."

"I'd go anywhere with you."

The one place he really wanted to take her was to the altar, but that had to wait.

CHAPTER 16

BLAKE WINCED WHEN HE saw Hez sitting in the chair beside the hospital bed. One side of his head had no hair, and the shaved scalp held bruises. "This could wait, buddy."

Dressed in khaki pants and a light blue shirt, his cousin waved a folder in his direction. "This couldn't wait. Shut the door. I don't want to be overheard."

Blake and Paradise exchanged a troubled glance, and she shut the door behind them before walking closer to Hez. "You should be resting."

"I'm tired of resting, and the fog is finally lifting where I can think. This is incredible news." Hez opened the folder to extract a sheaf of papers. "There are some gas and oil on the property, but they don't mean much."

Blake's optimism faltered, and he stepped forward to study the report. "I'd hoped they might help our financial situation."

"This other discovery means much more than oil or gas deposits, and you'll want to keep it quiet, at least for now." Hez touched a finger to a paragraph near the bottom of the report. "There are rare earth elements here, guys. And they're worth more money than you can even imagine."

"What are rare earth elements?" Paradise asked. "It's a vaguely familiar phrase, but I can't quite remember what it means."

"There are seventeen heavy metals that are extremely valuable because they're used in a lot of electronic components. They aren't really rare—but it took a long time to isolate them. Right now 81 percent of the world's rare earth is mined in China, so finding some in the US is a big deal."

Blake struggled to understand it all, but the dawning joy on Paradise's face was more important than anything right now. She clung to his hand, and he looked down at her with the hope that their marriage might not have to be put off too much longer.

Blake took the paper and read through it. "What do you think it's worth?"

"Many millions."

Blake's chest squeezed, and he glanced at Paradise. "But we'd have to sell the property."

"Yes, but you'd be able to buy more property outright and build it out to your specs. A discovery like this changes everything."

"I'm not sure Mom would want to sell and move. It's not like packing up a household and moving a few miles way. We're talking hundreds of wild animals. The construction at the new place boggles the mind to think about."

"True, but I've heard you complain about outdated buildings and security features. You could have state-of-the-art everything." Hez's blue eyes flashed with enthusiasm until he winced and touched his head. "I need to not get so excited, but it's hard when I think about what this means for Aunt Jenna and the boys. You, too, of course, but I worry about her."

"I'll tell her, but Mom's idea of the expedient road is to wait on God, and I have a feeling this won't be any different. The Almighty himself might have to speak in an audible voice before she'd sell the place. I could be wrong, but we'll see."

Hez's color waned by the moment, and Blake took Paradise's hand. "Savannah would skin us alive if she saw you out of bed. If we want to live, we'd better let you rest."

"I might need a nap." Hez gave a half smile.

Blake might need a nap before he told his mom about this.

Hez's bombshell rattled Paradise. She couldn't imagine leaving this place now. "I can fix a salad." The sounds of cartoons playing on TV came faintly from the living room. Blake's deep voice explained the history of the old Popeye cartoons to his little brothers. He hadn't told Jenna about the rare earth yet, but Paradise planned to.

"Blake did it. It's in the fridge." Jenna set a pan of lasagna on the counter. "So what did Jane say about Adams being here opening the gates?"

The breather of another topic appealed to Paradise as well. She stayed close to the oven to be able to check the breadsticks in another couple of minutes. "She doesn't have jurisdiction here, so she can only ask for information. She's going to check with Rod about the investigation. Greene was there for hours with his same innuendos and sneers. I didn't want to call him, but we had no choice." She hadn't dared to tell Blake what she wanted to do, but Jenna might understand. "I thought about going to see Adams myself."

Jenna set down the stack of plates in her hands. "Paradise,

that would be so hard. Have you talked to him since you left here?"

"I haven't seen him since CPS removed me from his house. Well, at least in person. Seeing his face on the video shook me."

"He was trespassing on our property, and that's likely the least of his crimes. If he unlocked the gate, it's likely he also shot Ivy with the tranquilizer gun. What would you gain by talking to him?"

Paradise shrugged. "Closure maybe. I'm not sure why I want to talk to him."

"Have you been able to find out anything about him since he left town?"

"Blake thought he and his wife broke up, but if that's true, they must have gotten back together. They're both listed as owners of a house in Birmingham."

Jenna touched Paradise's hand. "I hear the fear in your voice. I know you hoped never to face him again."

"I don't want to now, but I think the shock might shake some truth out of him that he wouldn't tell anyone else."

"I'm sure he thought no one had seen him."

Paradise checked the breadsticks, which were golden brown and perfect. She opened the oven and put them on top of the stove. She'd skipped lunch, and the yeasty-garlicky odor made her mouth water.

Blake had suggested she tell Jenna the news about the rare earth. He didn't want it to apply pressure to his mom. "Jenna, Hez dropped some news. There are minerals under your land, something called rare earth, and they're worth a lot of money."

"I've never heard of rare earth." She listened to Paradise's abbreviated explanation and what it could mean for The Sanctuary. "I'm not sure I believe it."

"Hez thought you'd be excited," Paradise said.

Jenna added more oregano to the sauce. "I don't know what to think. If it's incredibly valuable, The Sanctuary will be saved for generations. But we'd have to move to get it. There are a lot of things to consider."

Paradise handed her the salt. "I know you're very attached to this place—I am too—but there are large tracts of land you could buy and develop for the animals if you needed to. You'd have the money to build from scratch."

Jenna's gaze went out the window toward the buildings in the distance. "Hank and I built this together. I don't know if I could leave it."

"I'll bet Frank would help you find the right property if it became necessary. You two have been seeing each other a little while now. It seems to be going well."

Jenna's cheeks reddened. "I enjoy being with Frank, but I feel guilty about it sometimes. I loved Hank so much."

"You're still young, Jenna. Hank would want you to have a happy, fulfilled life."

"I have my boys."

"And they're great—I love them, too, all three of them. But your little ones will be grown before you can blink. They'll always love you, but the house will be empty. There's nothing wrong with finding someone to share your life with."

Jenna smiled. "And what about your plans if this rare earth thing pans out? Blake isn't fooling me with his 'need to take it slow' talk. He'd swoop you up and marry you in a heartbeat if he wasn't worried about providing for me and the boys. I see the financials, and I know how thin our margins are. My boy doesn't even cash all his checks—he plows most of his earnings back into the business, and what he does cash, he spends on groceries around here."

This time Paradise's cheeks warmed. "I don't want to get married until I find out what happened to my parents. It's important to me, and if I start a new life, I'm afraid I'll forget all about it."

"Maybe that's for the best, Paradise. You may never be able to get to the truth. I'd hate to see you put the brakes on your life while you're searching for something you may never find."

Paradise moved the breadsticks to a plate and carried it to the table. How would she feel if she never knew the truth? "I don't know if I can live like that, Jenna. Never sure if the killer will strike at me next. Blake and I want kids. How could we bring children into a world where some nameless, faceless maniac might strike in the night?" She shuddered and hugged herself. "I have to find out what happened."

"I get it, Paradise. I've suffered through my share of loss as well. When Blake's father died, I was mad at God and bitter at life. I vowed never to go through that again, but if I'd let that fear paralyze me, I wouldn't have had those years with Hank. The thought of more children terrified me, too, but Hank showed me each day is a gift and so is life. I should have been the one to go first since Hank was younger than me, but that's not what happened. If we let fear control us, we miss out on the day-to-day things that make life rich and meaningful. Don't let that happen to you. You and Blake are so good together."

Paradise's tongue felt stuck to the roof of her mouth. Jenna had put her finger on the past fifteen years of Paradise's life. The fortress she'd built around her had been impenetrable to everyone but Blake, who knew how to scale the walls. She needed to dismantle them and welcome in whatever experiences God sent her way. But could she give up her quest? Maybe not even for Blake.

CHAPTER 17

THE RED FIREPOT HID along a small walkable alley, which explained why Blake didn't know of its existence in Nova Cambridge. Several candles emitting a patchouli scent fluttered from the breeze when he and Paradise stepped onto the tile floors of the shop. Colorful pottery lined open shelves and display cases throughout the small space. Pottery appeared to be sold here, not created.

Two women stood at the checkout talking to an older woman with red hair. Paradise nudged him. "That's the woman who used to play cards with my mom. What luck!"

"We'll browse while we wait for her to be free." He wandered over to a display of blue mugs. "I like these."

"Me too." She picked one up and showed him the attached tag. "The owner made them. Trisha Miller. I remember that name now. Mom called her Trish, and her husband was Wes. He called her Red. Maybe that's how she came up with the name of the pottery shop."

He set the mug back on the shelf. "I don't think I've met her."

The two women carried their bubble-wrapped pottery out of

the store with contented expressions, and Blake headed for the counter with Paradise. "Are you Trisha Miller?"

"Sure am."

Paradise inched forward with a smile. "I'm Paradise Alden, Becky's daughter."

Trisha gasped and came out from behind the counter. "My goodness, no wonder you looked familiar to me when you came in. You look so much like your mom. She was a great friend, and Wes and I still miss playing euchre with your parents. Those were great days. I saw the newspaper article about you opening Pawsome Paws. I planned to bring my dog Buster in for a checkup."

"I'd love to see him." Paradise fidgeted, then straightened. "How long were you and Mom friends?"

"Gosh, honey, years. We went to high school together. Wes and your daddy played football at USA together."

The University of South Alabama in Mobile played in NCAA Division I sports, so Granger Alden must have been a good athlete. And since the couple had been friends for years, Trisha might spill good information for Paradise. Blake kept quiet and let her lead the conversation, though he itched to pepper Trisha with questions. She might have an idea who killed Paradise's parents.

Paradise laced her fingers together. "Then you might know about something I recently discovered. Mom gave up a son for adoption."

The smile vanished from Trisha's face. "I've never talked about that, and it's not something I'm comfortable discussing. Your mom is gone, and there's no reason to dig up dirt."

"My parents are *dead*, Trish, and I have a brother out there. That's a big deal to me. It's not dirt on my mom—it's about finding my family."

"I promised your mom I wouldn't talk about it, not ever." Trisha moved back behind the counter.

"Do you know who adopted my brother? His name is Andrew. If Mom didn't want anyone to know, why would she keep all the information in a box? I think she planned to tell me someday."

"I doubt it. It would be too dangerous." Trisha's brown eyes went wide as if she wished she could call back the words.

"Dangerous? To whom?"

The older woman bit her lip. "Your brother's dad came from money, and talking about it wouldn't be wise. That's all I can say."

"I don't have to know who Andrew's father is—I just want to connect with him. Do you know where he lived growing up? Even a hint of how to find him would be wonderful."

"I'm sorry, Paradise." Trisha glanced at the clock on the wall. "I need to tend to some things in the back. I'm sorry I couldn't be helpful, but you should forget about it."

She would bolt any minute. Blake cleared his throat. "Did Becky ever talk about leaving Granger? We've heard rumors she might have been having an affair."

"You're not investigating that old murder by yourselves, are you? You must have a death wish. I don't want to be involved in any of it." She hustled toward the door to the back without a backward glance.

⁓

Another dead end. Paradise and Blake exited the alley, and she pointed out University Grounds. "I could use a pick-me-up. I'd hoped for a lot more from her." What kind of family connection could be so terrifying to Trish?

The aroma of espresso and steamed milk felt like a warm hug

when Paradise stepped into the coffee shop. They placed their orders and took their drinks outside to a patio table on the wide front porch. Paradise nursed her mocha with tiny sips while she contemplated what to do next. A customer across the street waved at her and another one honked as he drove by. Little by little she was becoming part of the community again.

She set her cup on the black iron table. "Every door I go through to try to find my brother gets slammed in my face. I don't get it."

Blake's brows rose. "That same thought crossed my mind. It feels like our efforts are scattered right now too. Do we find your brother or work on tracking down who killed your parents?"

Paradise ran her finger around the rim of her cup. She wanted both things, but it made sense to focus on one. "We have the murder at the park to figure out too—Greene won't get anywhere. And finding out Adams was the one who sabotaged the fence changed everything, don't you think? It feels like someone is trying to drive me away before I remember the night my parents were murdered. At first I thought someone didn't want me to find my brother, but maybe that's not it." She rubbed her head. "It's all so confusing."

Blake reached out and took her hand. "The attacks keep coming. I'm weary, and I know you are, too, but we have to keep going and figure this out. Someone wants you gone and the park closed. Why? We have to know or this won't end."

What he wasn't saying was that Greene seemed determined to pin a crime on Blake. The attacks on her were meant to scare her away. If Blake ended up being charged with murder, he wouldn't have the luxury of moving away and leaving it all behind. "The priority is the park. I got distracted by the crazy things like the snake in my car and creepy music. That's probably what the intruder wanted. The future of the park rests on finding out who killed Ivy. Greene will have you charged, tried, and convicted if we don't figure it out. Let's not lose our focus."

"I'm not so sure the person after you isn't dangerous though, babe. The snake wasn't a prank but an effort to harm you. I'd give up the park before I stood back and let someone hurt you. I'd even go to jail first."

She returned his squeeze on her fingers, and her eyes burned with the effort not to cry. Blake always put the people he loved first. His example of selflessness was something she wanted to follow. "I've come through it all unscathed. Here are my priorities. One, make sure the park is safe. Two, find my brother. I can't bring back my parents, but I can build a relationship with my only sibling. Three, bring whoever killed my parents to justice."

"And four, we start a new life with all this behind us."

A smile curved her lips. "We can't get through the others fast enough for me. I'm ready to step past all this."

"Me too," he said. "Me too."

<hr />

Paradise squatted beside the large red wolf, Czar, she'd just sedated. The rest of the wolf pack watched through the fence separating her and Blake from the inner and outer perimeters of the enclosure, and the wind carried their musky scent toward her. The winner of the fight that had caused the gash on Czar's flank seemed particularly interested in what they were doing.

She sterilized the wound and began to suture it. "We'll need to keep him crated with a cone for a few days. He won't like that."

The call from Blake about the injured wolf had come in before six, and Paradise had rushed immediately to the enclosure. The injury was deep and four inches long. She finished the sutures and put a cone around his neck, then Blake eased him into the large crate. It was sheltered from the sun by a large oak tree. She filled a water bowl for him and planned to withhold food for a few hours until she was sure his tummy was okay from the anesthesia.

Blake embraced her and kissed the tip of her nose. "You do good work, Dr. Alden."

She smiled and gave him a real kiss, one she felt clear down to her toes. The man had a way with kisses. Someone called his name, and he released her with obvious reluctance to turn toward the male voice.

Clark rolled toward them in the Gator. There was a figure in the passenger seat, but the sun was in Paradise's face and she couldn't see much more than it was a woman until Clark braked and she recognized the private investigator who had pretended to be a student at TGU. Nicole Iverson held her chin up and met Paradise's gaze with a challenging glint in her green eyes. The green hair was gone, replaced with a more natural brown shade. And a pantsuit replaced the casual college attire she'd worn last time.

Clark stepped from the Gator. "I found this lady wandering around in the back pasture. She'd cut the fence." His big hands were fisted at his sides, ready for any threat to Blake or Paradise.

"Thanks, Clark, I'll take it from here." Blake's expression went grim as his gaze swung to the woman. "Still looking for oil and gas, Ms. Iverson?"

She flinched and her smile faded at his use of her real name. She got out of her seat and stood with her shoulders squared and her chin up. "Not gas or oil. I think you know what you have out there, Mr. Lawson. Rare earth elements."

Paradise bit back a gasp at the woman's knowledge of the report. Clark eyed them all before getting back in the Gator to return to his job.

Blake tensed beside her, but he studied Nicole for a long moment before he put his hands on his hips and took a step closer to her. "Did you break into the house and see the report?"

"What? Of course not. I got the information the same way you did—with a soil sample."

"If you already got a soil sample, why were you in the field again?"

"I wanted to see if you knew what you had yet. I saw where your soil sample had been taken, so I planned to come see you anyway before your goon grabbed me." She rubbed her forearm.

"Cut the act," Blake said. "There's nothing wrong with your arm. Clark is a good man and was doing exactly what he was hired to do, which is take care of the property."

Nicole dropped her hand back to her side and stared back coolly. "Is there somewhere we could go to discuss the offer I'm prepared to make?"

"An offer for what?" Blake reached out to pull Paradise to his side. "And you can say whatever you have to say in front of Paradise. I don't have any secrets from her."

Nicole pressed her lips together. "I have a serious offer to purchase your property. Fifteen million dollars."

Blake's arm tightened around Paradise, and she could feel the tension in his body. An offer that high had to be tempting. They could purchase other land and build animal sheds, barns, and the other things a park would need.

He stepped back. "We aren't interested in selling."

"I'm sure we could raise that offer a bit. And my employer realizes the park is not doing well financially."

"Who is your employer?"

"I'm not at liberty to say. Can you really afford to turn down an offer this high? Surely you at least want to present it to your mother."

"My mother wants to sell even less than I do. I don't think any offer will sway her, but I'll tell her about it, of course."

Nicole extracted a business card from her leather bag and held it out. "Here's my contact information if you change your mind. And if you get another offer, we'd like to have the opportunity to increase ours."

Blake took the card but stared at Nicole. "You've told others about the rare earth?"

She raised a brow. "Of course not, but whoever ran your tests could have told someone. News like this rarely stays secret." The woman slid the strap on her bag up on her shoulder and walked toward the parking lot with brisk steps.

"Well, that was a surprise," Blake said.

"Fifteen million dollars. That's crazy, Blake, especially since you only have 120 acres."

"I'd like to know who her employer is."

And Jenna would have to hear of this offer.

CHAPTER 18

THE FEBRUARY AIR WAS warm on Blake's arms today. It was going to be a great day. A call had come through from Governor Amelia George's aide this morning that she was bringing her grandson Jackson to the park. There would be photographers along as well as security. The governor was running for reelection, and the park would make a great photo op for her to show her family side. Blake didn't mind because it would also be a great promo for the park.

He had told his mother about Nicole's offer to purchase the property last night, and she had refused to discuss leaving The Sanctuary. The excitement of today's visit would help ease his constant dithering about what to do.

He stood next to the ticket office with Paradise and waved in the entourage as they entered. The stink of gasoline burned his nose. The governor had requested a private safari, and she'd given a large donation to offset the disturbance her visit would cause.

"Why am I here?" Paradise whispered.

"She asked for the vet to come along in case Jackson had questions. I guess he has an interest in becoming a zoo veterinarian." He gave her a quick hug. "I was quick to say yes as long as she came when you were done in town. We don't get time like this together very often."

She smiled and adjusted her hat. They both wore shorts and safari shirts with the accompanying hats. They might as well look the part for the pictures.

"Has the governor ever been here before?" she asked.

"Not that I know of. I've never met her."

"Me neither, and it's exciting to have all this going on."

A black SUV cruised to a stop, and the driver stepped out to open the door for an elegant woman in her late fifties. A boy about Levi's age climbed out behind her. Blake had only seen the governor on TV dressed in a navy suit and sensible pumps, but today she wore designer jeans with boots and a long-sleeved blouse. Gray streaked her dark hair, and her green eyes were striking. She'd accomplished a lot of good in Alabama, and she was often on the news expounding measures she supported. She didn't seem to mind the reporters lining the vehicle.

She extended her hand with a warm smile. Her voice was a husky purr that was easy to listen to. An orator's voice. "Good to meet you, Blake. This is my grandson, Jackson." She touched the boy's dark hair. "He's eight."

"My brothers are five and seven."

The governor's eyes lit. "I should have asked if there were children who could come along. I suppose your brothers are in school though."

"Mom homeschools my brothers. I'm sure she'd allow them to accompany us. I'll text her." He tapped out a quick message to his mother before resuming his conversation with the governor. "We have a fun time planned, Governor. I'll show you around the park as well as behind-the-scenes areas that most guests never see. We'll break for lunch at one and let the kids help feed the animals. Later this afternoon there will be an educational time with our ring-tailed lemurs."

"I love lemurs!" Jackson said, beaming. "I told Gram I hoped you had lemurs."

Squeals of excitement came from behind them, and Blake didn't have to turn to know his brothers were rushing their way. They'd be thrilled about spending the day at the park. The boys reached the group, and Blake introduced the kids. Jackson began to pepper them with questions about living on an animal preserve.

Blake glanced around at the adults. The governor had brought two bodyguards, a photographer, and a woman the governor introduced as her aide, Angela Burns. He clasped her hand. "Ms. Burns." He guessed her age to be around sixty with her soft white hair that lay in a cap around her angular face.

Her shrewd blue eyes took in everything around her with keen interest. "Thank you for accommodating our last-minute request. Jackson is very excited. A visit here was the one thing he wanted for his eighth birthday."

"We're honored to hear that." He waited a few minutes while members of the press snapped pictures as well. "Everyone here?"

"Yes, we're ready when you are." The governor nodded at the man with the camera and tripods. "Make sure you get plenty of pictures of me with Jackson."

"You got it, Governor."

Blake led them to his best safari truck, though that wasn't saying much. The seats were cracked from use in places, but he kept the vehicle clean and in good running order. He put the steps into place alongside the high door on the vehicle. Three long rows of seats ran from front to back. The governor ascended with no assistance and took a place on the middle one once the children commandeered the seats along the window openings. Blake had already loaded the truck with a cooler packed with snacks as well as a box of green leaves for the Serengeti animals. So far the governor seemed pleasant enough. She wasn't putting on airs or ordering him around.

He exchanged a glance with Paradise, and she inclined her head in approval before she climbed into the back with the guests while he got behind the wheel. He clicked on the intercom. "First off, we'll visit a small version of what you might see in the Serengeti. You'll get a chance to feed giraffes, zebras, and wildebeest. They're very friendly, but don't get too close to the zebras. They can bite if you aren't careful. Toss the leaves to them and don't give them a chance."

With the rumble of the big engine and the vehicle jolting over ruts in the road, Blake wouldn't be able to hear questions well until they stopped, so he didn't try to make conversation. He drove to the first gate, and Paradise jumped out to open and lock it again after he rolled through before letting him in the second gate.

Once they were inside the acres devoted to the Serengeti wildlife, he cut the engine and turned on his mic. "The giraffe on your left is Carla. She's our oldest giraffe at twenty-five. She's also our friendliest. She'll lick you if you give her a chance. If you're brave, get a photo of her sloppy kiss."

He cut the mic and listened. The governor appeared to be on a call with someone, and he overheard the term *rare earth*. Should he take the opportunity to ask the governor what she knew about the valuable resources that might be under this property?

～

Rare earth. Paradise's head swiveled at the term, but the governor didn't notice her interest. She caught Blake's wide eyes in the rearview mirror. He gave a nod, and she nodded back. Maybe she could dig up some information.

Governor George ended the call and dropped her phone into her Hermès bag. She leaned close to her grandson for a photo op as Jackson shrieked with laughter when Carla stuck her head through the glassless window and licked him with her enormous tongue.

Her smile still in place, the governor moved out of reach from the dripping saliva. The photographer dodged the seats to catch shots from different angles and even stood on top of the back of the seat opposite the giraffe. Ms. Burns jotted several things down in a leather notebook.

The photographer looked at his camera and gave a thumbs-up. "Great pics, Governor."

She smiled and settled back on the middle seat, leaving the boys to clamber from opening to opening with food for the animals. Her grandson was enthralled with the peafowl spreading their feathers in a brilliant display.

"What do you call a group of peafowl?" Paradise asked.

Jackson frowned. "Peafowl?"

"Peacocks."

His brow cleared. "I don't know."

"They're called an ostentation or a muster. The female is called a peahen, and the male is the peacock. He's the most colorful one."

"I wish I could get a feather." Jackson leaned back on the seat.

"I'll see if I can find one when we get back," Paradise promised.

Blake started the engine and rolled slowly through the various wildlife to exit the enclosure. "We're going to stop at the lemur enclosure next."

"Yay!" all three boys yelled. They high-fived one another and rushed to the windows.

Blake drove to the next stop while Paradise tried to figure out how to ask the governor about her call. The older woman consulted her phone several times and tapped out a few texts while the children chattered around her. They'd quickly become friends and had exchanged a few Pokémon cards from their pockets. Isaac had even brought his card holder, and Jackson had bargained for Isaac's favorite card and succeeded in getting it just because he asked. Isaac was like that—his heart was as big as his big brother's.

The vehicle stopped before Paradise could ask the governor about rare earth. Maybe it was a sign she wasn't supposed to pry, but it felt like their best chance to find out something about what might be under the soil here. A woman like Governor George would know all about trade, worth, uses, and everything else they didn't know.

Paradise followed everyone out and prayed for the woman to mention the term again. The strong odor of the primates made her eyes water. The males must have had a stink fight.

Governor George posed for several pictures with her grandson, who was excitedly admiring the lemurs, before she settled on a bench and pulled out her phone when it rang. Paradise hovered close and nodded for Blake to keep an eye on the kids. She overheard that phrase again, and once the call ended, she sidled over and sat on the bench too.

"I couldn't help but overhear you mention something called rare earth. It sounds exotic."

The older woman smiled. "Rare earth elements are not as fancy as the term sounds. REE is used in things like batteries and magnets. They wouldn't be terribly important if China wasn't cornering the market on them. Such necessary elements put the US at a disadvantage for energy independence. Alabama is in a good position to be able to extract it from REE feedstocks like coal. We need new technology to do it though. It's costly to dig up and extract. We have to figure out cheaper ways to remove it from the earth and get it to market. It's one of the things I've been working on. You seem very interested."

"Just intrigued. I'd heard the term and wondered what it was." She wanted to reveal what they'd discovered, but it wasn't her news to share. If Blake or Jenna wanted to talk to the governor about it, they could. She'd make sure they knew Governor George had a particular interest in REE.

Paradise rose. "I have a surprise for the kids. There are new pups old enough to be handled. With your permission I'll let Jackson hold one."

"Wonderful!" The governor snapped her fingers at her aide and the photographer. "Get ready, she's getting a baby lemur for Jackson."

Paradise went to the barn where the babies were in a pen with their mother and grabbed a crate. "We won't hurt your little ones, Mama. You can come with us to make sure." Loki adored Levi. She would probably leave her babies to be with him.

The boys' eyes widened when they saw the pups in the carrier and Loki loping along with Paradise into the petting arena.

Levi leaped to his feet and made a call that sounded amazingly like the noise Loki made the instant she saw him. Paradise opened the gate for the boys to come in, and the mama lemur immediately loped to Levi.

He petted Loki with a gentle hand. "I haven't seen her in forever, Paradise. She didn't forget me."

"Of course she didn't. You're her favorite." The other boys squatted by the pups, who proceeded to crawl onto their shoes.

The photographer was snapping pictures constantly, and he

gestured for Governor George to join her grandson. Paradise let her in, and she settled on the ground with the pups around her. Paradise spotted the grin on Blake's face and knew he was thinking about the great PR this segment would bring. They might weather this storm after all.

"Paradise, this has your name on it," Levi called.

She turned to see him holding a music box with a monkey on top with cymbals. Her name was scrawled on a note on the side. "Where'd you find it?" It looked like one she used to own from *The Phantom of the Opera*, and it sent a sinister shudder down her back even though she'd loved the movie for years. She supposed there were many replicas.

"Loki found it and gave it to me."

Paradise hesitated before she took it. "Thanks." Opening it would have to wait until she was away from the children in case it contained something dangerous. For an instant she wanted to toss it into the bushes, but she couldn't do that. Why did it frighten her so much?

CHAPTER 19

LOBLOLLY PINE TREES SWAYED in the wind behind Blake and Paradise and showered them with their scent. Their guests had gone to enjoy the gourmet lunch the park had arranged for them. Blake stared at the music box in Paradise's hand. The paint was battered and old. The trinket shouldn't have filled him with trepidation, but his hand trembled when he reached for it. "It might be dangerous to open. Let me do it."

She took a step back, moving closer to the trees. "I'll do it, Blake." Her voice held a sharp edge.

Was he smothering her again? He curled his fingers into fists and bit back a reminder that he'd been in the midst of bullets flying and knew how to handle explosions. Why did she struggle so much against letting him take care of her? It wasn't that he felt she wasn't strong and capable—it was that he had more experience with objects that could turn dangerous.

She exhaled. "I'm sorry I snapped at you. This might be an important clue, and I want to see it for myself. At the end of the day, I want to know I did everything I could to get to the truth.

If I'm going to rid myself of the guilt that constantly haunts me, I have to do this myself. It's my burden, not yours."

They'd had such different upbringings—she'd been tossed from home to home, dragging her garbage bag of belongings with her. He'd always had the stability of his mother's love, while Paradise had never been sure of anything, even where she would sleep the next night. It was no wonder she felt she had to prove her worth.

He put his hands behind his back and nodded. "Is it heavy?"

She hefted it gently in her hand and nodded. "But the monkey with the cymbals is the heavy part."

"At least it's likely not a bomb then. Go ahead." Despite his outward show of confidence, he breathed a prayer for safety.

She turned it upside down. Taped to the bottom was an envelope with her name on it. Inside were two tickets, and Blake couldn't see them well enough to identify them. He held his peace and waited until Paradise smoothed them out on her palm.

"*The Phantom of the Opera* was playing in New Orleans, and I went with my mom. I watched the movie over and over again. I can still quote it by heart."

"Are the tickets from the showing in New Orleans?"

"No, they're from Broadway. I've always wanted to see it there."

"Whoever has been using the songs from the musical has to know how much you love it."

"That would be Abby and maybe Brittany."

"Brittany?"

"Caster. I heard she moved away for college and never came back."

"We could talk to Abby at the bank. Maybe she's heard something about Adams."

Paradise pulled out her phone and called up the Notes app.

"Here's what I know about the musical. It was developed by Andrew Lloyd Webber. The original stars were Michael Crawford and Sarah Brightman, who was married to Webber at the time. Steve Barton played Raoul. It opened at the West End in London in 1986 and on Broadway in 1988. I watched all the movies made from the novel. Lloyd wrote the score."

Blake didn't know much about the musical, but he tried to follow her details. "Webber went by Lloyd?"

"Yes, why?"

"Not a common name, and I immediately thought of Adams."

Her eyes went wide. "I always think of him as Mr. Adams. I never called him by his first name. He couldn't have anything to do with this, could he? And if he did, why would he point to himself?"

"It's probably nothing."

"Your suggestion to talk to Abby is great." She glanced at her watch. "She knows everyone in town, and she might know something about Adams. Lunch break is almost over, and she gets off at six. I'll be waiting outside the bank to talk to her."

"You might want to set up a private meeting so she's not Bad paragraph break.

"You're right. I wouldn't want her in a bull's-eye. I'll call the bank and see if we can meet."

"Maybe along the picnic area at Mary Ann Nelson Park, there by the bridge."

She nodded. "There's a big tree that screens the area from people driving by. And it wouldn't be out of her way home since she lives down near Pelican Harbor."

He loved the way light glinted in her eyes when she was excited. Having a direction had given her new purpose. The murky aspects of this ordeal had taken a toll on her.

He touched her chin and lifted her lips to meet his. "I think we have a little time to linger."

———

Abby Dillard McClellan still looked like the girl Paradise had learned to ride horses with at the Dillard Ranch. Her curly hair was more auburn than fiery red like her daughter, Quinn's. Paradise had seen her in passing at the bank, but they hadn't had a chance to really reconnect. Today that mane of hair was stuffed under a hat, and she wore sunglasses. Abby had suggested an alternate meeting place, a remote road that led to a park near the tea plantation.

"It's beautiful here. I can't remember the last time I came out this way." Live oak trees festooned with moss filtered the sunlight, and birds sang from their branches. Egrets hunted in the tall grass along the ditch. It was peaceful—and empty. "I don't know how you still look about sixteen. Are you in disguise?"

Abby stuffed a wayward curl back under her hat and glanced around. "I'll admit I took a few steps to hide my identity. Things have been weird, Paradise, really weird. The things I've overheard . . ." The smile she sent toward Paradise was like sunshine. "But first I want to say I'm so glad you called. I've wanted to get together with you since you got back to town. I've never forgotten my best friend."

Paradise winced at the reminder she'd been so self-absorbed she'd neglected her only real friend from her teens. "I'm sorry, Abby. I should have called you to get together sooner. You were a loyal friend when we were in school. Can you forgive me?"

"Of course. You came back with a quest, and I understand."

"Let me tell you my weird things first." Paradise ticked off the excrement left in her car and the scare with the snake. "Someone doesn't want me here. Have you heard anything?"

Abby removed her sunglasses. "You can't tell anyone what I'm about to say, Paradise. Lloyd Adams is back in town."

"I know Adams is here."

"How do you know?"

"Blake and I saw him on video. He left a gate unlocked in the park, and the action led to Ivy's death. Maybe he even killed her. He's a monster."

Abby swallowed hard. "Adams is part of the attacks going on at the park. It has something to do with rare earth. That's all I know. I like Blake and Jenna so much, and I couldn't stand by while someone stole something they don't know they have."

Rare earth. Who else knew what treasure was under the land? "How do you know this?"

"I can't tell you that."

"Who had the report?"

"I'm not certain. Just warn Blake and Jenna not to sell the land off dirt cheap. I see their accounts at the bank, and I know the park is teetering on the verge of failure. They might be tempted to sell it off for a ridiculously low offer, but they need to hold steady. Someone is trying to ruin the park's reputation so they can swoop in and grab it cheap."

It made perfect sense. Ever since she'd gotten here, the rumors had spread about the park. None of them were true, and all along it had been an organized campaign. It wasn't anything to do with a developer. "I'll make sure Blake and Jenna know."

"I don't think the attacks on you are related to the rare earth thing. The park doesn't belong to you, and you have no control over what happens there. I'm scared for you. Maybe it's a vendetta by Adams. His reputation was ruined."

Paradise hugged herself against the breeze. "I talked it over with Blake, and we think someone is afraid I might remember more of the night my parents were murdered."

Abby bit her lip. "I don't like this, Paradise. Maybe you should leave town for now."

"I would never leave Blake and Jenna to face this alone. With so much at stake, whoever is behind the attacks must be very rich and powerful."

Abby fiddled with the sunglasses in her hands. "That's a fair statement."

"Would your dad know more about it? I could talk with him. There isn't much that goes on around here that he's unaware of."

"Dad's had a lot on his plate lately. Getting him involved might not be the best thing. I've been worried he's sick, like seriously ill."

"I hate to hear that."

Where had Abby learned all this? At the bank? It would make sense she didn't want to reveal information she'd overheard there.

CHAPTER 20

BLAKE CLOSED THE BOOK he'd been reading to the boys and tip-toed out of the bedroom. He paused to switch off the light, then closed the door behind him. He'd been on edge ever since Para-dise got back and he'd heard her whispered comment about putting off the discussion until the boys were in bed. Her amber eyes were shadowed and her mouth drawn, so whatever she'd learned from Abby had been troubling.

He went down the hall and found both of the women in his life in the living room. Mom had lit a fire, and the warm glow and smoky scent made the home feel welcoming. They all loved this little shotgun cottage with its quirky hiding places and cramped rooms. It was home, and the thought of having to leave it hurt. Mom had given him the bad news that paying their employees would be a challenge this month. They might have to take out a loan.

He needed wisdom for what to do.

A cinnamon-scented candle flickered on the stand at the end of the sofa by Paradise. He settled beside her and took her hand. "I could tell you got troubling news from Abby today. Spill it."

"Adams is part of some plot to pick up the park for a song."

His gut clenched as he listened to what Abby had told her. "I wonder if PI Nicole Iverson was checking for rare earth and not gas or oil deposits all along. The smear campaign against the park started with Danielle Mason's body found in the horse trailer the day you arrived here."

"And it hasn't stopped yet." His mother ran her hand through her dark brown bob. Her blue eyes were shadowed and damp.

He'd been unable to stop events from shoving them into this tight spot. Seeing his mother so broken was almost more than he could bear. What could he do? How could he fix this?

"She said to hold firm and not sell."

"I'm not sure how we can do that when we're teetering on the edge here." His mother's voice wobbled.

Paradise laced her fingers with his. "At least we know about the rare earth. If you're ever forced to sell, you could advertise that value to prospective buyers."

Blake squeezed her hand gently. "It sounds like extracting the rare earth elements is a big challenge. We may not have many takers."

"Someone is taking steps to keep it quiet, so I think there's likely to be more interest than we realize."

His mother rose and paced the floor. "I admit I was a tiny bit tempted when I heard how valuable the rare earth elements were, especially when I did the books late last night and realized how dire things are. But I don't want to leave here. This is home for us. It would be more than the boys could handle to yank them away from here. We have to get on top of these rumors and innuendos circulating about us." She swiped tears from her eyes. "I just don't know what to do."

Everything Blake had worked for was disintegrating in his hands, and a sense of failure crushed his shoulders. "I'll talk to Hez. Maybe we could sell just the rare earth rights to the unimproved land, and it would give us running capital."

"It would have us landlocked though, with no room for expansion." His mom sank back into her chair. "There aren't any easy answers."

A tear slipped down Paradise's cheek, and she leaned her head against Blake's shoulder. The enormity of what lay before them was an unexpected blow. Until today he'd been optimistic about the chances of turning things around. Now he wasn't so sure. How would they meet payroll?

He pressed a kiss to Paradise's forehead. "Did Abby have anything else to say?"

"She'd heard about the scare with the snake and the vandalism to my car. She's worried about me."

His phone sounded, and he showed Jane's name on the screen to Paradise and his mom. "Blake here."

"Sorry to call so late, Blake, but I finally got ahold of Chad at the place that ran your DNA. I had quite the time finding anyone to talk to me."

"Thanks for being so persistent. What did he say about the disappearing results?"

"He said they'd discovered they'd been hacked and were making efforts to shore up their online security. He apologized for the trouble, then claimed they'd traced the break-in to somewhere in DC, though he didn't know more than that. No name or company behind the hacking."

"Was anything else in the database changed?"

"That's the strange part. Only that particular result had been tampered with. It's very odd, and even he admitted he didn't know what to make of it. At any rate, he says the results have been uploaded and Paradise should be able to message any of the possible family connections that show up now."

"That's good news," Blake said. "I'll have her check the DNA portal. Any word on fingerprints or DNA on the binoculars?"

"We lifted prints and have a match, but I'm sure you won't be surprised to learn they were used by Lloyd Adams. I'm sharing the results with the sheriff's office, and I'm sure they'll pick him up. If nothing else, he was trespassing and sabotaging an animal enclosure, but I think it's likely he killed Ivy. And we also got DNA off the USB drive found in Paradise's car the night of the snake incident. It also belongs to Adams."

So Abby was right—Adams was involved in more than the sabotage incidents at the park. Blake heard a child whining in the background. "Sounds like Dolly is still up."

"Sleep regression. The bane of my existence. Hang on." Jane's voice held humor and not anger, and she called to her daughter. "Coming, sweet girl. Mama will be right there."

Blake grinned when she signed off. Even a police chief dealt with fractious toddlers.

———

Blake followed Paradise to her apartment, and he checked closets and bedrooms while she made a charcuterie board of crackers, cheese, pepperoni, prosciutto, nuts, and mango chutney. It might not be a professional job, but it made her mouth water.

With glasses of sweet tea, it would make a nice treat to eat with a movie. She'd let Blake choose tonight's selection, which meant she had no idea what it would be. He had eclectic tastes that ranged from war movies to sci-fi and fantasy.

All that mattered was she'd be snuggled against his side, right where she wanted to be after the crazy day.

"All clear." Blake dropped onto the sofa beside her and reached for a cracker. "This looks amazing. I don't even know how to spell what kind of board it is."

"I just remember *char* like a steak and *cuterie* like it's cute. But it's hard to spell for sure."

"Why not just call it a snack board? Or cracker board? Who came up with a word like *charcuterie* anyway?"

"It's French." She slathered chutney on a cracker and stacked it with meat and cheese. "So what are we watching tonight?"

"I'd rather watch you than the TV." He coiled a strand of her hair around his finger. "It feels like we haven't had much alone time lately. I want to hear how Pawsome Pets is doing. All we've done is talk about The Sanctuary. Any interesting cases?"

"My hours are starting to fill up, and someone brought in a pet otter a couple of days ago. The poor thing didn't have the right habitat, and I had to lecture the owner on how to do better. I think she might be considering bringing the otter to the park. They are super cute, but it takes a lot of dedication to provide the right space."

"Levi would love another otter. That kid is obsessed with them."

"And a litter of puppies got dropped off. Part Lab and part mongrel but very cute." Merlin stared at her with disdain at the mention of the dogs, then hopped up on her lap to remind her she belonged to him. "I got lucky and the next family in that day took all three."

"Mom will thank you. The boys would want them too." His embrace pulled her closer. "Enough talk."

His mouth covered hers and she forgot all about the problems they faced. She found herself on his lap with her arms wound around his neck. His breath was ragged when he pulled away and so was hers. "Whose idea was it to wait awhile to get married?" he whispered.

"That would be all your fault, big guy."

He leaned his head against hers. "I don't even know what to do, babe. It feels like the park is slipping away from us. Mom keeps the books, so I hadn't really looked into our finances. I was floored when she admitted we'd have trouble meeting payroll on Friday. I often don't even cash my check, but it's still not enough. I could make a lot more money as a paramedic. Maybe I should get another job and hire someone to drive the safari truck."

Her stomach bottomed out. "Don't pay me this week. Pawsome Pets is paying for itself, and the payments should be a good revenue stream for you guys eventually. What can I do to help?" She had a little money in savings she'd tucked away for their wedding, but she knew better than to offer it up. Blake would never take it. "I'm practically part of the family—it's okay to hold my check just like yours."

His eyes narrowed. "I'm not taking your money. I'd thought about trying to get a loan, but I'm not sure the bank would go for it with our current balance sheet. I could get a little cash advance on a credit card, but the interest rate is crazy and it would only bail us out for a week. I own my truck free and clear. I could get a loan with it as collateral for probably twenty thousand." He rubbed his head. "But that just creates more debt. If we could just get more donors, but the bad PR is scaring them away."

"Let's pray about it, right now." It wasn't a comment she'd ever thought she'd hear coming out of her mouth, but she'd found herself turning to God more and more since she'd quit blaming him for every bad thing that had happened in her life.

He lifted his head, and his blue eyes were tender. "Could you repeat that? I'm not sure I heard you."

She elbowed him. "You heard me all right. You pray and I'll add an amen."

CHAPTER 21

THE MORNING NEWS PLAYED on the television when Blake got up. Governor George's smiling face filled the screen with her grandson Jackson beside her. They sat on the ground while the lemurs rambled around them. The reporter oohed and aahed about the cubs and the playful mama. George's smiling face and windblown hair added to the sense of good time the clip showed.

The governor turned to fully face the camera. "We had the best time at The Sanctuary Wildlife Preserve. The animals were so happy and well taken care of. If you haven't visited this amazing park, I urge you to do so. What do you say, Jackson?"

"It was the best time ever, Grammy! I want to live there. Oh, and vote for my grandma for governor. She's the best!"

Governor George chuckled. "That wasn't quite what I meant, Jackson, but thank you for the plug."

Her easy manner would gain her votes, and Blake hoped it would result in new visitors. He and Paradise had prayed last night, and he was grateful God had showed up this morning with the great interview. There was one last segment of Paradise finding a peacock feather and presenting it to Jackson. The entire interview was heartwarming and would do wonders for the park.

He followed the enticing aroma of pancakes and warm maple syrup to the kitchen, where he found his mother taking breakfast off the stove. "There was an awesome segment on TV just now about Governor George at the park. How's the day look?"

She straightened and a smile lifted the sadness in her expression. "That's great news. It probably played late last night, too, and would explain how all the safari tours are sold out for the day. And there are three behind-the-scenes ones at a thousand dollars each. Let's pray it keeps up."

"I am." He took the plate of pancakes she offered and poured maple syrup from the warm pitcher onto them. "I'm starving. The boys still asleep?"

"I heard them stirring a little, so I expect them any minute." She slid a cup of coffee his way. "Did you get any rest?"

"Not much. Worry will do that to you."

"This shouldn't be your burden, and it grieves me that you have to be part of all of it. I'm the mom—I should be taking care of you."

"I'm a grown man, and I love you and the boys."

"But it's keeping you from having a fulfilling life." She broke off in a choked voice. "You should be slipping a ring on Paradise's finger and planning a wedding. You should be dreaming of your own sons and not helping raise your brothers. I've messed up everything."

"Mom, stop it." He went around the peninsula and hugged her. "I have a great life. We're a close family, and I love it that way. There's time for me and Paradise to get engaged and plan that wedding. She's only been back in town a few months, and she wants to take it slowly anyway. She's got plenty on her plate with her search for who murdered her parents. She's not pushing for that ring."

And the realization of that stung a little. He'd hoped she would be as eager to be with him as he was to be with her. She loved him—he didn't doubt that. But he didn't sense the same urgency he felt. Was she worried he might let her down again? He'd messed up badly all those years ago, and maybe she didn't fully trust him.

"I have an idea. I don't know how you feel about it or how she would feel, but I have a beautiful emerald necklace your dad gave me before he left on that final tour of duty. You could have it made into a gorgeous engagement ring, and the color would suit her so well. Does she like emeralds?"

A lump formed in his throat at the thought of giving Paradise something so special to his family. He had a few happy memories of his dad. His dad's voice encouraging him to get the rubber ball. Being tossed in the air and staring down into his dad's face, that image now dim with time. "I would love that, Mom. It would be special to me and to her, too, I'm sure."

"I'll get it and see what you think. I told him at the time he paid way too much money for it, but now I'm glad, because she's worth it." She left him in the kitchen and went down the hall toward her bedroom.

He settled at the table and ate his breakfast while he waited for her to return. The sound of cartoons filtered from the boys' bedroom, and contentment settled through his bones. He didn't need much, just a family who loved him with Paradise by his side. They could build a great life here, and after that TV segment, he felt hopeful for the first time in months.

His mother was smiling when she returned. "I'd forgotten how perfect these emeralds are. I can't wait to see a ring on Paradise's finger. I love that girl like she's my own and always have." She placed the necklace in his hand.

The stones caught the light streaming through the kitchen window. They were almost as gorgeous as Paradise's eyes. He instantly imagined a ring that would do them justice. It would take some time to get it designed and created, but it would be worth the wait.

———

Paradise wandered the apartment on Thursday after work. Blake had a meeting with the bank and had promised to take the boys fishing later, so she opted to have an evening to herself to think. Her emotions were so jumbled she found it hard to land on a plan to figure things out.

The music box sat on a shelf of the bookcase in the living room, and she caught a glimpse of it as she paced the floor with Merlin in her arms. A few people knew about how much she loved *The Phantom of the Opera*. Her cousins. She hadn't seen her older cousin Lily in over a month. Paradise glanced at the clock on the wall. She could be at Lily's by seven. Or she could have a chat with Molly, her cousin Rod's sister. A visit with Molly would be more fun, but one with Lily might be more productive. She and Mom had been close, close enough that Paradise had been hurt when Lily refused to care for her and had let CPS take her.

Cowardice never resulted in a victory. Paradise put the kitten down and grabbed her purse. Lily lived on the outskirts of town, and it only took ten minutes to drive to the older two-story home with a Southern porch complete with a swing. Lily had always loved working outside, and Paradise spotted her yanking weeds out of the flower bed in the yard. When the car pulled into her drive, Lily stood and wiped the perspiration from her forehead. Her scowl didn't change when Paradise got out of the vehicle.

"Hi, Lily. I hope I'm not interrupting anything."

"I was about done. I could use some sweet tea—how about you?"

At least she maintained her Southern hospitality. Paradise smiled. "That sounds great." She followed her cousin to the porch with its painted floor and haint blue ceiling.

Lily pointed to the swing. "Have a seat while I wash my hands and get the tea."

It was a gorgeous evening. Paradise settled on the old swing and gave it a nudge with her foot. The gentle swaying reminded her of sitting in this very spot with her mom so many years ago.

Lily returned with glasses of sweet tea and a small plate of lemon bars. "I made these this morning."

"I haven't had lemon bars in forever." Paradise selected one.

"I suppose you have more questions about your mother." Lily sounded resigned.

"I'm always interested in hearing any memories about Mom, but this time my questions have to do with that off-Broadway musical I went to in New Orleans with Mom. *The Phantom of the Opera.* Do you remember?"

"That's all you talked about for weeks. I never saw a girl so obsessed with a movie." Lily took a lemon bar and bit into it.

"Someone has been trying to scare me out of town by having the music play on my phone and in my car. Someone hid a music box similar to the one in the movie in the lemur habitat. I wondered if Mom might have told someone how much I loved it."

"Well, sure. Your mom talked about you all the time. You were the smartest, prettiest, most perfect daughter there ever was." Lily's tone held a trace of contempt. "But then, whatever Becky cared about was *all* she cared about. She didn't like listening to me talk about my kids."

Pain flared in Paradise's soul. Mom loved her, sure, but Paradise had never realized her mom bragged about her to her friends. "Do you know the names of people she might have told?"

"Your eighth birthday party had a Phantom theme. Friends, family, kids from the neighborhood and school. Your dad grilled burgers and hot dogs for several hours to feed all the people."

"I—I don't remember the party." With a start Paradise realized her birthday was in five days. It had been years since she'd even gotten a card to celebrate. Not many people knew the date. All of it had been buried by the murder of her parents.

Lily's gaze softened. "It's coming right up. Next week, isn't it?"

"Y-yes."

"I'll be the first one to wish you happy birthday."

Maybe the only one. It wasn't a day she usually thought about, much less celebrated. When the calendar flipped to February, Paradise struggled to get through every day, an hour at a time. Her thoughts usually didn't clear until April.

"Many here in town know how much you loved that weekend with your mom. She showed pictures of it at the party. And since you're so determined to dredge up the past, I have a box of stuff I bought from the sale after your parents died. It's in the attic. Let me get it for you."

If she'd loved it so much, why did that music box fill her with such dread? She should have been thrilled to see it. There was more here than she understood.

CHAPTER 22

FRANK ELLIS PATTED HIS stomach, still taut at his age. "That was the best lasagna I've ever had."

Jenna blushed and tucked a strand of dark hair behind her ear. "I'm glad you enjoyed it. Paradise made that Italian bread for the cheese toast from scratch."

Blake's respect for the builder had grown over the past few weeks his mom had been seeing him. Frank knew a lot about business—maybe he'd have some ideas on how to save the park.

The boys had cleaned their plates and run off to play with their kittens, leaving the adults at the kitchen table. The sound of *Minecraft* joined the distant animal noises. They'd had their biggest visitor count ever this week, thanks to the governor. The revenue would allow them to cut paychecks for the next month, but Blake was pragmatic enough to know the surge might not last.

It had been a squeeze to get six of them seated in the small space, but Frank hadn't seemed to mind the homey little room. Blake liked seeing his mom blush like a high schooler and send little glances Frank's way. They both seemed smitten. Maybe losing the park wouldn't matter so much if Blake knew Mom was settled with someone who would love her and the boys. Frank's kids were grown, but he knew how to talk to Levi and Isaac, and the boys already liked him.

Blake gave a slight shake of his head. It was way too soon to be thinking like that. Anyone could put on a front for a while, but it took time to get to know a man's heart and character. Frank hadn't been in his mom's life for a long time, and he might not be the same as the kid she knew in high school. Only time would tell. The present problem was Blake's to figure out.

Frank leaned back in his chair, and his blond hair fell away from his forehead. "There's been a somber mood around here tonight. Is something wrong? I thought there would be jubilation all around after that great interview with Governor George."

"It helped for sure," Blake said. "But it's not enough to offset the ongoing attacks on us that are having an adverse impact. We're hopeful things might start to turn around now though."

"Then what's with the doom and gloom?"

Blake exchanged a glance with his mother. Frank would probably know about rare earth elements. Maybe he could advise them. His mom inclined her head like it was up to Blake to make that decision. What did they have to lose?

"There are people out there who seem determined to force us into bankruptcy so they can buy the land, Frank. We found out some interesting news about what's under our ground." He rose and grabbed the report from his jacket hanging on a hook by the back door. It was creased from constant folding and unfolding.

Frank took it and read it over. His brows lifted. "Whoa, I wasn't expecting this. You're sitting on a gold mine—no, better than a gold mine. If you make this known, you'll have plenty of companies willing to pay you top dollar. You don't have to settle for being forced off the property."

Mom wrung her hands. "But we don't want to sell. What we're doing here is important, Frank. The animals are happy, and we love our spot here."

Frank nodded. "I get it, Jenna. When I was younger, success was the main goal, and while I always tried to be ethical and fair in my business practices, I kept an eye on the bottom line. I'm older and wiser now. Some things are priceless and no amount of money is worth their loss. Only you can decide that."

Paradise glanced at Blake, then back to Frank. "We have 120 acres. There's a 22-acre area we haven't developed at all. Would it make sense to sell off that portion?"

Frank shrugged. "Maybe, but it takes a huge area to mine. Whoever bought it would want all of your acreage plus more all around. And something you might not know is that mining creates a huge environmental impact. Toxic water must be disposed of somehow, and there are other major problems. There have been numerous spills over the years that have had major negative consequences on communities. And even if this site becomes only a mine where the ore is dug out and sent elsewhere to extract the rare earth elements, a mining operation so close to the ocean could spread contamination. I doubt that's something you want to do. New methods are in development though, and maybe an investor would be content to buy it and wait for the safer extraction methods."

"I wouldn't want to see the beautiful spot here become a gaping hole in the earth."

"I wouldn't either." Frank nodded. "This is a great park. Maybe a donor campaign would be worth doing. I can pull together a list if it would help."

"That would be wonderful, Frank, thank you." Mom's voice wobbled, and she stood to begin to clear the table. "Let's put our glum thoughts away. God will provide, and if he doesn't intervene and we lose the park, he has something else planned for us. He's walked me through some dark times, and I know he will do the same with this problem."

Blake's faith was strong, too, but the problem was, he didn't *want* to let go of the park. Would God even ask it of them when they'd poured so much of their lives into this place? How could they walk away from their life's work? He had no doubt he could place the animals in zoos or other refuges, but The Sanctuary was unique, and the animals had so much room to roam. He hated to think of them in cages or tight quarters.

Glancing at Paradise's face, he knew she felt the same.

It was Paradise's birthday, and it felt worse than usual for it to be unacknowledged this year. In previous years it didn't matter because she wasn't with people she loved. Why did it feel wrong that she'd worked at the park all afternoon without anyone wishing her a good day? She'd felt on the verge of tears all day.

She forced a smile and headed to Jenna's cottage. She hadn't seen the boys for several days, and they would cheer her up. Their smiles would make her day better. Jenna didn't like her to knock but to go on in like Blake did, so she opened the screen door and stepped into the living room. The place felt quiet and empty. Where was everyone? Blake would have gotten off half an hour ago.

"Blake? Boys?" She walked on through the cottage but found it empty. Maybe they were out on the back deck. When she pushed open the back door, she caught the scent of grilling steaks and spotted Blake flipping meat.

Her gaze skipped over him to the crowd milling around the

backyard. Mason and Clark waved to her and she waved back. Honey and Evan were here with their kids, who were playing in the sandbox with Isaac and Levi. Her cousins were here too— Lily, Molly, and Rod as well as their kids. The yard was full of people in party hats.

Jenna turned and saw her. "You're early."

"I—I finished a little early." Over Jenna's shoulder Paradise spotted a long table with a banner that read *Happy Birthday*. A cake and all kinds of sweets weighed down the white tablecloth. Was this for *her*?

Blake put down the tongs and left the grill to embrace her. "Happy birthday, babe. We couldn't let the big 3–0 pass without a celebration."

He kissed her, and suddenly feeling woozy, she clung to him. "You remembered?"

"All these years I wished you were here for your birthday, and now you are. I knew the boys would blab it, so I kept them away from you for the last few days."

She'd thought no one ever gave her birthday a thought, and yet Blake had remembered for the past fifteen years. If only they hadn't lost all that time.

"Paradise, it's your birthday!" Isaac ran toward her with a noise-maker. He blew it, and his eyes grew larger when the streamers flew out. "Did you see that?" He climbed her like a monkey.

"I sure did. Good job."

Chocolate around his mouth, Levi rushed her. "We got you peanut M&M's."

"I think you ate them all."

"I left you some." He clung to her leg. "I made you a card. So did Isaac."

"I can't wait to see them." She put Isaac down and the boys ran to fetch their presents. She turned to find Blake watching with a smile. "I can't believe you planned this and I didn't know."

"Mom helped." He nodded toward the group. "You'd better greet your guests."

She hardly knew what to say as she wandered from person to person exchanging hugs and receiving well-wishes. One minute spooled into the next until they'd all eaten and she'd blown out the candle and admired the boys' handiwork. Sunset came before she was ready for the party to be over, but she walked to the parking lot with her guests. The night air couldn't cool the warmth in her heart from the amazing few hours.

No wonder people liked birthday parties. She hadn't had one since her parents died, but maybe this was the beginning of an every-year occurrence.

Blake stood with his arm around her waist, and they waved goodbye to Abby, who was the last one to pull out of the lot. He pressed a kiss to her temple. "I hope it was a fun night."

"The absolute best," Paradise said.

"I haven't given you my present yet." He fumbled in his pocket and pulled out a satin pouch.

She opened the drawstring and drew out a silver locket, clearly vintage, with filigree on the outside. "Oh, I love it. Are there pictures inside?" She opened it and discovered a picture of Blake and her together on one side. On the other was one of Levi and Isaac with her. Tears stung her eyes. "I have a family now, Blake. I'm not alone. This is the first birthday celebration since my parents died."

His smile disappeared. "You didn't have a party at all during this whole time?"

"No one even knew. It's been a wonderful night." Her gaze went back to the locket. "Where'd you get this? It's so unique."

"It belonged to my great-grandma. Grandpa gave it to her when she turned thirty. I could have gotten something new, but I wanted to show you what an integral part of our family you are."

She threw her arms around his neck and pulled his head down for a kiss. All her loneliness and heartache of the past fifteen years vanished as she put all she felt into that kiss. His arms tightened around her, and she spiraled into a vortex of passion and love.

Something whipped past her ear, and Blake tore his mouth away to push her to the ground and cover her with himself. "Keep your head down!"

She could feel his heart pounding against her, and she didn't move. She hadn't heard a gunshot. What had so narrowly missed her head?

Squealing tires followed the roar of an engine tearing off, and Blake cautiously got up. He lifted her to her feet. "Go inside until I'm sure they're gone."

She turned and saw an arrow on the ground. A paper fluttered at the end of it. "Blake."

He turned and saw it, then stooped to peer at the paper without touching it. She knelt beside him to read the words *Your last birthday if you don't leave.*

A jolt of fear shivered down her back until she got it under control. Adams was an archer. Was he out there amping up his fear tactics? "No one will scare me away."

"I wish you'd stay with us until this is resolved."

"I'm not going to run. They want me gone for a reason—and I'm going to find out what that is."

CHAPTER 23

WHAT A DAY. PARADISE'S morning had been packed full of pets, including a sick iguana. She'd had to research notes from a distant college class about the creatures to treat it. Her neck ached, and a faint headache pulsed at her forehead. Her belly signaled she'd skipped lunch, which was probably the source of the pain in her head.

She opened the refrigerator and pulled out the chicken salad she'd picked up at the grocery store last night. She wanted nothing more than to fill her tummy and veg out with the newest Denise Hunter novel. Blake was watching the boys so Jenna could attend a fundraising event with Frank, who'd pulled it together in a week. Paradise had offered to babysit so Blake could go, too, but he'd insisted his mom's pretty face would win over the donors better than he could, and he wanted a boys' night out to play mini golf in Gulf Shores with the kids.

She made a chicken salad sandwich, threw some carrots onto her plate, and called it a healthy meal. The kittens curled up beside her while she ate, and the stress of the day melted away as she opened her book.

She'd just finished her meal and was on the second chapter of her novel when her doorbell rang. It was probably a surprise visit by the boys, and she went to the door with a smile forming. Her breath caught when she spotted Mary Steerforth standing on the small deck at the top of the steps outside her entry. She was crying, and the scars on her face were florid from whatever had caused her distress.

Paradise threw open the door and took Mary's hand. "Mary, what's wrong?"

The older woman swiped at the moisture on her face and stumbled across the threshold. "I need to sit down a minute. I'm so sorry to bother you, Paradise, but Blake and Jenna weren't home. I didn't know who else to turn to."

Paradise led her to the kitchen table and poured two glasses of sweet tea. She handed one to Mary, then pulled out a chair and sat beside her. The woman was still distraught and kept choking back sobs.

Mary took a sip and shuddered. "I still can't believe it."

Paradise took her hand. "Tell me what's wrong. I'll do whatever I can." Maybe she should call Blake, but she hated to interrupt his fun evening with the boys. They thrived on the time they got to spend with their big brother.

Mary clutched Paradise's hand in a painful grip. "It's Dean. I—I think he killed Allen."

Paradise set down her glass of tea. Blake had suspected that Allen Steerforth's death hadn't been an accident. "Did Dean admit he ran Allen off the road? Or did you discover something about drugs?"

Mary downed a gulp of her tea. She took a deep breath and her tears slowed. "Allen and I went through a hard spell after the tiger attack. It was mostly my fault. I pushed him away because I felt ugly. I couldn't believe he could love me in spite of my scars and told him to move out. He was angry but he went. He moved in with Dean for a while."

Paradise's fingers crept to the ridge of scars on her shoulder. A traumatic injury could mess with anyone. "How long were you separated?"

"A year. Too long really. I knew I'd made a mistake three months in, but my stupid pride wouldn't let me go crawling back to him. In that time he changed his will and left everything to Dean. Or so Dean says. Dean said he saw a signed copy. No will was found when Allen died though."

"But could he even do that? Didn't you own the property jointly?"

Mary wiped condensation from the glass. "Allen inherited it from his parents free and clear, and we never bothered adding me to the title. I never dreamed . . ." She broke off and shook her head. "And maybe it's not true." She lifted her gaze to Paradise's. "But it *feels* true."

"Dean just told you this out of the blue?"

"He was drunk, raging around and yelling at me that I needed to hand over the will. That it was all my fault he didn't get the money he'd expected, and he had to have it. I think he's in trouble with gambling, but I'm not sure."

"What about Allen's death?"

Mary took another gulp of tea. "He said something like, 'If I'd known the will would be missing, I never would have—' He broke off and didn't say the rest, but I—I could fill in the rest of it. He never would have run Allen off the road and injected him with meth."

That was a stretch. He could have finished that sentence various ways. Maybe he wouldn't have gambled if he didn't know he was getting the money. Still, Mary might have a point.

"I can see you're not sure if Dean is capable of murder, but you don't know what else he's done. He's convinced that Allen hid the will on Sanctuary property for safekeeping and told me he's been searching the property to try to find the will. I shudder to think what he would do to the boys if they walked in on him. You have to be careful!"

Paradise swallowed down a bitter taste in her mouth and followed it with a gulp of sweet tea. "But you already sold the refuge property. What can he do now?"

"He can submit the will within five years of probate and it could reverse everything. If he can find the will in the next month, we're all in trouble."

"B-but what about the money Jenna paid you for it?"

"I don't know how it all works, but the refuge would be gone. Maybe I'd have to pay back the money, but it's gone, so I wouldn't be able to." Mary wrung her hands. "I don't know what to do."

Neither did Paradise. She glanced at the clock on the wall. In another two hours she could take it to Blake.

Blake pulled the door shut as he backed out of the boys' bedroom. It hadn't taken long to get them to sleep. They'd been tuckered out from miniature golf, pizza, and go-carts. He yawned himself. It had been a full day, but he grabbed his phone to call Paradise. He'd missed her tonight.

Lights swept across the picture window, and a vehicle parked in front of the cottage. Paradise's green Kia. He smiled. Maybe she'd missed him as much as he'd missed her. Mom wouldn't be home for at least a couple of hours.

He opened the door before she could ring the bell. His welcoming smile faded at the worry on her face. He reached out to take her hand. "What's wrong?"

She raked her hand through her mane of hair and went past him to the small living room, leaving her plumeria scent behind. "It's crazy. I need coffee."

"I'll make it. Come with me and tell me what's going on." Blake went to the kitchen and tossed beans into the grinder.

"The park is in serious jeopardy," she began.

Over the sound of the grinder, he listened to her story of Mary's visit and Dean's obsession with a will. He punched on the coffeepot. "That sounds unbelievable. You can't roll back the clock on a sale when the will wasn't found at the right time."

She hugged herself. "Call Hez and find out."

He'd do it to appease her, but it didn't make sense. His chest was tight when he placed the call to Hez. This had to be wrong. He hated to bother him while he was still recovering, especially when he was dealing with some issues at TGU for Savannah, but his cousin would know whether the law was on the park's side or not. Blake turned on the speakerphone.

Hez answered on the first ring. "Hey, Blake."

"How you doing, buddy?"

"Pretty well. The headaches are improving, so that's good. I can't drive for a while, so that's bad. You sound upset."

"Can a sale of property be invalidated if an unknown will is found after the place is sold?"

"Whoa, that's a loaded question. What's going on?"

Blake spilled out everything he'd heard. "That can't be true, right?"

"It's not an easy question to answer since there are some layers to it. Alabama law says a good faith purchaser is protected after a year, and you've had it longer than that. But if the will is found within five years and your mom knew there was a will, the purchase could be invalidated. Mary Steerforth would be required to pay back the money. If she doesn't have it, which seems likely, you guys might be out of luck. You could sue, but it could take a long time to be repaid, and you'd still lose the property."

"I'm sure Mom didn't know anything about a will, but I'll ask her and find out for sure." Blake poured two mugs of coffee and handed one to Paradise. They both sat at the table with the phone between them still on speakerphone. "I was told he has a month to find the will or it'll be too late. In a month it will be five years since we bought it."

"That's also correct. But if the will hasn't turned up by now, it probably won't. I would guess Dean has checked with town attorneys."

Blake glanced at Paradise to verify. She shrugged. "I would guess so," she said. "He was drunk when all this came out to Mary, and he seemed frustrated. Mary thinks he might have killed Allen."

"Whoa, that's a piece of info I wasn't expecting." Hez's voice rose. "Does she have any proof? Murder would mean he couldn't inherit."

"Just a suspicious comment he never finished." Paradise told him what Mary had said.

"You might dig for proof just in case the will shows up at the last minute. And if he did kill his uncle, he needs to be brought to justice even if the will never surfaces."

Though Hez's comment was meant to reassure him, Blake

pressed his hand against his forehead. "Not sure how to go about investigating something that happened so long ago."

"Mary believes Allen was run off the road, correct? Ask her if she still has the vehicle he was driving at the time of his death. If he was forced off the road, there might be damage on it. And talk to Dean's friends. If he spilled something while drunk, he might have said something to one of them. I can try to get a copy of the accident details. There might be something suspicious in them."

Paradise took a sip of her coffee. "The authorities didn't suspect foul play at the time, though Mary tried to get them to consider it when the drug screen showed methamphetamine in Allen's blood. She says he hated drugs of any kind after their son died of an overdose."

A kitten twined around Blake's ankles, and he picked it up. The contact settled his agitation. "So someone, presumably Dean Steerforth, drugged Allen, then forced him off the road."

A long pause followed before Hez replied. "Or maybe he was drugged up and ran off the road by himself. He could have had a heart attack or some other effect of a drug overdose like a seizure or disorientation. It would still be murder. It's odd the detectives didn't take Mary's statement into account about how unlikely it was that he'd taken a drug."

Everything Blake needed to do crashed in with an overwhelming weight. Not only did he have to figure out how to save the refuge, but now he had to prove Allen was murdered. With the way things had been going, he didn't dare assume the will would stay missing.

CHAPTER 24

PARADISE DIDN'T KNOW HOW to settle Blake down as they waited for Jenna to come home. His knee jiggered up and down as he sat beside her on the sofa, and he looked pale and drawn. The weight of everything rested on his shoulders. His commitment to those he loved was one of the many reasons she adored him. He wouldn't be Blake Lawson without that huge heart.

She took his hand and brought it to her lips. "We'll get through this, babe." His nod was jerky, but at least it was there. She touched his cheek to turn his face her way. "Look at me."

His gaze focused on her and she nearly flinched at the misery in his blue eyes. He was hurting so much, and she was helpless to help him. She cupped his face in her hands and kissed him with all the love in her heart. He clung to her and pulled her close against his chest. The tension eased out of his shoulders as he kissed her like a drowning man looking for air. She held him until he finally pulled back.

"What would I do without you?"

"Thankfully you'll never know."

Lights from a car outside flooded the living room with light.

"There they are," he said in a tight voice, the stress instantly back on his face. He rose to face the door as his mother walked in with Frank. They were smiling and holding hands. Frank had a contented grin that made Paradise smile, too, even though she still feared for their future. Frank was good for Jenna, and Paradise loved him for the way he wanted to care for her.

Jenna did a fist pump when she saw them. She looked beautiful in her black cocktail dress and heels. Her dark hair was in an updo, and she was radiant when she glanced at Frank. "We raised over three thousand dollars tonight, kids! I can't believe it. Frank is a genius." Her jubilant smile faded when her gaze landed on Blake, and her hand went to her throat. "Are the boys okay?"

"They're fine, Mom. They're asleep. Sit down. This will take a little time to explain."

Frowning, Frank led Jenna to the sofa and nudged her down, then perched on the sofa cushion beside her. He turned to stare at Blake and Paradise. "Do you want me to leave?"

"No," Paradise said quickly. "Jenna needs your support right now." She gulped and swallowed the lump in her throat. Should she tell her or let Blake do it?

Blake plunged in before she could decide what to do. "Mom, it appears Allen Steerforth may have a will floating out there that would negate the sale of The Sanctuary to us. If it's found, we won't own the park any longer."

"W-what? Mary assured me there was no will." Her blue eyes grew wide as Blake laid out what they knew about the situation. "But it hasn't been found yet, so we're fine, right?" She turned toward Frank with a bewildered plea on her face.

He took her hand and held it in both of his. "I'm sure there's more to the story. Stay calm, honey."

"If a month passes without it turning up, we're clear," Blake said. "But I don't think we can assume it won't be found. We need to be proactive. Hez says we should try to find out if Dean killed Allen."

"Mary has always believed it was murder."

Frank glanced around the living room. "It seems one avenue is to find the will yourself. You could make sure he doesn't find it that way."

"But wouldn't we be obligated to turn it over?" Blake asked.

"I don't know what the law says about that. I doubt it requires a found will to be turned in to anyone."

It might not be required, but what was the right thing to do? What a dilemma. Did they find a will and turn it over to a murderer? That didn't seem right either. This Christian walk wasn't as black-and-white as Paradise had thought. What *was* the right thing to do? Didn't justice matter? Maybe they needed to pray it was never found.

Blake let out a harsh breath. "I'm not sure I want to face what God might require if we find the will."

"I get it," Frank said. "It doesn't feel like justice to reward a murderer for his crime."

"If he really *is* a murderer. We don't know if that's true."

"Mary seemed certain," Paradise whispered. She was too new at this faith thing to know what was right. And it wasn't her fight—they could figure it out and do what they thought best. But she still planned to pray nothing would happen, that the park would go on saving the wildlife with this new influx of cash.

If they lost the park, it might be years before Blake felt stable enough to start a new life with her. That shouldn't matter to her, but it did, and she had begun to feel like in the list of things important to Blake, she was third or fourth place. But hadn't she encouraged him to take things slow, to get the park on firm footing? It had been a joint decision, but it was one she was beginning to regret. The day-to-day life of running back and forth from town and getting only snippets of time with Blake was wearing her down.

She gave a slight shake of her head. It was her fatigue talking from the brutal day and the stress of learning about the dire situation. She would never want to come between Blake and his family—they were all important to her too. It wasn't a choice between her or them; it was all of them together. Her chronic feeling of being displaced and unloved was attacking now. And she wasn't about to let those feelings win.

Blake rubbed gritty eyes, then made a mug of coffee in his Keurig and carried it down the stairs from his apartment. Dew dampened his feet as he crossed to the back deck of the house. He'd tossed and turned—and prayed—trying to figure out the best course of action. Sunrise over the park touched everything with a glow that smoothed out the rough edges. The view and the scent of pine combined with his mom's narcissi growing along the side of the yard soothed his agitation. A bald eagle perched in the tall branches of an oak tree and watched for mice or other small rodents.

"I thought I'd find you out here."

He turned at Paradise's voice. Her hair was up in a ponytail, and shadows bloomed under her eyes. She hadn't left until after midnight, and he doubted she'd slept much either. "Want some coffee? I can make you a mug."

"Not yet. It doesn't look like your mom and the boys are up, and I don't want to wake them." She crossed the cedar planks to his side and palmed his cheek as she kissed him.

Her soft touch and sweet breath were the balm he needed. He pulled her into his arms for a real kiss before he drew back, resting his forehead on hers. "Not sure what to do, babe." The feel of her in his arms and her unmistakable scent were what he needed in this moment.

"I think we first need to see if there's any truth to Mary's belief that Dean killed Allen. Hez was going to try to get the accident report. Maybe he'll get that today. In the meantime we can go see Mary and ask more about Dean and the situation. She might be able to give us the names of some of his friends. And if there's an old girlfriend, she might be bitter enough to give us some information."

"You're incredible. Those are great ideas." He reached for his phone. "I'll text Hez. He's an early riser."

An answer to his reminder to Hez about the file came back almost immediately. *Sent out request last night. I hope to hear later this morning. I'll be in touch.*

Blake thanked him and set his phone back on the arm of the deck chair. "I think we have a busy day today. Saturdays are always crazy. What's on your plate?"

"Pawsome Pets is closed. I'll check in with Warren and see if our animals are all healthy today. If there's nothing that needs my attention, I could go collect any information Mary might have. Once you're free, we can make the rounds to any friends or girlfriends she might suggest."

"I'm not crazy about you doing it by yourself. What if Dean figures out we're snooping around? You could be in danger."

She stiffened and sighed before sliding off his lap. "I'm a grown woman, not a child. I don't need to be coddled and protected from all possibility of harm. You're a natural-born protector, but you have to quit acting like the sky is falling if I'm out of your sight for five minutes."

He stuffed down his anger before he could say something he regretted. "I know you are, babe. I think I react that way because the losses started early in life for me. They've trained me to always be expecting the next one. Losing you would be more than I could take."

Her frown smoothed and a smile curved her lips. "I tend to overreact to things like that."

How did other men do it? He wasn't the only male who wanted to protect those he loved. Women could be hard to figure out sometimes. "I'll work on it."

Her gaze softened even more. "I love that you're protective, Blake, but you have to learn the line between protection and smothering. I can make a perfectly normal visit with a friend to ask questions without alarm bells going off for you."

She tapped his chest. "If we have kids, will you put a leash on them and make sure they're safe every moment? Life isn't safe. Things happen, bad things. We can't control them, but we can temper how we react to them. Our kids will have to learn to deal with issues and discover for themselves that they're strong enough to handle life. Don't steal that strength from them or from me."

He searched her gaze and nodded. "I see your point."

The back door opened, and his mom joined them. "Good morning. You're both up bright and early." She looked as tired as the two of them. "I'm making coffee and breakfast."

"I can help." Paradise went toward the door. "I feel like biscuits and gravy. I'll make the biscuits if you do the gravy. Mine usually turns out like wallpaper paste."

Blake rose to follow them. "I doubt that. You're a great cook, Paradise."

She drilled him with an amused glance. "I can bake if it's easy. Tricky recipes are still a trial, but I'm trying."

"I'll show you how I do it," Mom said.

"I can make the coffee," Blake said.

It might take a while for Paradise to thaw today. He wasn't sure how to keep the protective side of his nature in check. His mom and brothers were used to the way he stepped out to help keep them safe, but the woman he loved valued her independence in ways he couldn't quite come to grips with yet. But if they were going to build a life together, they had to figure out a happy compromise.

CHAPTER 25

THE OCEAN WAS AS turbulent as Paradise felt this morning. An overnight storm had churned up the shallow water along the Fort Morgan peninsula, and the normally blue water was brown. A sprinkle of rain fell as she mounted the steps to the elevated deck and crossed to Mary's front door. Gulls squawked overhead, and she ducked as one dive-bombed her.

The obstacles felt overwhelming. What if they lost The Sanctuary? She took a couple of deep breaths and pressed the bell. Only Mary's blue Chevy was parked in the area under the house, so Paradise wouldn't have to deal with Dean.

Mary answered the door with no makeup, and the scars from the big cat mauling looked red and inflamed in the morning sun. "Good morning. I was glad to get your text. This is serious." She stepped out of the way. "I have fresh coffee."

Paradise followed her inside. "I'd love a cup. Black, please."

The large kitchen was open to the living room, and the windows on the Gulf side of the house displayed a terrific panoramic view of the water and white sand beach. Another deck on that side of the home was elevated on pilings. The furnishings were a mishmash of various chairs, sofas, hutches, and tables Mary must have collected over the years. Though nothing matched, it felt welcoming. Various collectible cookie jars lined the tops of the cabinets, and a display cabinet held pieces of carnival glass.

"I love your home. It feels homey."

Mary limped to the pot and poured coffee, then handed her a mug. "Allen hated what he called my hoarding tendencies. Most of the pieces came from my mother, and they make me happy." She gestured to the blue plaid sofa. "Have a seat."

Paradise settled on the misshapen cushion and took a sip of coffee. A calico cat jumped up beside her, and she let it crawl on her lap. "I told Jenna and Blake about the problem. Blake's cousin Hez is looking into things. We thought we should investigate whether Dean killed Allen. Hez will try to get the case file to examine, but is there any evidence a vehicle hit Allen's truck?"

"I don't know. I told the police he had to have been run off the road, but no one listened. But I don't think you should poke around in that—it might be dangerous."

Too late to ignore that possibility. "Was the truck totaled?"

Mary shrugged. "There was very little damage. Allen was thrown from the truck, but the police didn't investigate it much when his tox report came back with methamphetamine in his blood. They couldn't be bothered with listening to me."

Proving he was drugged would be harder than finding out if he'd been run off the road. But maybe both things had happened. "Where's the truck now?"

Mary fiddled with the hem of her blouse. "Dean has it."

"Did he ever get it repainted or repaired?"

"No. It still has a dent in the driver's door, and it's the same color, pale blue. It's a Ford with an eight-foot bed."

"Where's Dean now?"

"Probably at work, at the barbecue place in Nova Cambridge."

Near Paradise's vet clinic. "Do you know how long he'll be at work today?"

"Probably until ten. They close at nine, and he stays to clean up. Are you going to look at the truck?"

"It wouldn't hurt to see if there's another color on it. It's been five years since the accident, but if he hasn't done anything to it, there might still be evidence on it."

Mary's expression was skeptical, but she said nothing. "Dean used to do drugs. That's why he and Allen had a falling out. Allen was living with Dean while we were separated, but he left when he found Dean cooking meth in the kitchen. He said he wasn't going to find another dead boy."

"Did you tell the police about that?"

"I should have, but I didn't want to point the finger at Dean. I never suspected him of lying to hurt Allen. I thought he loved him." Mary's voice trembled, and she stared down at her hands. "I thought it was someone who wanted our land."

"You mentioned once when Blake and I talked to you that you suspected Frank Ellis."

"He'd tried to buy us out several times, and Allen disliked him, so that was my first thought. But I was wrong. I'm sure Dean killed Allen."

But how did they go about proving it? Paradise finished her coffee and thanked Mary. By the time she got to Nova Cambridge, it would be lunch hour and she should be able to examine the truck while Dean was busy with customers. It would be unlikely she would be seen. Blake would want to be with her, but he'd left for a little while to take pictures of Hez asking Savannah to marry him. Paradise would've liked to have watched that herself.

As she drove back north she thought of Blake's stricken face when she'd told him he was smothering her and wished she'd been a little gentler. But if she loved him—and she did—she had to make sure he understood how important this was. His protective instincts sparked too strongly when he loved someone. Since she'd come back here, she realized more and more that bad things were going to happen to everyone. None of them were exempt.

Certainly not her parents.

The familiar guilt rose in her chest and she recognized it as the same behavior she'd just pointed out to Blake. They both felt life ought to be able to be steered, and they were both wrong.

She slowed as she entered Nova Cambridge's town limits. Her car knew the way to her place, and she decided to park behind the building like usual and walk over to Chet's BBQ. There was a small lot across the street from the restaurant, but there was no blue truck, so she walked around to the back of the building where employees might park. The blue truck with its full-size bed was the first vehicle.

She walked around the truck and spotted the dent in the driver's side where it had hit something. There was no transferred paint, so she examined the passenger door and found a swipe of white paint. She moved to the rear bumper and spotted another touch of white paint. She took out her phone and snapped a picture of it. It could be anything though, and she wasn't sure this line of research would yield any results.

⸻

After helping feed the animals, Blake scraped mud and dung off his boots in the grass outside the snack shack. The odor of lemur clung to his hair, and he couldn't wait to take a shower. His mom didn't need his help tonight, and he planned to spend the evening with Paradise.

Clark spotted him and came his way with two sodas in hand. Clark had thrived since he'd come to live on the property. He'd been an invaluable help at the wildlife park as well as a good friend to Blake once they'd laid the bitter past to rest.

He offered a drink to Blake. "Looks like you could use one. I got you a root beer."

The coldness of the glass was nearly as refreshing as his first gulp. "You must have read my mind."

"Like a book. You look like a man with a lot on his mind. Things going okay?"

Clark was just as perceptive and caring now as his twin brother, Kent, had been. "We have a big problem, buddy. Have you seen anyone skulking around the property?" Blake told him about Dean's search for the will and what it might mean if they found one.

"I haven't seen anyone, but I'll be vigilant." Clark clapped him on the shoulder. "And I'll be praying for protection for The Sanctuary. You're doing a good work here, and we can't let that guy destroy it. Have you thought about talking to him about it directly?"

"I wasn't sure if it would escalate the situation."

Over Clark's shoulder, Blake spotted Mason in his wheelchair with the drone controls in his hands. The boy's head was tipped back as he watched the drone fly over the park's landscape. "You know, I was looking at drone footage for clues of the murder, but if I could find a picture of Dean trespassing, I could file charges and end this."

"You still have the video?"

"Detective Greene took the originals, but I made copies. And there might be more footage, including the most recent break-in. It's a good place to start." Blake clapped his hand on Clark's broad shoulder. "I'll talk to you later." He walked across the grass to Mason, who beamed a smile his way at his approach. "Got anything good?"

Mason turned the camera around to show Blake. "Great footage of the white tigers. Paradise wanted some she could use for social media. And I got some cute scenes of the lemurs. They're very popular right now. And those black bear cubs are adorbs. I think they'll bring in some visitors."

"Your drone takes great video. I think I need to take a look at your recordings again." Blake told the boy about the break-ins. "I have copies of the first videos, but I'd like to see anything else you've recorded since."

Mason reached for his phone. "Dad should be about ready to leave to come get me, and he can grab them on his way out." He shot off a text, and the answer came back almost immediately. "Dad's getting them. He'll be here in ten minutes."

"Thanks for your help. And not just for the recordings. These pictures and videos you're getting will help the park in lots of ways."

"I love the park." The teenager's hands stroked the arms of his chair. "It's helped me feel part of something bigger, and I don't feel so trapped by my chair anymore. I'm glad I can do something for you."

They chatted a few minutes until Mason's dad, Randy, showed up with the footage. With the small box of SD cards tucked under his arm, Blake headed for his truck and tossed it onto the passenger floorboard before heading to his apartment to shower. He took the stairs two at a time and reached the landing outside his door in record time. He touched the doorknob, and the hinges creaked open. The place was unlocked, and he knew it had been secure when he left this morning. He'd been on high alert after hearing about Dean's plans.

He opened the door with his foot the rest of the way and paused. Should he grab his gun from the truck? He gave a slight shake of his head. One of the boys could have come up here to get something, and he wouldn't want to scare them. He grabbed a baseball bat from the corner of the tiny living room as he entered.

"Levi? Isaac?" he called. No answer. So he walked through the tiny space and down the hall to the bedroom.

His bedding was still taut and smooth. Old military habits died hard, and he couldn't leave his bed in disarray. The closet door stood open, and he'd left it shut. He pushed the bat in between the clothes hanging on the rod. Nothing. His boots and shoes had been disturbed though. They'd been lined up on the floor and were now jumbled in a pile as if someone had picked them up and looked them over. The boys wouldn't do this.

He pulled out his phone and called up the camera app to retrieve any video triggered by movement. A figure in a black ski mask came up the stairs. From the walk and movements, Blake was sure it was a guy. He bent over the doorknob for several minutes until he managed to get inside. Blake studied the jeans, boots, and hoodie the man wore, but they were all nondescript and common with no telltale lettering. The guy was Dean's build, but men of that height and medium build were common. There was no way to identify him.

His hands were bare, though, so Blake grabbed his phone and called Jane. Maybe there would be fingerprints.

CHAPTER 26

PARADISE TURNED INTO THE Sanctuary's parking lot and inhaled at the sight of Nora's forensic van. *Something else has happened.*

She parked her green Kia beside the van and hopped out. Blake, walking with Nora, waved to her as they strode away from Jenna's cottage. He left Nora and walked ahead to join Paradise. Her tension eased at the casual way he came toward her. Whatever it was, it seemed everything was mostly okay.

He slung his arm around her. "Someone broke into my apartment. Jane sent Nora out to check for DNA and fingerprints. There's touch DNA she can check for. If whoever broke in touched anything. She and I checked out Mason's other SD cards too. There's a good shot of Dean at the back door, but we have no proof he broke in." Nora reached them, and he thanked her as she climbed into the forensic van and drove off.

Paradise's heart rate dropped to its normal level. "You think it was Dean?"

"Probably. I have more video for us to examine to find proof of Dean's breaking and entering. If we could get him arrested, this might be over soon. He only has a month to find anything, and we could put this behind us."

"Any word on proving Adams killed Ivy?"

"Jane was closemouthed about it. Greene talked to all our employees, and they've got Mason's videos, but I don't think they have enough evidence yet. They want to question Adams, but they haven't been able to find him."

She leaned against him and caught a whiff of lemur scent. "Did the boys have another scent fight?"

"Is it that bad?"

She poked him. "I've smelled worse, but I'll wait while you shower. Where are we going tonight?"

"I thought we'd go to Mac's. I'm in the mood for shepherd's pie."

They hadn't been to the Irish pub in Pelican Harbor in quite a while, and she smiled at the thought of an evening alone with him. "You shower and I'll go chat with your mom and brothers."

"I'll expect a warmer welcome when I smell better."

He brushed his lips across hers, and she wanted to pretend to recoil at the odor, but she couldn't resist him and wrapped her arms around his neck and sank into the tenderness of his kiss. She palmed his face and relished the slight rasp of his whiskers that would soon be replaced by a smooth-shaven cheek.

He released her with obvious reluctance, and they walked back to Jenna's cottage. "I'll be right back."

She watched him bound up the stairs before she climbed the stairs to the porch of the cottage. Jenna spotted her through the window and opened the door before she could knock. "The boys were just asking about you."

Both boys rushed to greet her, and Isaac climbed into her arms. "I missed you both," she told them. "How was your day?"

"We saw bear cubs," Isaac said. "And the lemurs had a stink fight."

"I think your brother was in the middle of it."

Levi wrinkled his nose. "He didn't smell very good."

She set Isaac back on the ground, and both boys went back to their homework. "I could use a sweet tea." She and Jenna went to the kitchen and Jenna filled two glasses with ice and tea.

Jenna handed her a glass. "I meant to ask Blake if he talked to Hez about the will situation."

"He called him as soon as I told him about Mary. Hez is concerned, but as long as you didn't know about the will, we should be okay." She told Jenna what could happen if she'd bought the property knowing a will existed.

"Mary said Allen might have had a will once, but it had never been found. She said he'd left everything to her, which was normal, so I didn't worry about it."

Was that enough? "Hopefully Nora can find evidence that Dean has been trespassing. If we get him behind bars, this will be over. He has less than a month to track it down. If there's even anything to track down. We only have Dean's word that Allen left a will in his favor."

"Mary wouldn't be able to pay us back. She put the sale money into her house. I don't know what we would do."

Mary could be forced to sell her house to pay off the debt, and Paradise hated to think of the older woman being without a place to call home. It was all such a mess, but if the will was never found, the issue was done.

"I went to see Mary today. And I checked out Allen's truck, the one that was in the accident."

His hair still damp from the shower, Blake came in the back door. "I heard that. Where did you find the truck?"

"Dean has it. Mary gave it to him after the accident."

"You went to Dean's? What if he saw you poking around?"

"I went to Chet's BBQ during lunch-hour rush. I saw the line out the front door, and he would have been too busy to see me in the lot behind the restaurant."

Blake's frown deepened. "You have to be careful, babe. I think he's dangerous."

Paradise ignored his comment and pulled out her phone and showed him the picture she'd taken. "There was white paint on the back bumper. Dean could have hit him from behind and knocked him into the ditch. While Allen was unconscious, he could have injected him with meth."

Blake studied the picture. "What kind of vehicle did Dean drive at the time?"

"I didn't get a chance to ask Mary yet." She took back her phone and shot off a text to Mary, who answered immediately.

A white pickup. I never saw it after I gave him Allen's truck. Dean said the engine went out on it.

She turned her phone around so Blake and Jenna could see the text. "What if we could find that old truck? It could be in a junkyard."

Blake shrugged. "Or crushed up by now. But it's worth a try."

———

The server placed the steaming bowl of shepherd's pie in front of Paradise, then slid one in front of Blake as well. The deep, meaty fragrance of slow-cooked ground lamb mingled with the aromas of rosemary, garlic, onion, carrot, and celery. She couldn't wait for the first taste of the buttery mashed potatoes on top.

She took a tiny bite of the top. "Yum. I felt a little guilty leaving the boys. They wanted to come with us so badly."

His blue eyes were warm with love and he reached his hand across the table to take hers. "They get our attention all the time. I wanted to be able to look across the table at my gorgeous girl without a kid distracting me. We don't have enough time together. I can't wait until there are no problems to deal with."

If that day ever came. The problems seemed to multiply exponentially. She gave an answering squeeze to his hand. His strong grip was a reminder of how he held fast to those he loved. "Just when it seemed the money troubles might be lifting, we got that news about the will. Have you heard anything from Hez?"

His smile faltered. "I thought he might call tonight."

She released his hand and scooped up the first savory bite of meat and gravy. "I wish I could get this recipe."

They could pick up beignets for dessert, then take a walk along the water. She'd rinse the powdered sugar from her fingers in seawater and listen to the boats blow their horns out on the bay. It sounded idyllic, but that state of mind felt unattainable with this cloud of foreboding hanging over her head.

They tucked into their food for a few minutes, then Paradise reached for a hot yeast roll. While they were walking, maybe Hez would call.

Blake scooped up a spoonful of gravy and potato. "I still can't believe we have to worry about a will surfacing."

"When the auction started for the property, had you heard anything about a possible will?"

"I was still in the Marines and was overseas. I wired money to Mom to help cover the down payment, but I wasn't in on the initial property evaluation. I remembered the place, of course. You and I both came over a lot when the Steerforths had the roadside zoo. I thought it was an unbelievable stroke of luck that we had the chance to acquire it. But I left the details to Mom and Hank, and Hank was one of those guys who researched everything. You probably remember that about him. I'm sure he wouldn't have moved forward unless he was positive things were in order." Blake took a roll and broke it open to slather it with butter.

She tensed and moved a carrot around in her bowl. How did she bring up that his mom had heard mention of a will?

His brows rose, and he set his roll on his plate. "Are you worried about something, Simba?"

Had Jenna even mentioned Mary's concern about a will to Hank? This didn't look good, but how did she tell Blake without making it seem like his mom had done something wrong? She knew Jenna well enough to be sure she wouldn't have purchased the property if she'd thought there could be a problem, but would a judge believe it?

It felt like she was throwing her friend under the bus, but she set down her spoon. "I told your mom what Hez said, and she mentioned Mary had told her she'd thought there might be a will, but it never surfaced. After failing to find it, Mary went ahead with the sale. She said the will left everything to her anyway."

"Did Mom and Hank consult an attorney about it?"

"Your mom didn't mention doing any other research, so I don't know."

"I doubt Hank would have bought it without doing some checking. At least I hope that's true." Blake slumped in his chair. "Babe, this isn't good. If Mom admitted she'd heard there was a will, would she have been required to make sure before purchasing the property?"

"That seems crazy. She's not a private investigator or anything. How could she find a missing will?"

"When I talk to Hez, I'll mention it, but you're right—it wouldn't make sense for the court to put the burden of proof on Mom."

Though she could see him make a conscious effort to shrug off his worry, clouds gathered in his blue eyes. His phone sounded with a message, and he glanced at it. "Hez says to come by the condo when we're done with dinner. I'd hoped for a romantic walk along the water." Blake grinned. "And I suspect Savannah wants to show you her engagement ring."

"We can do both. Hez can tell us what he's found out, and we can walk to the pier when we're done. Our romantic evening isn't ruined."

But his attention felt far away from her, and the new distraction of the threat to the park's ownership had derailed her as well. Would they ever get a chance to talk about their own future?

CHAPTER 27

HOLDING PARADISE BY THE hand, Blake walked the two blocks to Hez's condo with her. Smiling people surged along the sidewalks toward seafood tents down along the water, but the party atmosphere failed to rouse him from his funk. Even the aroma wafting from Petite Charms didn't draw him out of his worry.

Paradise tugged him toward the entry door. "Let's take some beignets to Hez and Savannah."

He allowed her to guide him in that direction, but the thought of eating anything else turned his stomach. He bought a dozen beignets, and then they turned left out the door to access the black iron staircase up to Hez's condo above the bakery.

Savannah met them at the entry, and the dogs crowded behind her to greet them as they stepped into the great room with its white kitchen. The remnants of a pepperoni pizza was on the breakfast bar, and its aroma lingered in the air. Savannah's nephew Simon and Hez sat at the dining room table with dominoes scattered on the tabletop. Simon had been living with Savannah since his mother died in a car explosion. He began to put the tiles away in a metal tin as Hez rose to meet them.

Savannah's welcoming smile faded when her green eyes took in the box of beignets and their expressions. "If it's bad enough to bribe Hez, I'm glad I made coffee to go with those." She closed the door behind them.

Hez accepted the box of pastries Blake offered and set it on the table. "You just saved me from a whupping. Simon plays a mean game of dominoes."

The boy did a fist pump and strutted toward the living room like he'd just scored a touchdown. The dogs bounced after him. Savannah carried mugs of coffee to the table, then returned with small dessert plates. With her auburn hair up in a ponytail, she looked younger and more vulnerable. Love had relaxed her full lips into gentler lines, and Blake glanced at Paradise. Since the two of them had reconciled, she wore the same content expression he saw on Savannah's face.

Blake warmed his hands on the cup and inhaled the strong coffee aroma. "Paradise gleaned some information from Mom today. Go ahead, babe."

Paradise perched on the edge of a chair and took a sip of coffee. "Jenna heard something about a will before they bought the property." She laid out the information she'd gotten from his mom.

Hez absorbed the news quietly. His expression gave nothing away, but Blake knew his cousin was too professional to show any dismay. Hearing Paradise recite it again ramped up Blake's anxiety though.

Hez reached for a beignet and set it on his plate. A fine dusting of powdered sugar coated his fingers and scattered on the plate. "Rumors are like this powdered sugar. They can dirty anyone around and cover the truth. If that will is found, you might be implicated, Blake. Aunt Jenna will need to be very clear on what she heard, where she heard it, and what she did to make sure she was purchasing the property legally."

"Or we lose everything." Though the words were bleak, Blake's heart felt even worse. If the court found that Mom bought the property knowing it might be fraudulent, they'd have no recourse. There would be no way to recover the money spent. Worse, the animals would all have to be rehomed in zoos and other refuges, which would be a huge task. Those that couldn't be given or sold to other places would have to be euthanized. His gaze locked with Paradise's, and he saw the same despair in her amber eyes.

He gathered his composure. "How do we prove Mom believed it was a legitimate sale?"

Hez swiped some powdered sugar off the plate. "How do you squelch rumors? It's hard. The best thing you can do is go on the offensive. For justice you need to get at the truth. Find out if Dean killed his uncle. Talk to Mary and find out what she did to try to find the will. See if your mom called attorneys herself or at least consulted an attorney. I don't think she did. I would have been the one she would have asked about this, and she never mentioned it to me."

That grim summation of the purchase was enough to elevate Blake's blood pressure. Mom wouldn't have talked to anyone but Hez. He was always the first one she turned to, other than Blake himself. And she hadn't mentioned any of this to him either. He'd been deployed, but they'd had a chance to talk about the sale before it happened, and she hadn't mentioned any possible problem with the purchase.

"I'll talk to her," he said. "And to Mary. Paradise found out Dean has Allen's truck, and she discovered white paint on the passenger door and back bumper. We thought we'd check junk-yards to see if we can find what happened to Dean's old white pickup."

"If he was smart, he put it in storage somewhere," Hez said. "He'd want to hide it. Does Mary have any other property with an extra garage around?"

"I'll ask," Paradise said. "Anything else we should work on?"

Hez steepled his fingers. "What about the will? Dean seems to think it's on your property. Could he be right?"

"I haven't looked." Blake didn't want to try to find it because he wouldn't like what God would tell him he needed to do if he found it. He'd need to turn it in even if it meant losing everything.

His gaze turned to the woman he loved more than his own life. If they had to start all over, he'd be helping his mom and brothers longer than he'd planned. The necklace his mother had given him was with a jeweler friend now, and he hoped to have a ring for Paradise in another month or so. He wasn't sure he could bear more years of waiting to start their life together.

───

Savannah always made Paradise feel welcome and wanted. The sparkle in Savannah's eyes matched the ring on her finger—a halo of rubies around a gorgeous diamond. While Hez and Blake went to get Allen's accident report in the office, Paradise went into the kitchen with Savannah to wash the powdered sugar from their fingers. She took one final lick of the sweet stuff, then washed her hands with something that smelled like coconut.

Paradise dried her hands on a blue kitchen towel. "Your ring is gorgeous."

Savannah displayed it under the overhead light. "The diamond is from my original engagement ring, but the rubies and the design are new. I love it."

"Blake said he took pictures of Hez popping the question. Wedding plans are underway?"

"If we can ever get there." Savannah dried her hands. "There's been so much to do at TGU, but things will settle down soon and I'll be able to concentrate. Hez has been consumed with keeping us all safe too."

"The cousins are so much alike. Blake is still a Marine at heart and wants to wrap me in cotton."

"It sounds like you're not sure that's a good thing."

"It's a little stifling at times."

"Sometimes it takes a while to settle into a relationship and find the balance. I've seen the way Blake looks at you, and you're the center of his universe."

"I share the spot with his mom and brothers. I'm not sure when we'll be able to make plans for the future. There are so many problems at the park."

"Everything doesn't have to be perfect before you make a life together. Sometimes you have to reach the realization that plans are overrated. Things are far from perfect with us, too, but we're bobbing in the currents as best as we can. At least we're doing it together, just like you and Blake are. The waves might get high, but you're holding fast to each other."

Paradise hadn't thought of it like that, but Savannah was right. Blake had worked at trying to make things better for all of them, and he'd made sure they had time together even in the midst of the tsunami of bad news crashing over them. He'd managed to keep them all afloat.

The guys returned with a cardboard box that Hez began to unload on the kitchen table, and Paradise followed Savannah over to join them. "I haven't had a chance to go through the evidence yet since I picked this up two hours ago."

There was a file of pictures, and Paradise quickly glanced away from the autopsy photos and skipped to the report. Blake handed the pictures to Hez, who leafed through them. The report was straightforward. "The coroner found an injection mark in Allen's left antecubital fossa, a common site for meth users."

"English?" Blake asked with a smile.

"His left elbow vein," Hez clarified. "The coroner found no scarring though. If he was a frequent user, there should have been evidence of that. You'd think the police would have flagged that as suspicious."

She glanced at Hez. "Anything surprising in the police report?"

"The most surprising thing is how skimpy it is. I think some pages might be missing. There's no mention of Mary's assertion that she told the detective she suspected foul play and nothing about her belief that Allen had been forced off the road. No record of interviews with Dean or Mary at all. Didn't she say she even told the detective she suspected Frank?"

"That's what she told me," Paradise said.

"Do we know who investigated Allen's death?" Blake asked.

Hez flipped to the first page again, and his jaw hardened. "Greene, of course. He's completely incompetent. Or intentionally covering something," Hez said. "There's something about that guy that sticks in my craw. I think he's dirty."

Blake riffled through the papers. "But how do we prove it? Rod doesn't see it. He thinks he's overworked, not incompetent or on the take. Is there anything in here we can take to Rod and ask for a fresh investigation?"

Hez frowned. "Do you want to do that though? He'll want

to know why you're interested after five years. The fewer people who know you're worried about a will showing up, the better. We don't know what Dean is trying to pull behind the scenes. And with Aunt Jenna now implicated in hiding what she knew about the will, it could be problematic."

Paradise wished she'd never said anything. Jenna would never hide something on purpose. "She didn't really know anything. Mary assured her it was fine."

"And Mary had something to gain from the sale. A court might believe Mary rushed it to sale and Aunt Jenna was in on it. Since Dean is looking so hard for that will, I have to believe there's some truth behind it. He wouldn't risk being arrested for breaking and entering if he wasn't sure he could find the will."

"If it was a legitimate will, wouldn't an attorney have a copy? That's the part I don't understand," Paradise said. "He could call around and try to find it that way."

Hez put the loose papers back in the green folder. "There's no database where wills are recorded. He would have to call every attorney in the country. It's possible Allen used an online source and had it notarized, then hid it."

The best they could hope for was that the will stayed hidden. If there was a will.

CHAPTER 28

PARADISE HAD FALLEN ASLEEP on the way to Nova Cambridge, and Blake kept stealing glances at her in the moonlight with her long lashes fanned against her cheeks. She made several soft noises and he reached over to take her hand in case she was having a nightmare. Everything lately had been about the refuge, and he hated that he hadn't been able to help her find the person who killed her parents.

They both kept thinking things would calm and there'd be time to focus on the reason she'd come back to Alabama, but that *someday* hadn't yet materialized. He had to move past his problems and see to hers. He loved her too much to let her stay in limbo with all of it. She hadn't even contacted her brother yet. Blake knew she was trying to help him first. That was love.

He parked at the side of Pawsome Pets and shut off the engine. She looked so peaceful sleeping with her head resting on the door and the light shining on her beautiful face. Someday he'd wake up in the night and find her sleeping beside him, but right now it seemed an impossible dream.

She cried out and her head thrashed back and forth. "No, no," she moaned.

He leaned over and brushed her hair back off her cheek. "Babe, we're home. It's okay—I'm right here."

She moaned again and opened her eyes. "Blake." She bolted upright in the seat and reached for him.

He leaned over the console and pulled her to his side. "I think you were having a nightmare."

"I remembered." Her voice vibrated with desolation. "It was my fault. I let him in."

He pressed his lips against the side of her head. "It was just a nightmare, my love. Let it go."

She gulped in air. "It was the monkey. I knew there was something about the monkey that scared me. It was in my dream, but it was real."

"Are you sure it's a memory and not remnants of the nightmare? Do you want to go inside, maybe get something to drink?"

"I—I think so. I need to process it all."

He released her and climbed out of the truck, but before he could get around to the other side to open her door, she was out and at the hood of the vehicle. She grabbed his hand in a death grip, and her hand trembled in his. Whatever she'd dreamed had scared her badly.

He led her up the steps and unlocked the door. Both kittens met them when they entered. He flipped on the light in the kitchen and went to get her something to drink. "Tea?"

She nodded, and he dispensed hot water from the fridge, then dropped a chamomile tea bag into the steaming cup. He made another one for himself and carried them both to the living room. He put the tea on the coffee table before settling on the sofa and pulling her into his lap. "You're still shaking."

"It was all my fault. No wonder I felt so guilty."

"Babe, you were a kid. No matter what happened, you didn't kill your parents. Some maniac did." She buried her face in his neck, and her tears dampened his skin. He held her close, murmuring consoling noises, but she still trembled.

He'd never seen her in such a desolate state, and he didn't want to rush her into telling him before she was ready. If he could take her pain, he would, but all he could do was hold her and try to absorb as much of it as possible. It didn't feel like enough.

She lifted her head and swiped at her wet cheeks. Tears still swam in her reddened eyes, and despair twisted her features. "In my dream I couldn't see who was at the door, but I threw it open for him because he had a music box with a monkey with cymbals, just like the one in *The Phantom of the Opera*. I couldn't wait to see one in real life. I can still remember how it felt to hold it and the way the monkey seemed to smile with glee as he crashed the cymbals toward each other. I smiled, too, and barely noticed when he moved past me into the house. He said he'd found it on the doorstep and was just there to take a look at our cable box."

"Did he look at your TV?"

"I think so, but I can't remember. I was too excited about the music box. I took it to my bedroom and played it until it was bedtime."

"So you never saw him leave? Babe, that might not have even been the murderer. It might really have been a cable repair guy who fixed your box and left."

"And he might have been lurking in one of the bedrooms until he was ready to make his move."

He grabbed a tissue from the box on the end table and dabbed at the tears on her face, then mopped the moisture from his neck. "I think your mom would have noticed."

She took the tissue and dabbed at her eyes herself. "She was hanging clothes on the line in the backyard."

"Maybe someone really did leave the monkey on the porch."

"Who would have done that?" She jerked another tissue from the box. "Now that I'm starting to remember, maybe I'll be able to recall what he looked like. And this opens the pool of suspects. If it was a stranger I let in, I might not have known him."

She sank back against him, and he pulled her close. He wasn't sure he wanted her to remember something that might put her in the bull's-eye of a madman.

———

Paradise studied the music box in front of her on the booth's table inside University Grounds where she waited for Abby. The monkey's mocking smile made her shudder, but it was her imagination making it appear malevolent. It was just a music box, not some supernatural trinket that cursed the owner.

The hiss of the steamer wand and the comforting scent of coffee and cinnamon filled the space and began to ease the tension she'd felt ever since her nightmare. Though Blake had wondered if her memory was just a remnant of her nightmare, she was positive it had really happened.

Abby arrived with her auburn hair windblown but still beautiful. She smiled when she spotted Paradise, who held up the cup of coffee she'd already purchased for her friend. She slid the cup across the table when Abby approached. "A caramel macchiato, extra hot."

"Perfect. You'd think I would vary my choice, but I like routine." Abby settled on the booth bench across from Paradise. Her attention went to the music box. "I wasn't expecting to see this little guy. What's up? Your text sounded mysterious and upset."

Paradise touched the monkey's cymbal. "When my parents died, do you remember me having a music box like this? I think I called you when someone gave me one."

Abby took a sip of her drink. "I think this is that same music box, Paradise. It looks just like it. Your signature should be on it." She picked up the music box and turned it upside down, then peeled off the envelope where Paradise had found the tickets. "There it is."

She flipped it around to show Paradise. "Look, you wrote your name in blue marker. When you went to foster care, the belongings in the house were auctioned off. My dad bought it for me." She made a face. "I wanted to give it to you, but my dad thought it would make you sad so I delayed, and over the years it got buried in a box in our basement. I forgot all about it. How'd you get it? I thought it was still in the basement at Dad's ranch."

Paradise stared at her name in a childish cursive. "I had a nightmare yesterday and remembered a cable guy handing this to me and coming inside the night my parents died. When I woke I knew it was true."

"It was. You called me very excited about it, and I came over to see it. The tune drove your mom crazy, and she made you put it up after a couple of hours. You don't remember me coming over?"

Paradise rubbed her forehead. "My memories of the weeks just before and after that day are very vague and jumbled. I wish I could pluck them out of the fog."

"I'm happy to share mine with you." Abby's smile reached deep into her brown eyes. "I was at your house the week before, and we helped your mom make cupcakes, chocolate and vanilla."

"With sprinkles," Paradise whispered.

"And you made faces out of chocolate chips on some of them. I got to spend the night, and we watched *The Phantom of the Opera*. I hid my face through a lot of it and couldn't understand why you loved it so much." Abby turned on the music box and it tinkled out the tune to "Masquerade" before she shut it off again. A few patrons turned their way. "Someone had to have known you loved that movie."

"I hadn't thought that through, but you're right." Paradise took a sip of her mocha, a splurge from her usual black coffee. "Maybe it really was a cable guy, and he found it on the step. Someone could have put it there and hoped I'd leave the door unlocked after finding it."

"Maybe. I doubt there are service records from that long ago. It's been twenty years since they died."

Twenty years yet the pain was still fresh. Paradise could see her parents' faces so clearly in her mind, though their voices had begun to fade from her memory. When she got a chance, she'd search the box Evan had found in his attic.

Abby set the music box back on the table. "I have to wonder why anyone would give this to you. It's a little creepy. Why not give you the soundtrack or maybe a masquerade mask?"

"It's an important part of the movie though. The music plays in the Phantom's lair, and it's sold at the auction when the movie begins." But that didn't explain why someone would give it to her. "Did I ever ask for one as a gift?"

"You didn't mention it, but then, you might not have wanted to tell me because I thought it was beyond creepy. Not to change the subject, but what did Blake say about Lloyd Adams?"

"I—I haven't told him. I want to face Adams myself, and Blake would be upset and worried. Not that it matters at this point since I can't find him. The police are looking for Adams but he's vanished. That priority has moved to the bottom of the list with all the problems at the park." At Abby's questioning expression, Paradise wished she hadn't mentioned it. The whole thing with the will needed to be kept under wraps. "You know about those." Abby would assume it was only the money troubles.

"You can't let Adams get away with his smear campaign." Abby bit her lip and looked down at her hands. "I probably shouldn't mention it, but I saw his truck parked in front of Bea Davis's house."

The former sheriff's widow had implicated her dead husband as a possible suspect in the murders. "Bea seemed to think her husband was having an affair with Mom, but there's no proof." There were so many clues Paradise needed to investigate, but there'd been no time.

Abby frowned. "I don't think that's true, Paradise." She clapped her hand over her mouth. "Before Mom died I promised her I wouldn't say anything."

Abby knew something. Was it about the adoption? "You can't leave me hanging. If it's about my missing half brother, I already know about him."

Abby exhaled. "Oh good. My mom said she thought Becky's former boyfriend had started coming back around before your parents died."

Paradise forgot to breathe. "Who was he?"

"Mom would never tell me. She said it would be dangerous for me to know."

And she was gone now. How could Paradise find someone who might know the identity of that mystery man in Mom's life?

CHAPTER 29

MARY'S OLD BARN OUT on Marcella Trail near Foley still held a few flecks of red paint. The battered metal roof had a missing panel, but a new lock shone on the sliding glass door. Blake hadn't expected to have a problem getting in. Mary had told them nothing was out here on the old property, but he and Paradise decided to check. Mary hadn't been out here in years.

Paradise's expression mirrored his disappointment. "Now what?"

Blake stepped to the lock and yanked on it, but it refused to budge. "Maybe there's another door. You go around the west side to the back and I'll go this way." He walked the length of the barn and down the east side. He passed two fly-speckled windows on this end, so he held out hope there was a door along the back, but he and Paradise found no door, just a long expanse of weathered gray boards.

"The windows might not be locked." He started with the closest one, and it stood open half an inch. "Let's try this one." He shoved it up and the earthy smell of hay and dirt rushed out to meet him. He examined the opening. "I don't think I can get my shoulders through this."

Paradise stepped in front of him. "Hoist me up."

"I don't know what's in there. Let's look at the other windows. I suspect none of them are locked." After walking around the building, he found he was right—but they were all the same tiny dimensions. And too filthy to be able to make out much beyond their grimy glass.

"I'm perfectly capable of getting in there. Maybe there's a key inside that fits the lock."

He wanted to argue but he caught the stubborn tilt of her chin and the flash of independence in her eyes. She called it smothering her, and while he didn't understand how his protection was a bad thing, he had promised to do better, so he dropped to his hands and knees. "Stand on my back and slide in feetfirst. Who knows what you might find under the window, so don't risk going headfirst."

She climbed onto his back and grabbed the top of the window casing before standing on the sill and shining the flashlight app on her phone into the dark space. "I can get in okay. I'll try to find a light." She slid feetfirst into the interior.

He heard something metal clatter. "You okay?"

"I'm fine." Her voice echoed off the high ceilings inside. "The place is littered with Coke cans."

A light came on and he spotted her moving past a pickup to the wall by the door. He squinted through the window. A rack held rakes and tack gear as well as old Folgers coffee cans with who knew what in them. Paradise ran her hands along the shelf and the hooks by the door. He turned his attention to the truck, but he couldn't make out much detail. A tarp covered most of the cab, and only the bed showed it was white.

Mary had been right about the color. He tamped down his excitement. They still had no proof of anything.

Paradise turned to face him with a key ring dangling from her hand. "There's a key!" She retraced her steps to the window and handed him the ring. "See if it fits."

There were several keys on the ring. One belonged to a Ford vehicle, but one appeared to be the right size. He jogged around the side of the barn to the front and went to the sliding door. The small key clicked into it and unlocked it. "I'm in!"

He removed the lock and slid open the door. Dust motes flickered in the dying sunlight flooding into the opening. The interior smelled of old wood, and he stepped onto the floor's wide wooden planks. There were animal stalls to his left with a hayloft overhead. The open space where the truck was stored vaulted to the top of the roofline.

"Get your camera ready," he said.

Paradise nodded and turned her phone to face the vehicle while Blake grabbed one end of the tarp and pulled it off. Dust flew into the air, and he coughed. The truck under the tarp was a white Ford, probably around a 1995. Rust crusted the wheel wells he could see, and a few dents crinkled the driver's side.

He shone his phone flashlight at the damage. "There's blue paint. I'll have Nora get a sample. She'll want to collect it herself."

Paradise snapped several pictures, then moved to the front of the truck. "I'll check the bumper." She bent over to examine it and snapped another couple of photos. "There's a dent here but no paint."

"Let's pray the sample matches what's on Allen's truck."

She rejoined him. "But even if it does, the accident report says he died of a drug overdose. How do we prove Dean killed Allen—especially when we don't trust Greene to investigate it properly?"

"What about talking to Rod? He might light a fire under Greene." Blake went to the open window and closed it as far as it would go, leaving a small gap like before. He followed Paradise outside under the darkening skies. "Let's go grab some barbecue and take it home for dinner. Maybe Dean will be there, and we can see how he acts." He opened the passenger door of his truck for her, and she climbed in.

Paradise hadn't been very talkative since he picked her up after work today. He'd tried to give her space until she was ready to mention the reason, but he sensed a worry that ran deeper than the truck investigation.

He got behind the wheel and started the engine. "Did you have a rough day at work?"

She fastened her seat belt. "Just normal stuff. I had coffee with Abby before I opened the clinic. There's so much I don't remember, but she does. I should have talked to her sooner. That monkey music box we found in the lemur enclosure? It was the same one the man gave me when my parents were killed."

He had started to pull away from the barn, but he braked. "Abby recognized it?"

"Her parents bought it at auction after the murders, and it's been at Dillard Ranch all this time in the basement. Abby filled in some gaps in my memory. She has no idea how it got from her dad's to the lemur habitat. Oh, and get this—she saw Adams's pickup in front of Bea Davis's house."

He pulled onto the road and listened to Abby's memories of the day before the murder. This long after the murders, there would be no way to trace where the music box had been purchased—or by whom.

The aroma of beef brisket wafted through Jenna's kitchen as Paradise cleaned up the remnants of the barbecue meal. The boys had demolished their plates plus what was left of the cornbread, leaving only crumbs, before running off to get ready for bed. Blake had polished off the rest of the baked beans. She carried the dirty plates to the sink, scraped the leavings into the garbage disposal, then loaded the dishwasher.

If only they could have talked to Dean tonight, but he'd left fifteen minutes before they stopped to buy food.

Before she could start the dishwasher, Blake embraced her from behind and buried his face in her hair. "Yum, you smell like barbecue with a side of delectable skin and kissable lips."

"It's more likely the odor is that of old barn and manure." She turned around to hug him. His broad hands ran over her back and settled at her waist, where he paused to pull her close for a kiss. His firm lips coaxed a response from her, and she wrapped her arms around his neck and released her need for him. He palmed her cheek with one hand and deepened the kiss.

When it ended, she rested her forehead against his chin. "You're really amazing, you know. Always supportive, always ready to catch me when I stumble, always my one constant when the ground under me seems to be turning to quicksand. I don't deserve you, but I'm glad you're mine."

His biceps flexed around her as he pulled her tighter against him, and his pulse quickened under her ear. "I love you so much, babe. I'll hold tight to you the rest of my life."

The light flipped on overhead, and Paradise jumped and started to pull away. "It's just Mom." He pressed his lips against her hair and turned her loose to face Jenna's amused expression. "Are the boys ready for their story?"

"Almost. I told them they could play on their iPads for half an hour. I wanted to catch up on what you found out from Hez today."

Paradise shot a glance at Blake before deciding she should handle this. Jenna had mentioned the will to her, not Blake, and if anyone took the heat for revealing the facts to Hez, it should be Paradise. "Hez is concerned that you'd heard about a will. He doesn't believe you consulted an attorney—correct?"

Jenna's smile vanished, and her gaze darted to Blake before landing back on Paradise's face. "He's right, of course. It didn't seem important. I mean, Mary said the will had likely been destroyed. Was I supposed to tell her I didn't believe her? What did Hez think I should have done if I was told there was no will?"

Paradise shut the dishwasher door and turned it on. "He says a judge might ask if you made any calls to try to find the truth about the will."

"Who was I supposed to call? Lots of people I know do an online will and get it notarized at the bank. Does he really think anyone would suspect me of fraud in buying the property? I didn't have the first idea about how to find a missing will."

"Did you call anyone at all?" Blake asked.

"No. I didn't even call Hez. It didn't seem important. Even at the auction, no one questioned Mary's right to sell the property."

Blake approached his mom and hugged her. "Don't let this bug you, Mom. I don't think there's a will out there. When no will was found, Mary would have had an attorney appoint her as executor. I would guess the attorney would have done at least a cursory search for a will."

Paradise didn't want to upset Jenna by contradicting Blake,

but Mary might have told the attorney they didn't have a will. A lot of people didn't. She couldn't see an attorney doing an extensive search for a missing will if the spouse said there was none.

Jenna's chest heaved a sigh. "I've been praying about this, Blake, and I think we have to search for the will ourselves. It's the right thing to do."

"Jenna, that's crazy!" Paradise waved her hand around the cute cottage Jenna had infused with so much warmth. "Even if there is a will, Dean killed his own uncle."

"We don't know that." Jenna pulled a chair out from the table and sank into it as if her legs wouldn't hold her any longer. "These are just things. If we try not to face the truth, it will hang over our heads forever. We'll always wonder what the right thing to do was. We have to keep our hearts pure."

Blake dropped into a chair and put his head in his hands. "Mom's right. I've been struggling with it too—that's why I've been so desperate to find out if Dean killed Allen. If he's a murderer, the law is clear on what happens next. He's not allowed to benefit from the will, and he'll go to jail."

"But what about Mary? She'd have to pay back the purchase price, and I don't think she has the money."

"She could make payments." Jenna sighed and rubbed her forehead. "If a judge believes I wasn't to blame in some way. That's for the law to figure out though. Our job is to do what's right in God's eyes, not our eyes."

"But that's so hard," Paradise burst out. "What about real justice?"

"God's in charge of that detail." Blake straightened and pulled Paradise down on his lap. "We have to take it one step at a time and see where things lead. Believe me, I'm praying we can prove Dean killed Allen, but we also need to take the next step to walking our own straight path and not let our desire to have our own way lead us along a crooked path."

This was all over Paradise's head. There was so much about the faith walk she didn't understand yet, but if God took everything from these people she loved, she wasn't sure she could live with it.

Jenna smiled at them snuggled together. "I'll leave you two lovebirds alone and go read."

The man she loved exuded strength in so many ways—not just his muscular build. Paradise leaned her face against Blake's and realized she could do something about this. "I don't want to wait any longer, Blake. Let's get married right away. I don't need a big wedding. We can get a marriage license and have a simple wedding at the church with your family."

She felt his surprise radiate through his sinews and muscles, tightening along the length of his form where she sat pressed against him. Her enthusiasm for the idea amped up a notch. "I have the apartment, and we can squeeze everyone in. I can redo the second bedroom for your mom and the boys. There's enough room to put in a bunk bed and another bed."

He palmed her face and stared into her eyes for a long moment. The joy in his expression gradually morphed into disappointment. "I see what you're doing, babe. You think we're going to lose everything, and you want us to have a place to stay, don't you?"

His hands came down on her shoulders, and he gently slid her off his lap to rise and pace the living room. "It's sweet of you to offer, but this isn't how I want our life together to start." He swept his hand around the living room. "It's hard enough getting alone time with you here. With us all crammed into your apartment, what kind of beginning to a marriage would that be?"

He was turning her down? The shock left her speechless.

CHAPTER 30

BLAKE AND PARADISE STOOD at the edge of the pond with the visitors who had disembarked on the safari truck. The group was from a local middle school. Bertha had noticed them, and the hippo's eyes and nostrils were the only part of her visible above the water. Blake glanced around to make sure everyone had crowded close for Paradise's lecture. She was in her element when talking about animals.

He still couldn't believe her marriage proposal last night, but he didn't want to start a new life with all of them packed into her tiny apartment. He didn't want her pity.

Paradise turned toward the group with a smile. "You might wonder why there's a strong fence between us. Bertha is a very friendly hippo and would never hurt someone on purpose—at least we've never seen any sign of aggression from her—but hippos are the second-largest land mammal in the world. Only elephants are larger. Bertha's bite is three times the strength of a lion's, and her teeth are formidable. You don't want to get a nibble from her. Hippos are social creatures, but Bertha has been here by herself. We recently learned we will be receiving a male hippo in a few weeks, and we think Bertha will be happy with the addition. A group of hippos is called a bloat or a pod. Or sometimes just a herd, but I like the other terms better."

A teenage boy at the front of the group waved his hand. "Does she live in the water all the time?"

"Hippos have no sweat glands, so they have to be in the water quite a lot," a girl next to him said. "Right?"

"That's right. And they can hold their breath for five minutes. They often sleep underwater—we call that rafting. She'll often do that with her nostrils sticking above the water's surface."

Blake let them ooh and aah over Bertha and walked away to check his phone. Hez was supposed to call with an update on his research into the probate case surrounding the Steerforth property. *Call me* was in a text from his cousin. Blake held up his phone to Paradise, who nodded that she'd keep the group together. He returned Hez's call.

"Hey, that was fast," Hez said. "I'll be brief since I know you're working. Dean contested the probate, but he had no evidence other than his own word. Mary claimed she'd looked for the will and couldn't find it. In a deposition, she said the only person who claimed Allen had made a will was Dean. She'd signed Allen's truck over to Dean before he contested the probate, and they had a sharp argument about it. She kicked him out of the house, and he left town when the court denied his petition. The judge found no compelling evidence to believe him."

"What does that mean for us?" Blake asked.

"If the will is found, Dean would reopen probate to have the sale set aside. Mary would have to repay him, but you're still out of the property. The court would kick everything back to being between Mary and Dean. Your mom isn't automatically protected as a good-faith buyer, though the judge could still find she had no responsibility to find the will. It's all speculative. Even if she's found not liable, she'd have to wait to be repaid once this all played out. Property costs more today, so finding another place could be problematic."

"Would it be possible for Mary to give Dean what she received for the sale and let us keep the property?"

"That would have to be negotiated on their own. I have my doubts Dean would agree to that, but I could be wrong."

"I could try to talk to Dean and see what he intends. Mom thinks we should search the property for the will." A long pause ensued, and Blake pulled his phone back from his ear to see if the call was still connected. It was. "Hez, you there?"

"I'm absorbing that crazy news. I should have expected Aunt Jenna would come to that conclusion. Her integrity is admirable, but I can't say I agree with a move like that. It's not her responsibility to ensure Allen's wishes are carried out. Especially with the cloud of suspicion Dean is under."

"I've been torn about it," Blake admitted. "It's hard to know what's the right thing to do, but I'm going to search and whatever happens is God's will. In the meantime I'll talk to Dean and let him know we know about his assertions and ask what he intends to do if we find it. I might be able to get a feel for his guilt or innocence in Allen's death. I have good instincts that tell me when someone is lying."

Blake saw several guests move toward the safari truck. "I'd better go. It's time to head to the next safari stop. Thanks for your work on this, Hez. I'm sure we'll owe you for more than our standard free hours."

"Not in this lifetime." Hez's chuckle was low and relaxed. "I'm not about to trample on people I love when they're hanging by a thread."

Blake thanked him and ended the call. *Hanging by a thread.* That was a good way to put it. What did the future hold if they lost the park? The loss would affect all their employees and volunteers—people he cared about like Clark and Mason, not just his family. It felt like a doomsday event was heading their way, and he couldn't figure out how to move them all to safety.

———

Blake parked his truck behind Paradise's building and shut off the engine. "I thought we'd walk over from here. Mary said Dean usually gets off around eight, so we should head that way."

Paradise unfastened her seat belt and opened her door. She took his hand and they crossed the street. She hadn't said much when he told her what Hez had discovered about the probate case. Jenna hadn't either. There was no point in discussing what might be coming until they got a sense of Dean's intentions. Paradise's mind worried the situation like one of her kittens with a catnip mouse.

She still felt blindsided by his rejection of her marriage proposal. Did he not love her enough to make a plan to do something unconventional?

Uncertainty was her usual state of mind with the way she'd had to expect circumstances to change on a day-to-day basis. Even after her stint in foster care, she'd never stayed at a job more than three years for various reasons. Her shoulder gave her a sympathetic twinge, and she rubbed it.

They stood off to one side in the back lot of Chet's BBQ and waited for Dean to make an appearance. The aroma of smoked meats wafted toward them, mingling with sweet scents from the bakery on the next street over. But she wasn't hungry, not when the coming confrontation would tell them what to expect.

Blake gave her fingers a comforting squeeze. "This will be over soon."

The word *over* felt ominous when she knew what the changes could mean, but she nodded. Learning to trust anyone, even Blake, came hard to her, and after his reaction last night, she was even more uncertain of their future.

The wooden screen door in the back opened and banged shut. Dean carried a take-out bag and wore a smile that vanished when he spotted them. The wind blew his curly brown hair onto his forehead, and he approached with a cautious expression.

"Hey, Dean, you have a minute?" Blake's tone was friendly and easygoing.

"That's about all I have. My girlfriend's waiting at my apartment."

"We won't keep you long. Your aunt told me you'd been looking around for a will you think might be stashed at the property. And my camera caught you entering my apartment. Touch DNA showed it was you."

Dean's brown eyes darted away and his jaw slackened for a long moment before he took a step back. "Uh, I'm not sure what she's talking about. I mean, yeah, I contested the probate when Uncle Allen died."

He doesn't want to admit he's trespassed.

Paradise saw the same realization dawn on Blake's face. She clung to his hand and squeezed his fingers. Dean's reluctance to admit the truth might be something Blake could use.

"If you do find the will, I wondered if you'd be amenable to your aunt Mary paying you what we paid for the land."

Paradise watched Dean's thought process and the accompanying emotions flicker across his face. Fear, disbelief, calculation, and finally hope. "Well, I don't know. It's worth a lot more now."

"Not that much. If you sold it elsewhere, you'd have to figure out what to do with the animals. Some of those came with the property. Some lions and a tiger and other big animals."

Dean shrugged, and his brown eyes went hard. "I'd just shoot them."

Blake's jaw flexed, but his voice was even when he spoke. "And where would you bury them? You can't just let them rot on the ground."

"Oh, yeah, I guess that's right. You'd have to take them."

"Some of them aren't ours," Blake reminded him. "They originally belonged to your aunt and uncle."

"Whoever buys the land for the rare earth could deal with it." The second the words were out of his mouth, Dean gritted his teeth and exhaled. He hadn't meant to say that.

Blake recoiled and glanced at Paradise. "Rare earth?"

"Never mind. I'll figure it out. But you shouldn't count on keeping the property."

"*If* there was a will," Paradise added.

"Oh, there's a will, all right. I saw it with my own two eyes."

"The probate court didn't find any evidence of one."

"Says who?"

"My attorney checked it out. You were unable to bring any proof to the court."

"That doesn't mean the will doesn't exist. I know it does, and I'll find it."

"Maybe your uncle destroyed it."

"He didn't have ti—" Dean broke off and brushed past them on his way to the truck.

Blake clung to Paradise's hand, and they watched him go. "Did he start to say Allen didn't have time?" Paradise whispered when Dean's tires spit gravel in his urgency to get away from them.

"I think it's likely." Blake rubbed his head. "I think he killed his uncle. I wasn't sure before, but I can sense his desperation. He's found out about the rare earth somehow, and that's driving this new determination to find the will."

"I think so too." She walked with him back to her building. "I've got some steaks I can grill for dinner."

He hesitated. "I probably should go home and tell Mom what happened. Not only is Dean determined to find that will, but he plans to sell it and have the property destroyed by mining. He has no care for neighbors or the land."

"I'll grab them and meet you at the house then. I'll fix dinner and you can talk to your mom. Do you think she'll still be determined to look for the will?"

"Probably. Honestly, I don't know what's right. Do we actively try to turn the property over to someone who plans to destroy everything around us, someone who's a murderer as well? He has no conscience. I could sense it."

Paradise could, too, but she didn't want to sway him if he had a strong conviction on what to do. She tried to imagine the animals dispersed across the country and the land with gaping holes. The buildings would be gone. And what about their neighbors? How could allowing such destruction be the right thing to do?

The bright future she'd envisioned seemed more and more elusive.

CHAPTER 31

THE AROMA OF GRILLING steak mingled with the scent of freshly mown grass. Blake relished watching Paradise flip the steaks. She was altogether too beautiful for him to be able to drag his gaze away. With her cheeks flushed and her hair a halo around her head, he wished they were alone so he could have her all to himself.

He hadn't had a chance to tell her or Mom that Jane had called to tell him preliminary results from the paint chips showed a match between the white and blue trucks. But she'd also warned him that with the official cause of death a drug overdose, it wouldn't change much. They had to prove Dean had injected his uncle with meth.

Clark had joined them for dinner, and Blake forced himself to pull his attention from Paradise. He handed Clark the first plate of food. "Yard looks good," he told him. He wished he could give his friend a raise. He was worth so much more than Blake could pay. The fences were in great shape with Clark's welding skills, and so were the zip lines. Bringing him here had been a real boon to the park.

"Thanks." Clark set the plate on a round patio table and took a seat.

Blake took his own plate and sat beside Clark. "You know the park about as well as anyone. Any ideas where something small might be hidden?"

Clark's brows rose. "Small as in a will? You're not going to look for it, are you?"

"I think we have to figure out where we stand."

Clark's chin came up and his brown eyes flashed. "You stand on firmer ground if that will is never found."

Blake couldn't deny that. Anxiety over their possible expulsion from The Sanctuary had mounted with every day they wrestled with this. It would be better to *know* what was coming than to worry and stress over it. Though he knew God was in control, it was hard to let go of his need to fix everything for those he loved.

He cut a piece of his steak and chewed it. "Great steak, babe," he called.

Clark hadn't touched his plate. "Tell me you aren't serious."

"Mom is determined too."

He glanced at his mother, who was sitting at the picnic table with Frank and the boys. Was her romance with Frank going to go anywhere? Even if it did, she'd mourn the loss of everything she knew here. She believed in the park and the work they did. She cared about every employee she'd ever hired and did her best to be a friend and mentor to them. All the unknowns had to be gnawing at her too.

He turned his attention back to Clark. "Any ideas on where I should look?"

Clark raised his gaze slowly to stare at Blake, and he didn't answer for a long moment. He exhaled. "You might check the hayloft in the big barn."

The bottom dropped out of Blake's stomach. "You found it?"

Clark's jaw flexed. "I don't like anything going on here that I don't know about, so I started paying attention to everywhere I went in the park. I was stacking hay bales in the loft, and there was a board sticking up under a layer of loose hay. I moved everything out of the way to repair it and realized it was hollow underneath. Several boards weren't nailed, so I lifted them up and checked it out. A metal box was screwed under the boards, and several things were inside, including the will."

Blake's mouth went dry and he swallowed hard. Paradise shut off the grill and closed the lid. She carried her plate of food toward him, and her amber eyes widened when she took in his face. He should have tried to control his expression better. He gave a jerky nod. "Did you read it?"

"Yeah. Not good. I wish I'd burned it."

Blake set his food aside. He wouldn't be able to eat until he'd faced this. Feeling as decrepit as an old man, he rose and headed for the deck stairs.

Paradise was beside him a moment later. "What's happened?"

"It feels like the world just ended, but I know it didn't." He told her about Clark's find.

She took his hand. "Oh, Blake. I—I can't quite believe it."

"Me neither." He clung to her fingers as they followed the oyster shell path that wound through the yard to the large barn by the Serengeti acreage. With every step his heart grew heavier. This would be so hard on his mom and brothers. On Paradise. On everyone.

The comforting press of her fingers clutched tightly to his steadied him. Was this the worst thing that had ever happened to him and Mom? No. They'd weathered worse when his dad died, when Kent had lost his life because of Blake's inattention, and when the boys had lost their dad. God had been their comfort in those times, and he'd see them through this too.

But there was no denying it would be hard. He tried not to think about losing the animals they loved. He'd find homes for them, good homes.

They reached the barn, and he led her inside to the sweet scent of fresh hay. The haymow was in the left back area, and he steadied the ladder for Paradise to go up. Once she reached the top, he put a boot on the first rung and forced himself to climb to face the doom of the dream his family had held on to for so many years.

Paradise had the box open and the will in her hands by the time he got to her. The document was in a small brown file, the kind a trifold paper would fit. He slid out the sheaf of papers and unfolded it.

Last Will and Testament

He skimmed it and handed it to Paradise. "Allen left everything to Dean, just like he said."

Paradise's thoughts were so jumbled she couldn't discern how to move forward. Jenna had realized something was wrong and had taken the boys inside to put them to bed a little early. Blake sat beside Paradise on the sofa with his head down as they waited for his mom to come back and hear the news.

How would they explain it to the boys? Her eyes burned at the thought of the little guys she loved so much facing such a huge upheaval. Wasn't it enough that they'd lost their dad? Did they have to lose their home now too?

It's not right, God!

Her faith was still too young and feeble to try to reason out why God would allow this. She'd felt this place was a sanctuary for all of them, not just the animals. To know it was about to be ripped away from them in such a horrible way was more than she could wrap her head around. Blake's mention of how gruesome the land would look made her wince. Would Dean even be allowed to sell it to a mining company? That was a question that hadn't been fully explored.

Jenna, blue eyes serene and expression calm, entered the room. "You found the will, didn't you?"

Blake raised his head and nodded. At his miserable expression, Paradise reached for his hand again, and his fingers gripped hers. He cared so much about his family. So did she, and she'd give all she had to make this better for Jenna and the boys.

Jenna walked closer and put her hand on Blake's dark hair. "It's all right, son. God is faithful, and if we lose this, he has something else for us."

Blake's face contorted. "I keep telling myself that, Mom, but it's not just us. It's the boys and our employees. It's the animals too. I can't see a way forward through the trees."

"I can't either," she admitted. "But let's take one thing at a time. The will leaves everything to Dean?"

"Yeah."

"I think we need to tell Hez first and learn the next step. Do we tell Mary or the court? Do we call Dean? I have no idea, but Hez will know." Jenna gave Blake's head a final pat. "Do you want me to call him?"

Blake reached for his phone. "I'll do it. We can all talk to him on speaker." He gave a few swipes to the phone and Hez's voice answered.

"Hey, Blake, everything okay?"

"It depends on what you mean by okay. If you mean without a problem, then no. We found the will." He told Hez about Clark telling them where to find the hidden metal box. "What do we do now?"

"I'd hoped you wouldn't find it. Is your mom there?"

"I'm here, Hez," Jenna said.

"This is a really hard spot, Aunt Jenna. Dean can reopen probate and contest the sale. He'll ask you to testify, and you'll tell the truth about having heard about the will. Even though you thought it was all okay, it will be all the proof he needs to invalidate the sale and gain ownership."

Jenna's gulp was audible. "What about the money we gave Mary?"

"You bought it at auction from the estate, so the estate would have to repay your money. How much did you pay for it?"

"One point five million. Hank had made some good investments, and Blake chipped in money, too, so we bought it outright."

"So you would eventually get that money back once Dean sold the property. But it would be tough to find a place for the animals until you could buy and build what you need elsewhere. Maybe Dean would give you some time. There's one more possible wrinkle." Hez's voice deepened as if he hated to be the bearer of bad news. "If Dean accuses you of conspiring with Mary to deprive him of his rightful inheritance, the court could find that to be the case and you'd never get your money back. At the very least, he could tie it up in court for years."

Paradise tried to wrap her head around the enormity of the catastrophe facing them. There was nothing she could do. The small savings she had was a pittance and wouldn't go far toward helping this family she loved so much. If she and Blake got married right away, he could share the master with her, and she could try to find enough space in the second bedroom for Jenna and the boys. She'd be glad to sandwich them into her apartment, but they'd have to throw air mattresses on the floor.

"Do I just hand the will over to the court?" Jenna's voice gained strength as she spoke.

"You're not an heir or executor of the Steerforth estate, so you can't address the probate court yourself. Mary or Dean would have to do that. Given the circumstances, you should probably give it to Mary and give Dean an official copy. Then it's out of your hands. They may come to a private agreement."

Blake let out a long exhale. "Paradise and I tried talking to Dean today about what might be done to let us keep the property. He has no interest in that and seems to know all about the rare earth here. I think that's what drove him to carry out a new search for the will."

"Interesting," Hez said. "How would he have discovered that?"

"He didn't say and seemed upset that he'd admitted he knew. I thought maybe he knew someone who worked in the mining field and had heard a rumor that brought him back here for more information. He and Mary hadn't spoken until he came back a few weeks ago."

"Find Dean's friends, even an old girlfriend. If he killed his uncle, someone probably knows."

Paradise had forgotten that possible avenue. She made a mental note to talk to Mary about that direction when they delivered the will. Mary's situation was even more dire than theirs—she wouldn't be entitled to anything and would have to pay back what she'd received. She'd likely spent at least some of it on the house where she lived. Would she be homeless too? She was older, and it wouldn't be easy to start again.

CHAPTER 32

AFTER CHURCH BLAKE PULLED onto the shoulder of the road before the drive that led to Mary's and evaluated her beautiful beach home. It was waterfront, and she'd probably put every penny she'd gotten for The Sanctuary property into it. He exchanged a long glance with Paradise, who sat with the document in her lap. The dread on her face reflected the same emotion churning inside him.

"I think I'd rather face a sniper right now than get out of this truck and give that will to Mary."

Paradise glanced down at her lap. "This will come as such a shock."

"Maybe not. She knows Dean broke into the house looking for it, so she might be prepared for the possibility."

"We *thought* we were prepared," she pointed out. "But none of us believed it would come to this."

"Good point." He squinted toward a car exiting the carport space under the pilings of Mary's house. "Someone is leaving, but that's not her car."

The white car, a Nissan Altima, turned out of the driveway and passed them on the road. The driver was on the phone and didn't glance their way as he went by. Even with tinted windows Blake recognized him.

Paradise leaned forward and stared after the car. "W-was that Adams?"

"Yep. The bigger question is, what was he doing at Mary's?"

Paradise whipped out her phone. "I'm texting Jane! Maybe they can apprehend him."

Blake moved his foot from the brake and accelerated toward Mary's house. "Something doesn't feel right about this, babe. He was sabotaging things at The Sanctuary, and we find him here hiding his car under her house? Most people park in front."

"We'll see how Mary acts." She grabbed her purse and slid the will into it. "I don't think we should give her the will until we figure out what's going on. What if she's in on this in some way?"

"What are you getting at?"

"What if there never was a will? Maybe Mary is working with Adams and Dean both? Maybe they tried to run us off by making the place appear unsafe. When that didn't work, they decided to plant a fake will to take back the property. The rare earth rights make it worth way more than what you paid for it."

Blake's forehead creased. "But Mary mentioned during probate there had been a will."

"Maybe it played out the way she said until Dean came back and told her how much they'd both stand to gain if she helped him regain the property and sell it for an insane amount of money. We know Adams is trying to shut us down. Nothing about his presence here makes sense unless they're working together. Maybe Dean planted the will at The Sanctuary."

He nodded. "You're probably right. I mean, why would Mary

act upset about the will if she was in on it?" He turned into Mary's drive and turned off the truck. "Six months ago I would have laughed at such a crazy idea. I'm not laughing now. Though I'm not convinced, it makes a sick kind of sense. We didn't have Allen's signature checked. I've been in that hayloft a thousand times and never found a cavity in the floor either. Let's use caution for now. We'll talk to Mary and then call Hez."

They got out of the truck and mounted the long staircase to the front door, shooing away the gulls that dive-bombed them. The sound of the waves was a soothing rhythm in the background.

Mary met them on the deck before Blake could ring the bell. Her cheeks were pink and her hands fluttered like a frightened bird. The scent of her perfume, something obnoxiously floral, mixed with the scent of the ocean. "Good morning."

When she didn't meet Blake's gaze, his suspicions ramped up more. Paradise was right—they needed to be careful here to make sure nothing underhanded was going on.

"I wasn't expecting you. I'm having lunch with a friend and don't have much time. What can I do for you?" Mary folded her arms across her chest expectantly without inviting them inside.

Paradise smiled and took a step closer to her. "This won't take long."

Mary glanced at her watch. "You had a question?"

Blake pulled out his phone and called up his Notes app. "Could you give me the names of some of Dean's friends? Does he have any old girlfriends?"

More color flooded Mary's already blotchy cheeks. "Oh my, that's a hard one. You know how young men can be—so secretive. He had a girlfriend a few years ago, but I'm not sure what happened to her or where she is now."

"What was her name?" he prodded.

Mary didn't answer for a moment, then finally shrugged. "Elowen Quintero."

"Unusual name."

"She said her first name was Cornish and her mother thought it sounded like a fairy. She was very sweet, much too nice for Dean." Mary's lips compressed in a disapproving grimace.

Blake put it in his note. "Any friends he usually hung around with?"

"They always varied. His best friend in high school was Wade Greene."

"Greene?" Paradise asked. "Is he related to Creed?"

"His brother."

Blake jotted down the name. Creed wouldn't welcome them interrogating his brother, but they couldn't let his disapproval deter them. Could there be some kind of connection? "Does he still live in the area?"

"I think he lives near Magnolia Springs." Mary glanced back toward the door behind her. "I really need to get going or I'll be late."

Paradise tensed beside Blake and touched Mary's arm. "One more question. Mr. Adams was here just before we arrived. We saw him leave. I didn't realize you knew him."

Mary's face flamed with more color before the red receded and left her pale. "He—he—I mean, we're seeing a little of each other." She glanced at her watch again. "I'm meeting him for lunch, so I really need to go." She backed away and slipped inside the house before she firmly shut the door in Blake's face.

He took Paradise's hand to walk back to the truck. "I don't buy it for a second. She's not seeing Adams. Why would she lie about that?"

"I think she was taken aback and it was the first thing that came to mind. She probably hoped we didn't see him."

Blake opened the passenger door for her to climb in. "Where to first? Adams or Wade?"

"Wade. We're more apt to get something useful out of him."

Maybe she wasn't ready to confront Adams. It might be a conversation Blake needed to have by himself with the man.

———

Blake had been quiet and reflective since the will had been found. Paradise shot him a glance as he drove to the address Jane had provided for Wade Greene. If only she could take some of the burden from him, but he wouldn't let her even if she could.

Things had been off between them since she'd suggested they get married, and she wasn't sure how to heal the breach.

The address on Bay Road wasn't far from Jesse's Restaurant. Children played in neatly kept yards, and Paradise admired the architecture of the older cottages. Live oaks draped with Spanish moss stretched their branches in a green arch over the roads, and the neighborhood's safe, family feel drew her. She could live here.

Blake pulled into the driveway of Wade's house and shut off the truck. "Jane said he's married now and has a two-year-old girl. He's a firefighter."

Paradise spotted movement in the side yard and saw a young couple with a toddler and a puppy heading toward the swing set. "There they are."

Blake got out, and Paradise joined him at the hood of his pickup. "Since his wife is with him, maybe you should ask the questions. Our sudden appearance might be less threatening that way."

She nodded and stepped out in front of him to head toward the little family. Wade had Creed's light brown hair, though Wade's wasn't thinning like Creed's, and Wade's smile spread across his face in a way she'd never seen on his brother's countenance. Creed was always stern and a little creepy, and this young man clearly delighted in the little girl and his wife. She instantly liked him.

His wife noticed them first, and she nudged Wade. The wind blew her long blonde hair, and her blue eyes tracked their approach. Paradise smiled at their little girl, a carbon copy of her mother. The puppy, a fat golden retriever, wiggled its behind and came toward them. Paradise leaned over to pet the soft fur. "Aren't you cute?" she crooned.

Wade turned. "Hi there, can I help you?"

Paradise straightened and took a step closer to him. "You're Wade Greene? I'm Paradise Alden and this is Blake Lawson. He owns The Sanctuary, and I'm the vet there."

"The wildlife park?" His wife's smile returned. "Tessa loves to go there. She's crazy about the otters." The woman wore a gauzy white blouse and a long blue skirt that flowed in ruffles to her ankles.

The little girl beamed when her mother mentioned the otters. "See otters!" She plopped on the grass and threw her arms around her puppy.

"I love the otters too." Paradise squatted in front of the toddler. "Next time you come, Tessa, I'll let you see the otter babies that were born recently." The girl's blue eyes widened, and she clapped her hands. Paradise stood and turned her attention back to Wade. "I'm sure you're wondering why we're here. Mary Steerforth told us you were Dean Steerforth's best friend."

He glanced at his wife. "*Was* would be the appropriate word.

He was dating Elowen, and I intervened when he hit her. We got into a fight, and I broke his nose." Satisfaction vibrated in his voice.

His wife took a step back. "What do you want to know about Dean?"

"You're Elowen?" When the woman nodded, Paradise floundered for the questions she needed to ask her. "We'd heard you had dated Dean and had planned to find you. How fortunate you're both here together."

Wade folded his arms across his chest. "We don't see him anymore. He's a violent jerk that I don't want around my family."

Paradise hoped their hostility meant he and Elowen would be more likely to reveal any secrets about Dean they might know. Paradise directed a commiserating look toward Elowen. "I'm sorry you had to endure that. Abuse should never happen. I grew up in foster care and experienced some of my own." When the blonde's expression softened, Paradise plunged ahead. "Did Dean ever mention his uncle had left him his property in a will?"

Wade snorted. "Not likely. Dean and Allen didn't get along. Allen was always pushing Dean to get a decent job, and they got into plenty of battles. Dean shoved his uncle once, and they didn't speak for several months."

"Yet they lived together for a while when Allen and Mary were separated," Paradise said.

"Only because Allen was trying to get him off drugs. Allen's boy died of a drug overdose, and when Allen found out Dean was shooting meth, he put aside his anger and tried to get him clean. He would have known better than to leave his property to Dean at that time. Allen came home one day and found Dean cooking meth in the kitchen. That was the final straw. Allen told Dean he couldn't find another dead boy and packed his things. He and Mary reconciled about then, so he just went home."

"So you never heard Dean talk about expecting to inherit anything?"

"Mary gave him Allen's truck when he died, but Dean never mentioned anything else." Wade glanced down at his wife. "Did he ever say anything to you?"

She bit her lip. "He filed a petition to contest the probate, but it was thrown out."

"Did you ever see a will?" Paradise asked.

Elowen glanced up at her husband, then bent to pick up their little girl. She didn't look at Blake or Paradise. "No."

She's lying.

And it was something she didn't want her husband to know. "Thank you for your time. I heard you're a firefighter, Wade. Thank you for your service to the community. I'm sure you're very proud of him, Elowen."

"Oh, I am!" Her expression went soft. "I love how much he cares about other people, and he's a great husband and dad. We decided before we got married that I would stay home and raise our children. He takes good care of us."

"Bring Tessa over to The Sanctuary this week when you have time. She'll love the otter babies."

Elowen shifted the toddler to her other hip. "I'll do that one day this week when Wade has to go back to work. Thank you!"

Paradise and Blake said goodbye and walked back to the truck. "When she brings Tessa by herself, I'll find out what she was lying about. She knows something about the will."

CHAPTER 33

ON SUNDAY NIGHT BLAKE sat out on the back deck listening to his mom and Paradise banging around in the kitchen as they cleaned up after dinner. The night sounds of nearby crickets and frogs mingling with the roars of the big cats out in the park reminded him how life went on even when it seemed impossible to find a way through the muck.

He buried his face in his hands and tried to pray for wisdom, but marshaling his thoughts and heart was impossible with the weight of responsibility bearing down on him. His mom hadn't been happy they hadn't turned over the will, but after talking to Wade and Elowen, he no longer believed it was real. God had brought up the right doubts at the right time, but had that been his decision because he wanted to believe it?

The slider onto the deck opened, and Paradise came to join him. Her plumeria scent enveloped him, and her presence strengthened his resolve to find out the truth and do the right thing.

She didn't wait to be pulled onto his lap but curled into her usual spot there with her head on his chest. "What's going on with you? I can see the wheels turning. Did your mom's reaction upset you?"

"A bit," he admitted. "I thought she'd see the wisdom in getting to the truth. We have a little time to figure this out. It's not like we had to turn that will over today. There are two weeks left. I think you're right though—this will isn't real."

"Could we get the signature checked for forgery?"

"Hez would probably know who to contact, but we'd have to get a copy of Allen's real signature. That might be difficult if Mary is in on this."

He buried his face in her hair and inhaled her sweet scent. How had he survived without her? He pulled his face back, cradled her in his arms, and kissed her. Her lips softened under his, and he drank in her love and passion until they were both breathless. "I'm glad you're with me to figure this out."

She palmed his face. "I wouldn't want to be anywhere else."

"Maybe you should talk to Abby about Mary. I could talk to her dad. The Dillards were neighbors of theirs for many years. They'd know Mary's character better than most. I don't want to accuse her without some evidence."

"Good idea. And maybe Roger would have a sample of Allen's handwriting. Over the years he could have sold him hay or something else for the animals."

Blake kissed her. "We can go over tomorrow after work."

"I hope Elowen brings Tessa soon. I want to hear what she knows that she's hiding from Wade."

"She may not tell you."

"I felt a kinship with her. I think she might if she knows how important it is."

He curled a strand of her hair around his finger. "You plan to tell her what's going on?"

"At least some of it." Her head cocked to one side when a big cat growled, and she frowned. "The cats are acting up tonight. Maybe we should check on them. They seem particularly upset."

He'd been so engulfed with questions he hadn't paid attention, but she was right. Roaring from tigers wasn't unusual, but growling usually meant they were warning off another animal or even a predator keeper. The tigers had already been fed for the night, so what was out there upsetting them?

She slipped off his lap and stood waiting for him. "I'll go with you."

"You don't have to." She still hadn't fully gotten over her fear of the big cats, though her terror had lessened as she'd tended to their health issues.

"I'm okay. Let's grab a tranq gun from the medical building, just in case."

He got up and opened the sliding door. "Mom, we're going to check on the cats. They're a little raucous tonight."

His mom sat at the table with a mug in her hand and her Bible open next to a plate of cheese and crackers. "I heard them and was going to ask you to check on them. Let me know if you need me for anything."

"Will do." Blake closed the door. At least she wasn't still mad at him. He took Paradise's hand, and they walked toward the medical compound. He left her at the door and grabbed two tranq guns and two big flashlights. When he returned she took one of each. The roaring of the tigers had increased by several decibels. Someone definitely had upset them.

He picked up the pace, and Paradise's long legs kept up with him. He smelled the big cats before they reached their enclosures. They'd been spraying, which meant they were marking their territory. None of the males were kept together since they were solitary animals, so either another predator had gotten in with a tiger or they sensed an intruder.

He paused at the outer fence and flipped on his big flashlight. The powerful beam probed the dark and highlighted the big cat growling on the inside of the fence. All seemed well and he spotted no breaks in the fence.

Did they have an intruder?

—◡—

The scent of the big cats and their growling set Paradise's nerves on edge. "Do you see any reason for them to be riled?"

"Nothing." He consulted his phone and frowned. "There's someone moving around by the barn. It could be an employee, but I can't tell. You go back with Mom and I'll walk over to check it out. I suspect it's someone unfamiliar to the cats, and they don't like it."

"You're not going by yourself. I can call for help if something happens."

He squeezed her hand. "I know better than to argue with you."

She walked with him toward the barn. The stars twinkled brightly in the dark sky, and the tigers had quieted. Lights shone out of the windows of the small employee cottages they passed, and it felt too peaceful for there to be much going on out here. Until an invisible hand shoved her.

Something lifted her feet off the red dirt and threw her to the ground on her backside.

Almost immediately a *boom* sounded and flames shot up ahead.

Dazed, she got up and searched for Blake, who had been tossed to the dirt as well. He had red mud on his face as he leaped up and rushed her way. "Are you all right?"

"I—I think so. What was that?" She turned toward the fireball and clutched Blake's hand. "That's Clark's trailer!" She escaped Blake's grip and ran toward the flames. "His propane tank exploded." She cupped her hands to her mouth. "Clark!" She yanked out her phone and dialed 911 to report the fire. She declined to stay on the line and ended the call.

Blake ran past her, shouting his friend's name, but the heat drove him back. Paradise watched for any movement from the trailer, which was nothing but burning rubble and twisted metal. She prayed that Clark wasn't inside. No one could survive a blast like that.

"Clark!" Blake shouted. His face was blackened with soot and mud, and he again attempted to move toward the destroyed hulk that used to be a home.

"I'm here," Clark said from behind them.

Paradise whirled and Blake leaped past her to grab Clark in a bear hug. He patted Blake awkwardly on the back with one hand while his other arm, holding a plastic bag, hung at his side.

Tears of relief stung her eyes. Clark didn't have a scratch on him and there wasn't so much as a smudge of soot on his face. "Where were you?"

Clark held up the sack. "Groceries." He stared at his former home. "It's all gone, and I didn't have insurance. My tent is still in my truck though." The words were matter-of-fact with no trace of self-pity.

Blake stepped back and wiped his streaming eyes. "I couldn't bear to lose you too, buddy. Praise God you're okay. And don't worry about the trailer. We have an empty cottage at the other end of the lane."

A self-conscious smile hovered on Clark's lips, and he looked down. "I haven't had a man hug me like that since Kent died."

Blake passed his hand over his eyes. "That brought back way too many bad memories." He turned and stared again at the remains of the trailer. "What happened?"

"The fire marshal might be able to figure it out," Clark said.

Paradise was finally able to get her knees to hold her, and still shaken, she walked to Blake's side. "Was it an accident or a diversion?"

Blake's mouth dropped open, and he turned to look at the barn. "Let's go find out."

CHAPTER 34

MURMURING AND EXCLAIMING, EMPLOYEES spilled out onto the lane in front of the cottages. Clark walked over to assure them he was all right, but most of the people continued to stare at the ravaged trailer.

Blake couldn't stop shaking. For a few moments he'd been right back there in the war and was trying—and failing—to save Kent. If Clark had died too . . . Blake shut down the graphic images in his head. His friend was alive and standing right next to him.

Blake's arm was around Paradise's waist, and he kissed the top of her head. "You can head back to the house before Mom packs up the boys and comes to see what's going on." He forced a chuckle. "You're shaking like me."

"That blast scared me to death. You can text her and tell her everyone is okay."

Blake soaked in the sight of Clark, who stood calmly watching everyone. He left the rest of the employees and came to join them. "You're a little pale, Blake."

Blake made an effort to compose himself. "You want to go tell Mom what happened?"

Clark nodded to a spot behind Blake. "Too late."

He turned around to see his mother hurrying toward him with both boys in tow. He intercepted them and scooped up Isaac, who was the sleepiest of the two. "Everyone's fine. The gas tank on Clark's trailer exploded. It was probably a gas leak."

Isaac wrapped his arms around Blake's neck. "I heard a big boom, but I didn't even cry. I went to make sure Mama was okay."

"You're a good protector." Blake set him down and ruffled his hair. "You guys can head back to bed. That was a rude awakening, wasn't it?"

"Can we get closer to the trailer? I want to see," Levi said. "I'm not sleepy."

"Tomorrow." Mom steered him back toward the house. "It's too dark to see much anyway."

Her backward glance at Blake was an unspoken question, and he smiled and nodded. "Everything is fine."

He waited until they were out of earshot. "Let's check the hayloft in the barn."

"The cavity I found with the will?" Clark asked.

"Yeah, I left a little trap for whoever left it there." An owl hooted from a branch above them, and the sounds of the park settling back into its nightly routine floated his way. A coyote yipped, and several wolves howled as if to assure him they were fine. Monkeys screeched in chorus with them.

The three of them reached the barn, and he eyed the door. It wasn't fully closed. "Were you in here?" he asked Clark.

"Nope. It was shut up tight when I passed this way to go to the grocery store."

Blake frowned and slid it open the rest of the way. The scent of hay made him sneeze. Could someone have been kicking it around? A light had been left on too. The ladder stood against the side the way he'd left it, and his boots were on the rungs before Paradise and Clark made it inside. He climbed to the loft and glanced around the dimly lit space. Hay still covered the cavity, but it was a thin layer instead of heaped high the way he'd left it.

Paradise came up the ladder and stepped onto the hay. "What are you looking for?" Clark scrambled up behind her.

"If Dean or Mary planted the will, they might be curious to see if anyone found it yet. Since Mary mentioned Dean was breaking in and searching park property, they might have needed a diversion tonight to get in here and look." He pointed at the area where they'd found the cavity. "I kept the original will but folded a copy and put it in the folder where we'd found it. I measured exactly where I laid it, and I put a quarter in the crack of the lid over the cavity so I could tell if anyone opened it. Someone has been in here. The light is on and the door was open."

He swiped the hay out of the way to reveal the wooden top over the cavity. "The quarter is missing." He spotted a silver glimmer and pointed it out. "It's there, right where it would have fallen if someone lifted off the lid." He knelt in the hay and pried up the board. "The folder is two inches lower than where I left it. Someone was definitely in here, and in a minute I'll know who it was." He pointed out the camera attached discreetly in the shadow of the barn ceiling.

He took out his phone, called up the camera app, and touched the recorded movements. Clenching his jaw, he turned it around for Paradise and Clark to see.

Dean's face was on the screen.

Blake uploaded the video and attached it to a message he sent off to Jane. "I sure hope this is enough to convince a court that something fishy is going on. He could have killed you tonight. Or one of the boys."

"Or you," she added. "I don't think he cares who he hurts. He's determined to get the property."

"He's not going to succeed." Blake clapped Clark on the shoulder. "Let me get you a key to the empty cottage and some clothes. We're about the same size, so some of my stuff will do for now."

———

The Dillard Ranch sprawled over three thousand acres and was one of the largest properties in Baldwin County. Paradise took in the green fields and grazing livestock, both cattle and horses. Picturesque red barns dotted the expansive grounds around the big brick home. The late-afternoon sky beyond the white paddocks added to the picture-perfect view.

"Roger has a beautiful property. I spent a lot of time here during my childhood with Abby. I haven't ridden a horse in ages."

"Roger would let you go horseback riding anytime you want." Blake maneuvered around the final curve to the sweeping driveway in front of the house. "You should plan to go with Abby sometime."

"I will." She hopped out when the truck stopped behind Abby's car. "I think it will be helpful to have her and Roger in one room as we try to figure this out."

Blake shut his door and joined her. They walked toward the porch together. The huge pillars were quintessential Southern Alabama, and warmth flooded Paradise as she mounted the familiar steps to the front door. The years fell away and she remembered how Abby's mom always hugged her when she came to visit, even more fiercely after Paradise's mom died. She'd died herself five years later, right after Paradise had been yanked from the Adamses' household.

Abby opened the door before Paradise could press the bell. She wore slim-fitting jeans with a flannel shirt and cowboy boots. Her red hair was in a ponytail that made her look about fifteen, but her brown eyes held heaviness. Paradise didn't think it had anything to do with the problems at The Sanctuary.

Abby hugged Paradise and held on longer than usual. "I came prepared to go riding, did you? I texted you to bring clothes."

"I didn't get the message." Her phone dinged, and Paradise glanced at it. "There it is now. Crazy cell service." She glanced down at her shorts and tee. Sandals instead of boots. "I think I'm underdressed."

"Luckily we wear the same size." She wagged a finger at Paradise. "Don't try to get out of it."

"I'd love to go. It's been ages since I was on a horse." She linked arms with Abby, and they passed through the foyer into the living room with Blake trailing them.

Abby's daughter, Quinn, was in jeans and boots as well. Her long red hair in a braid, she glanced up from where she sat cross-legged on the floor and gave a slight wave before going back to her phone. Typical fourteen-year-old behavior though she was only ten. She would be a real handful by the time she was in her teens. "Grandpa said I had to stay here with you in case I could help you with the questions. Mary used to babysit me. Grandpa will be here in a second. He was looking through paperwork." She waved at the coffee table. "I brought in a tray of sweet tea. Help yourselves."

Paradise and Blake settled on the sofa, and Abby perched on

one of two leather armchairs opposite them. Her gaze went to Quinn, and that worry line deepened. Paradise took a glass of iced tea, beaded with condensation. Blake grabbed one too.

Abby leaned forward. "I'm dying to hear what's going on, but we'll wait for Dad so you don't have to explain twice."

"Dad's right here," Roger grumbled as he entered the room. He carried a manila folder. "You can start that explanation anytime." The distinct odor of horse wafted from his jeans and pearl-button plaid shirt. His boots were worn and soft.

Blake leaned forward. "Dean Steerforth claims to have seen a will leaving The Sanctuary property to him. I'm concerned he might be trying to convince us all of a lie." He nodded at the file in Roger's hand. "I see you have some paperwork with you. Did you find anything with Allen's signature on it?"

Roger ran his hand over his grizzled head. "One of the employees signed most of the sales slips I have, and I have a few with Mary's signature. Sorry I can't be more helpful."

Quinn got up. "I have a card Allen sent me after I helped rescue one of his bears. He wrote all over it. I'll get it." Her thick red braid bounced as she rushed off to hurry up the stairs.

Roger frowned. "Wasn't expecting that," he muttered. "She must like you, and that's saying something when we often seem to merit only an eye roll."

Abby's expression was troubled. "I thought the danger to the park was over. Isn't it a little late to reverse the sale?"

"There's a chance it could be snatched away if a will is found in the next two weeks," Paradise said. "But it's all such a mess. You know Mary really well, even better than I did since you continued to volunteer at the zoo. Did you ever worry she might not be . . . ethical?" Paradise hated to plant any doubt around Mary's character, but she didn't know how to ask it any other way.

Abby's eyes narrowed. "You think she might be in on this with Dean?"

"We don't know. We have reason to believe the land might have much more value than what we paid her," Blake said.

Paradise took a sip of her tea. "I've always liked Mary, so it's hard to consider she might be partnering with Dean on this, but we don't know what to think."

Abby's gaze darted between Paradise and Blake. "You might look into her financial situation." She bit her lip and reached for a glass of tea.

"Abigail!" her dad growled. "You know better than to insinuate something like that. Working at the bank carries a lot of responsibility, and you need to keep your mouth shut."

"I know, Dad, but this is *Paradise*. I love The Sanctuary, and I can't sit back if she needs my help. I gave no details."

Roger's scowl deepened, but he said nothing. Quinn's boots clattered on the hardwood stairs, and she rejoined them with a card in her hand. "Here you go." She hesitated. "I'd like it back when you're done with it. Allen was my friend, and this card is special to me."

Paradise rose. "I'll make a copy right now and you can keep the original. You have a printer with a scanner, right?" she asked Abby.

"I'll show you." Abby patted her daughter on the arm as she passed.

The office felt quiet and secluded. "I thought about asking you to meet for coffee," Abby said. "I need someone to talk to." Her gaze darted to the open door.

"I'm here now." Paradise turned on the printer, then stepped to the door to hear Roger expound on the right way to train a horse. Blake and Quinn were still out there too. "What's wrong?"

Tears glimmered on Abby's lashes. "Jason's getting remarried. He's marrying my friend, the one he was having an affair with when he divorced me."

Paradise embraced her in a tight hug. "I'm so sorry, Abbs."

"Thanks. I had to tell someone." She pulled away and sniffled. "I haven't even told Dad yet. Or Quinn."

Paradise felt her friend's pain. Betrayal was hard.

CHAPTER 35

ASTRIDE A GENTLE BAY mare, Paradise galloped across the field beside Abby. The wind tore at Paradise's hair, but it stayed put in its braid. She drew in a breath of hayfields and horse. It should have relaxed her, but it was hard not to dwell on Abby's situation.

Abby reined in her black gelding and dismounted beside a pond surrounded by tupelo and oak trees, and Paradise did the same. They led their horses to the water for a drink, then Abby dug string cheese out of a pouch and handed a stick to Paradise. "I've got water too."

Paradise smoothed a few loose strands out of her eyes. "I'd forgotten how free I feel when riding. Like the horse and I are one creature exploring all-new territory. Thanks for making me do it." She turned to examine the pond and surrounding terrain. "We used to catch bream in the pond. Best fried fish in the world. I've missed this place."

Abby gave her a once-over from head to toe. "There's the country girl I remember. The jeans fit well. How are the boots?"

"I never want to take them off." She released her mare's lead and settled on a low wooden bench. "I needed this. Things have been, well, stressful."

Abby plopped beside her. "That's an understatement. You've been attacked from every direction, and The Sanctuary is teetering on the edge of destruction. It's a wonder you're not curled up in a corner somewhere refusing to talk."

Paradise ran her fingers through the soft grass and inhaled the aroma of the pond and trees, a fresh scent unlike any other. "I don't know what to do to help resolve all this. I've been putting up social media posts, trying to combat the continually bad press, and that seemed to be working—especially after Governor George's visit with her grandson hit the news. But this whole contested sale thing is monumental. We're all scrambling to figure out if it's even true, but it feels very ominous."

Abby reached down and picked several leaves of mint, then offered some to Paradise. "I hope you find out it's a forgery."

"Blake was going to take Allen's signature sample to Hez for him to get analyzed. I can't believe Mary would be part of trying to pull something like this, and I feel terrible that I suspect her. I mean, I *know* her. You and I spent a lot of time over at Steerforths' roadside zoo."

"You always want to believe the best in people. Even with all you've been through, you have hope in their better instincts."

Paradise chewed on a mint leaf and the tang sharpened her thoughts. There was an undercurrent in Abby's tone, a reserve that Paradise had never heard before. Or maybe she hadn't been listening closely enough. "You want to tell me something, but I'm not good at riddles. Just spit it out. Am I wrong to suspect Mary is involved?"

Abby rolled the mint leaves in her palm. "I think you're very astute. Go with your gut. I wish I could say more, Paradise, but it wouldn't be ethical. Your instincts are on target."

"But how do I find out? I know nothing about figuring out anyone's financial situation."

"Check out the online places that will do the work for you. It's not that expensive. Even a cursory look will—" She clamped her mouth shut, then tucked the mint leaves in her mouth. "Things are always changing in life." Her brown eyes took on a faraway expression. "I love the ranch so much, but even Dad is talking about it becoming too much for him. He doesn't say so, but I can see he's thinking of selling it. I don't know what I would do if he did, but I would adjust and adapt. We all do. Change is hard no matter how it happens."

Was Abby telling her she needed to stop trying to control things in life so tightly? Paradise had always known she tended to cling to the familiar because she'd experienced so much change when she was younger. The cataclysmic upheaval that could be barreling toward them wasn't anything any of them would welcome.

Paradise reached for more mint leaves. "I can't imagine your dad selling this place. It's such a wonderful haven."

"Something's up with him. He's aged quite a bit the last three months. I worry he's ill, like, seriously ill. But he's always kept his problems closely guarded, so it would take something unprecedented for him to tell me anything. But he's managed this ranch and this county by sheer force of will, and I don't think he could ever sign his name to a sale document. I'm probably worrying for nothing."

"Quinn is great. She's your only child?"

"She's ten going on fourteen. I think that says it all right now.

Friends assure me she'll be human again soon. Remembering the drama we went through at that age gives me hope."

"How will you handle telling her . . . about Jason's remarriage?"

Abby's smile faded. "I have no idea. She adores Jason and already feels like she doesn't see him enough. I have to do it today though. Confrontations are hard."

"They are. I need to talk to Adams, but I haven't been able to force myself to do it."

"That's a job you should delegate to Blake or Jenna. He probably sees you as that vulnerable fifteen-year-old and he wouldn't listen anyway. A big guy like Blake might be able to get him to back off."

"While you're right that he might underestimate me, that could be in our favor. He might think I'm no threat and tell me something he wouldn't if Blake cornered him. I need to be the one to confront him. Blake offered, but I told him he needed to let me stand on my own two feet."

"Independence is highly overrated. We are all stronger together. Blake loves you. I mean, he *really* loves you. He wouldn't change anything about you. That's so rare. It's not weakness for the two of you to bolster each other when you need to, to be the one who comes alongside and helps the other stand when your knees want to give out. I never felt that with Jason."

Paradise had never thought of it that way, but it made sense. She glanced at her phone. "I need to get back. I want to hear what Blake found out from Hez."

When Blake left the Dillard Ranch, Paradise had run off with Abby to change clothes and go on a horseback ride. He drove to

Tupelo Grove University and found Hez's office in Connor Hall. It was quitting time, but recovering or not, his workaholic cousin would still be in the office.

Blake parked in the lot near the pond and spotted the old gator Boo Radley sleeping in the grass. Students chatted in small groups and glanced his way as he entered the building and found the office for the Justice Chamber.

Hez hadn't been wrong to warn him that the tiny room was the second-worst office on campus. The scarred oak door stood open, and his cousin sat at a tiny desk with a computer that should have been in an antique store. A small printer perched on one corner of the desk, and a shiny coffeemaker, emitting the aroma of strong coffee, occupied another corner. Four mismatched chairs completed the room. Fluorescent lights buzzed overhead since the drafty trefoil window didn't do much to push back the shadows.

Hez hadn't seen him yet, and Blake studied the plaque on the wall behind the desk. He had to read it aloud. "'But let justice roll on like a river, righteousness like a never-failing stream!' Amos 5:24."

Hez glanced up and his harried expression morphed to a smile. He rose and came around the desk. "Blake, I wasn't expecting you." His shaved dark hair was beginning to grow back around the scar.

Blake gestured at the plaque. "I like the verse. I hope I'm not interrupting."

"You're saving me from digging deep into a case that makes no sense, but that's what we do at the Justice Chamber. The plaque was a gift from Savannah. I like it too. Have a seat."

Blake settled on a cracked plastic seat closest to the desk and handed over the envelope containing the copy of the card Quinn had found as well as the will. "We managed to get a sample of Allen's handwriting. I hope you'll be able to have the writing analyzed to see if the will is a forgery."

"Great thinking. We can start with scanning them and uploading them to an online program for preliminary scrutiny. If the program sniffs out a rat, we can go a step further." Hez took the card to the printer. He plugged in a USB drive. "I'll scan them and we'll see what we've got. Fingers crossed." The scanner hummed to life, and the light swept the underside of the printer top. When it was done, he plugged the USB drive into his computer to upload. "This will take a few minutes. Any other clues to this mess?"

Blake told him about the video of Dean at the park and about Clark's trailer exploding. "I told Jane that Abby had seen Adams's car at Bea Davis's house and that Paradise and I saw it at Mary's. They're looking hard for him."

Hez had winced at the news of the explosion. "Coffee?"

"Sure." He accepted the mug Hez handed him. "We went to see Mary after church yesterday morning. I didn't pull in right away but stopped down the street. Adams pulled out from under her house. Paradise was suspicious and started analyzing what we know. We decided not to tell Mary we'd found the will. Instead we asked her about Dean's friends and got a couple of names." Blake unloaded all the events of the last two days.

"I always knew I liked Paradise. This sounds very suspicious, Blake, and I'd proceed with caution. If Mary is working with Dean in a plot to defraud you of the property and split the proceeds between them, they will be formidable. The minute Mary gets that will, she's likely to address the probate court and throw her support behind overturning the sale. It would go right through, and Aunt Jenna would have to find somewhere else to go. If they would be this underhanded, they might even conspire to say she knew all along there was a will and chose to ignore it. She'd never get her money back."

Blake sank back in the chair. "That's my biggest fear. Abby suggested we check out Mary's finances. I'm not sure how we do that."

"A simple credit check would tell us a lot." Hez jiggled his mouse and stared at the screen, then typed a few words. "This won't take long." The seconds ticked by and a frown settled on his forehead. "She's got a terrible credit score and her house is in pre-foreclosure. She initially paid cash but got a mortgage a few years ago that's in default."

Blake absorbed the news. "If she joined in with Dean to regain the property, it could change everything for her too. They could split the millions and both end up with much more money than she got initially. It all makes sense."

The computer dinged and drew Hez's attention again. "This is what I'd hoped to see. The program thinks Allen's signature is a forgery. It will take time to get an expert to weigh in, but you'd have ammunition to go to Mary and Dean and tell them you know what they're trying to do."

"Should I do that or continue to investigate? I don't want Dean to get away with murdering Allen either. We spoke to Dean's former best friend and girlfriend, who happen to be married now." He told Hez about Elowen's behavior. "Paradise thinks she's hiding something, and she might be able to pry it out of her when she sees her without her husband."

Hez leaned back in his chair. "Creed Greene's brother—that's an interesting connection. Based on this new information, you should wait to talk to Mary or Dean and see what you can find out. In the meantime I'll get to work on finding an expert to give us an official opinion on the signature. We might be able to nip this at the source before we get mired in litigation."

Hez's buoyant expression lifted Blake's hope, which had been sagging about as low as a sow's belly. "I think I'll take the family somewhere to celebrate. The boys have been feeling the weight of our worry. We haven't told them, of course, but kids feel that stuff."

Hez nodded. "Simon's the same way. He picks up on the smallest things."

Blake swallowed the last of his coffee and stood. "I'm glad I got to see the famous Justice Chamber. Whoever attracts your attention is lucky you're working on their case. Me and Mom would be in manure as deep as the haymow if we didn't have you."

CHAPTER 36

MOISTURE FROM LAST NIGHT'S rain soaked Paradise's boots on her jog across the grass to the ticket booth to meet Elowen and Tessa. She sidestepped a skink that darted away from her feet. She smiled when she spotted Elowen's radiant smile. She held Tessa on her hip and pushed a stroller with her other hand.

"You made it." Paradise had paused long enough to grab a stuffed otter, and she held it out to the toddler.

Tessa let out a squeal that made the monkeys down the path screech back. "Otter!" She clutched the stuffie to her chest.

"What do you say?" her mother prodded.

"T'anks."

"You're welcome. The baby otters asked me if you were coming today, and I said I hoped so. Let's take a cart." She led Elowen and Tessa to an employee golf cart and got them seated, then folded the stroller and stuck it in the back. "Hang on."

Tessa's smile widened with the wind in her hair. She peered at the birds as they passed the aviary, and when the parrots squawked, she covered her ears. Paradise exchanged an amused glance with Elowen. They reached the otter enclosure, and Paradise stopped the cart.

"For the past few weeks we only watched via a camera so the little family could bond in seclusion, but the pups are eager to explore their new world, so they're being released for the public to see tomorrow. But I'm going to take you into their domain today before anyone else gets to encounter them."

"That's amazing. Thank you so much." Elowen scooped up Tessa and followed Paradise past the fences screened with murals announcing the upcoming arrival of the new family.

Paradise grabbed a cooler of crayfish. Inside the first perimeter, there were no posters screening the habitat from view. The otters frolicked in a pond surrounded by green grass and weeds. The babies spotted Paradise and came her way, emitting their characteristic chirps and squeaks.

"They associate me with food. They tend to get excited about their meals, so I can't let you give it to them. I don't want them to mistake your cute fingers for crayfish." Paradise opened the cooler and began to feed the otters. "We have five in this raft, which is what a group of otters is called, including the mama." The otter smell was strong from them marking their territory, but Tessa didn't seem to notice.

They spent half an hour watching the otters play and swim. Paradise couldn't decide if she should bring up her questions or wait and see if Elowen offered whatever secrets she might be holding. When the toddler made noises about going to see the other animals, Paradise decided she had to make a move. It was already nearly noon, and she had other animals to check on.

She led the way out of the enclosure and locked the gate behind her. "The petting zoo is right here. I'll bet Tessa would love to see the rabbits." She took them the short distance to the barnyard entrance.

Elowen let Tessa go in by herself to sit with the rabbits. "I wanted a moment with you," she said, glancing around. "You asked me and Wade if we'd ever heard anything about a will, and I—I lied. Wade is the best thing that's ever happened to me, and I didn't want him to be disappointed in me. There is a will out there, Paradise, but it's forged. Dean forged it."

Paradise put her hand to her mouth. "When was this?" They had proof, but if Elowen wouldn't testify, it wouldn't get them very far.

"When Dean came back a few weeks ago, I ran into him at the barbecue place where he works. I was carrying my take-out order to the car, and he waylaid me. I wasn't trying to see him or anything, but Wade might think I knew he was working there. I hadn't heard he was even back in town."

"You should tell Wade. It's not a good thing to keep secrets from the man you love. It makes complete sense that you'd go get food without knowing he was there."

Elowen tucked a lock of blonde hair behind her ear, and her blue eyes filled with tears. "I know, but he'd be so angry if he found out what Dean wanted."

"And what was that?" Paradise asked in a gentle voice.

"He wanted me to forge Allen's signature on a will Dean drew up."

Paradise took a quick peek at Tessa, who had a bunny on her lap, before turning back to Elowen. "That seems a strange request."

"I—I did some forgeries for him when we were together. I'm so ashamed of it, but I was afraid of him. He needed money for drugs, and he had me forge some checks of Allen and Mary's.

They passed right through the bank, so he thought this would be easy for me."

"Did he have access to meth?"

"He cooked it and sold it, so he had plenty of opportunity to use it. He was always so angry when he was high."

Paradise had to tread carefully here. "Did he ever talk about Allen's death? You were together after that, right?"

Elowen sank onto a nearby bench and stared down at the ground. "He killed him. He told me he slid a needle in his elbow, and the expression on Allen's face went from anger to surprise and then to contentment. He thought he did a good thing because Allen had cancer. Mary didn't know, so Dean never told her. It was pancreatic cancer, and he didn't have long. Dean claimed he was only helping him out, but I think he believed Mary would let him move back in and he'd have access to her money again. She didn't."

"Would you testify to this?"

Elowen put her head in her hands. "I don't want Wade to know. I wish I'd never told you."

Paradise gripped the younger woman's forearm. "He'll still love you, Elowen. I could see that he's a good man."

Tears pooled in Elowen's blue eyes. "But even a good man would recoil at what I've done."

Tessa ran back toward them with pink cheeks. "Lemurs!"

Elowen nodded and scooped her up. "I don't know what I'm going to do."

~

Paradise showered and washed her hair, then wrapped it in a towel. Snug in a tan terry robe, she stretched out on her bed with the kittens beside her and grabbed her laptop. Her hands trembled as she lifted the lid and went to the genealogy site.

Tonight was the night. She might not hear back from Drew tonight, but she could start the dialogue and see what happened. Not everyone who looked for their heritage wanted to hear from relatives, so it was possible he wouldn't respond at all. She had to keep that possibility in mind.

She inhaled. "This is it, Luna." The kitten pricked her ears at the sound of her name, then went back to playing with her toy mouse.

The cursor blinked on her screen, and she opened her message app. A bolded message caught her attention. She had something from a match. Was it Drew? The app allowed matches to correspond without giving out names and addresses until both parties felt safe. Maybe it was someone else, but she allowed the hope to settle a moment before she opened the message.

The title read *Match* and her mouth went dry.

> Hi, my name is Andrew James Bartley, but my friends call me Drew. I think we might share the same mother. I hope this isn't too much of a shock to you. I always knew I was adopted, and I sometimes got letters from our mother with your picture, so I always knew about you too. But my existence might be a shock to you, and if that's so, I apologize for the intrusion. I'd like to come see you on a matter that's very urgent. Would that be possible?

An urgent matter? Alarm bells began to go off at the phrase, and she snatched back her hands. She'd always heard these things progressed slowly, but this man was ready to hop a plane and get here right away. Was it a scam of some kind? There had been enough trouble getting her results that caution was in order. This could be whoever kept deleting the results of her test.

The blinking cursor seemed to mock her as her indecision rose. Cowardice wouldn't get her any closer to the truth, and she'd moved a lot of rocks in her quest so far. She inhaled and put her hands back on the keyboard.

> My name is Paradise Alden. I only found out I had a brother a couple of months ago when I discovered a box in the attic where I used to live. It belonged to our mother, and the information about you was in the box. That is why I had my DNA done. I was hoping to find you. I live in Alabama. Where are you?

She clicked Send and swallowed down a bitter taste in her mouth. Had this been a colossal mistake? She stared at the inbox. Would she be able to tell when it had been read? Maybe the app didn't have that capability. To kill time, she took the towel off her head and combed out the tangles before braiding it. There was still no answer, so she put on sweats and a tee and went in search of something to drink. She was already too wired for more caffeine, so she opted for orange juice and headed back to her bedroom.

Both cats were on the bed staring at the computer screen. Had it made a sound? Heart in her throat, she plopped onto the bed and saw another bolded message. She nearly spilled her juice in her eagerness to open and read what Drew had to say. If it even was Drew. She had to stay cautious.

> I'm glad I haven't shocked you. I'm sure you're worried about some complete stranger wanting to come

see you, but I really am your brother. Our mom's name was Becky, and she had a tiny tattoo of a humming-bird on her left shoulder. I'd heard she loved Hawaii. Is that why she named you Paradise?

To answer your question, I live in Atlanta, but I could be there tomorrow. Can you give me your location? We could meet at whatever safe place you want. I don't have to know your home address if you're cautious. And you should be, by the way. I make no judgment on caution. I'm a police detective, and I've seen what happens when women don't listen to their inner warning signals. So you pick the place.

She stared at the flow of information he'd given. Blake would tell her not to do it yet. He'd advise her to talk on the phone first and get a sense of who Drew was. But she couldn't let this chance slide by without embracing it. She had a *brother*. It seemed impossibly surreal. He knew about her mother's tattoo and her love of Hawaii. He'd even guessed why her parents had given her such a ridiculous name. And he was a police detective! That was a welcome piece of news. Maybe he would help her figure out what happened to their mother and her father. And she longed to know who his father was as well. It was all a piece of her mother's history Paradise knew nothing about.

I'm in the Gulf Shores area. Let's meet at the animal park where I work as a vet. It's called The Sanctuary Wildlife Preserve on Vernant Park Road.

She gave him the link to the park and waited. The orange juice was bitter on her tongue, but she drank it anyway.

I'll be there by nine in the morning if that's okay. And please bring a friend if it makes you more comfortable.

Blake was going to be shocked at all she'd found out tonight. She couldn't believe it either. It was nearly ten but he'd still be awake. Maybe she should drive out there and tell him in person. The news seemed too important to spill over the phone.

She closed her laptop to take it with her and bolted for the door.

CHAPTER 37

BLAKE LAY ON HIS side and wished he'd gone home with Paradise. He'd stayed around to put the boys to bed so Mom could run to town with Frank for a root beer float. The kids would have wanted to go if they'd heard the plans, but Blake had diverted their attention by getting out the Monopoly Junior game. He'd kept them entertained until he put them to bed, then had watched TV until Mom got back.

He'd been back in his apartment for an hour but still wasn't sleepy. He started to reach for the phone to call Paradise when he heard a noise on the steps to his apartment over the garage. It sounded like someone was climbing them. He leaped up and grabbed his gun before easing to the door and looking out the viewer. The stairwell was dark. Had the light gone out, or had someone turned off the power?

A light tap came at the door, then Paradise's voice softly called, "Blake, are you awake?"

He flung open the door and pulled her inside. "What are you doing skulking around in the dark so late? I could have shot you. Was the light out when you got here?" He pulled her into an embrace and felt her trembling. She smelled of fresh coconut shampoo. Her hair was back in a damp braid, and she wore the sweats and tee she usually slept in. "I'm sorry, did I scare you? You nearly gave me a heart attack."

"I didn't mean to." She nestled against his chest. "The light was out. I couldn't wait until tomorrow to tell you the news. My brother is coming tomorrow!"

He shut the door. "Whoa, hold on. Tell me what's happened." He led her into the tiny living room where they settled on the sofa and she showed him the messages from Drew. The unease that had begun to crawl up his spine subsided a bit at the news he was a detective. Or at least *claimed* to be.

He took her laptop and did a search for an Atlanta police detective named Bartley. The man popped up on the city's website, and Blake studied his face. "He's got your eyes and coloring. His hair is redder than yours, but I can see he's related to you." She went quiet, and he glanced down at her.

Her hands were clenched together, and she was taking deep breaths. "I—I was afraid to hope he was real, but he has Mom's eyes too." Her voice wobbled. "I have *family*, Blake. A real brother. I can't quite believe that after all this time of being alone, I have a brother who wants to see me. And he knew all about me. Why would they tell him about me but not say a word to me about having a brother? It doesn't seem right."

Her euphoria stung a little because he'd thought he was enough. But of course she wanted a connection with someone who was her own flesh and blood. Just like Levi and Isaac rooted and enriched him, her brother would fill an empty spot in her life. He wouldn't give up his little brothers for anything, and he wanted the best life possible for the woman who was everything to him.

"Maybe you'll learn more about that when he comes tomorrow." He studied the messages again. "Not a clue there about why he's so eager to see you in person. What kind of urgent matter would have him ready to hop a plane at a moment's notice?"

She shrugged as if it didn't matter. And maybe it didn't. The most important thing was he was coming to see her. She'd meet her brother for the first time, and he would get to see it. "I'll meet him with you. I assume he'll come to the registration window to ask for you."

"I gave him the address. I should give him my number too. I'm not afraid now that I've seen how we look alike. I'm glad you thought of doing a search for him." She took back her laptop and sent out a message with her phone number. He answered a minute later with his.

This was really happening. "I wonder if he knows about your mom and dad's murders. Maybe he's investigating them."

"Or maybe he's trying to find his birth father. He didn't mention him, and maybe he doesn't know his identity."

"That's possible, but it doesn't seem as urgent as a murder investigation."

"You think he's trying to track down the murderer too?" She tensed and edged away. "I'd love to have him help us, but what if it's dangerous? I wouldn't want to lose him as soon as I found him." Her voice took on a bite. "I wish I knew what he wanted to talk about."

"Babe, he's a police detective. He faces danger every day." He lifted her chin and leaned in for a lingering kiss. The tension eased out of her as she kissed him back, and he pulled her close. "Whatever it's about, we'll know in a few hours," he murmured against her mouth. When she was relaxed and pliable in his arms, he pulled back and cupped her face in his palms. "Let it go until tomorrow, babe. No sense in getting strung out over something we can't know."

She nodded. "You always do that." She pressed her lips against his neck. "You have a way of soaking the fear and anxiety right out of me with one touch. That's why I came tonight. I needed you."

The words struck a chord in his soul. He wanted to be the one she turned to, the one who anchored her and kept her safe. The one who held her when she cried or soothed her when she was afraid. Being with her did all those things for him too. Even when they faced the uncertainty of the park's future, he'd never envisioned a moment when she wasn't by his side, facing all these trials together.

He kissed her again. "I'll be grateful forever that you came back to town and gave me a second chance."

⌒

Paradise checked her hair in the window's reflection for at least the fifth time as she stood with Blake outside Jenna's cottage. She tried smoothing the flyaways, but it was a useless attempt. Why did her hair have to react like this in humidity? She'd texted Drew this morning and told him to meet her here at the house away from curious stares. They could sit on the porch and talk.

Blake slipped his arm around her waist. "Relax," he whispered. "You look gorgeous. He'll be proud to call you his sister."

She kissed him. "You always say the sweetest things. I want to invite him to stay for lunch—is that okay?"

"Of course. Mom will likely come out with the invitation herself. Or the boys will. You know they'll all be watching from the window."

She spotted them inside the house and waved. Jenna smiled and led the boys off for their lessons. While she was curious, she wasn't going to be obnoxious about it. Paradise's phone read 9:05 a.m. "He's a little late."

"Unfamiliar roads and traffic."

She nodded and caught sight of a white Toyota Sienna driving slowly toward where she stood with Blake. Her pulse moved up into her neck, and she couldn't breathe. It had to be him. The vehicle rolled to a stop and a tall, broad-shouldered man got out. Their gazes locked, and she saw the certainty in his eyes.

"D-Drew." She choked out the name. *My brother.*

"Paradise." His gaze never wavered as he came toward her.

He wore dark wash jeans that fit his muscular thighs well and a navy tee that showed off the biceps he'd likely hit the gym to maintain. Was he married? While she could have checked out his left hand, she couldn't look away from his awe-filled face. She couldn't wait to find out if she had a sister by marriage too. And maybe a niece or a nephew. The thought of an extended family hadn't crossed her mind—it had been enough to have a brother.

She didn't realize she'd stepped forward until they were a foot away from each other. Though she'd told herself she would be reserved and circumspect, she went into his arms without thinking. He hugged her back, a welcoming embrace that didn't want to let go.

Her eyes were wet when she stepped back. "We look alike, Drew."

"I noticed—I'm a detective, after all." His amber eyes twinkled with good humor and his gaze roamed over her face. "You still look like the last picture I got of you." He dug in the pocket of his shirt and pulled out a faded snapshot of her when she was about eight. Mom was French braiding her hair, and they were both laughing.

Pain and longing stole Paradise's breath. "She'd just hit me with the brush for squirming and told me I couldn't go to school looking like a ragamuffin. I didn't know what the word meant, so she started reciting the poem 'The Raggedy Man,' and it made me giggle every time she said, 'Raggedy! Raggedy! Raggedy Man!' I have no idea why. Mom loved poetry and would quote it every chance she got."

"I wish I'd known her," he said softly. He held out his hand to Blake. "Detective Drew Bartley."

"Blake Lawson."

"Blake is m-my fiancé." She stumbled over the word because he hadn't formally asked her to marry him yet, though they talked about the future often. She covered her left hand with her right and wished she hadn't said the word.

Blake must have sensed her discomfort because he slipped his arm around her waist. "We're glad you're here, Drew. Paradise has been overjoyed at the thought she has a brother."

Drew smiled and nodded toward the yellow cottage with its white trim and red door. "What a pretty cottage. Is it yours?"

"My mom lives here with my little brothers. We can sit on the porch and chat." Blake took Paradise's hand, and they walked to the house with Drew on her other side.

There was so much to discuss, but she couldn't articulate the words in her heart. She ached to hear of his life, of his family, to be part of all that she'd missed through the years. Maybe it was abnormal to feel such an immediate bond with a stranger, but somehow she *knew* him. Their souls had an instant recognition— that sounded insane but was authentic.

They went up the two steps to the porch and she settled onto the glider beside Blake. Drew stood with one sneaker resting on the bottom rung of the porch rail. "I think I'll stand for a few minutes. I've had to sit for several hours and I'm not used to it. I missed my gym workout this morning."

"I have so many questions," Paradise began.

Drew's smile faltered, and he gazed around the park. "I do, too, but how about we save it for over lunch? I have an urgent matter to talk about."

She sensed how important this was to him. "We have time."

He folded his arms over his chest. "I've been trying to find out who murdered my dad."

She gasped. "Your father was murdered, too, just like Mom and Dad?"

"He died just before they did. I think the murders might be connected."

"Who—who was he?"

"I don't know. I was hoping you did."

She studied his expression. "All I was able to gather about your dad was he was older than Mom and she got pregnant with you when she was still in high school. He drove in from out of town in a fancy car, so everyone assumed he had money. But if you don't know who he is, how do you know he was murdered?"

"My parents told me, but they wouldn't give me his name. I know the month he died, but that's all. My dad let that slip accidentally."

"It was suspected he was married and was sneaking around on his wife with Mom," Paradise said.

"That's what my parents said too. I find it way too suspicious they all died within a short time of each other."

"Do you know how your father died?" Blake asked.

"I was told he was bludgeoned to death, but I've combed

through the records and never found a report of a man being killed that way in the necessary time frame. But I did find the autopsy report for your parents. There's something here, and I mean to find out what it is."

An ally. Paradise rose. "Let me get the box of things from the attic. Maybe it will give you something I missed. You can take it with you to Atlanta."

By the time lunch was over, she knew he was single with no siblings, like her. He loved his job, and she had no doubt he would help her find her parents' murderer. She could wait for more direction from him and concentrate on saving The Sanctuary.

CHAPTER 38

"READY OR NOT, HERE I come!" Blake called out. The aroma of grilled brats and burgers wafted from the small grill his mom tended to on his tailgate. He opened his eyes and listened for the telltale giggle from Isaac. His littlest brother had trouble staying quiet during hide-and-seek.

He walked through the replicas of Stonehenge, called Bamahenge. The massive structure looked like the original, but the stones were made of fiberglass filled with cement. It was amazing to find this sight down a country road near Elberta. He hadn't brought the boys here in a while, and they wanted to explore the dinosaurs next.

He heard a giggle and whipped around to see Isaac duck back behind an upright block. "Found you. Now where are Paradise and Levi? I think they might be hard to find."

His dimple flashing, Isaac came to join in. "I know where they are."

"No cheating. I have to find them on my own." He lifted the five-year-old to his shoulders, and the little guy entwined his fingers in Blake's hair.

The sky held the magic of impending dusk, and Blake was ready to find his woman and enjoy dinner with the family. He and Isaac wandered from stone to stone and didn't catch a glimpse of them. "I might need your help after all," Blake said.

Mom called out that supper was ready. That should get a reaction from Levi, who was always hungry. There was no answering call or giggle from either of the two missing players.

"Levi was right there behind that tree." Isaac leaned down to direct Blake. "He must have moved."

Blake headed that direction and found the grass flattened where Levi had been. He lifted Isaac off his shoulders and set him down. Had they circled around to go back to the truck without being seen? Maybe this game hadn't been the best idea when Blake was already worrying about keeping everyone safe. "Let's check and see if Mom saw them dart off."

When he exited Bamahenge, he spotted Paradise coming from the direction of the stegosaurus. "Do you have Levi?" he called.

She shook her head and broke into a jog. Her expression was troubled when she reached him. "He was right there." She pointed out the same location Isaac had identified.

"He knows better than to wander off." Blake cupped his hands and shouted for his brother. "Time's up, Levi. Olly olly oxen free." No answering shout came back, and he turned toward the trees. "Isaac, you go help Mom while Paradise and I find your brother."

A tear slid down Isaac's cheek. "The T-Rex didn't eat him, did he? I knew that dino was dangerous."

Mom joined them, and she called for Levi too. "Levi, dinner!"

There was still no answer to Mom's shout, but maybe he was out of range to hear. That wasn't good, but it didn't mean anything had happened to him. Blake patted his teary-eyed little brother's head. "The dinosaur didn't eat him—they're pretend, remember?"

Isaac's lip trembled. "Maybe they came to life."

"Paradise and I will go look for him. Mom will feed you, and we'll go get ice cream later." He glanced at his mother and mouthed, *Keep him distracted.*

She bit her lip. "Paradise, you want to take Isaac? I'd like to look for Levi."

"Sure."

As Paradise started that way, Isaac started to wail. He clung to his mother. "I want you, Mommy. Hold me."

"We'll find him, Mom. I'm sure he's just out of earshot. He's fine." The words felt hollow, but his mother's frown eased and she carried Isaac toward the food.

Blake and Paradise walked toward the stones. He eyed the stone on top of two others. "I don't think he could climb up there." It was probably twenty feet tall, maybe more. There were no good climbing holds either.

He and Paradise walked around every stone and didn't find Levi. His little brother had never been able to hide for so long. He was still young enough to get bored if he wasn't found, so he'd make noise like a faint whistle or a sinister chuckle, but there'd been nothing. Blake didn't want to admit he was worried.

Paradise turned away from Bamahenge. "Let's check out the trees. He might have climbed one."

He followed her into the tree line, and they took turns shouting Levi's name. Blake tried checking the ground for prints, but it was too hard for any impressions to be made. They could be searching in the wrong direction. "Did he know you were at the dinosaurs?"

"I don't think so, and I know he didn't come with me. He was right there in the stones when I saw him last." She clutched his forearm. "Blake, I'm scared. I shouldn't have let him out of my sight with everything that's happened."

"Let's stay calm. He loves hiding in small, tight places. Like closets. I can't tell you how many times I've found him in one with the door shut. Are there any caves or dens around? Let's see what we can find." He didn't think there was anything like that in the area, but for all he knew, his brother could have wedged himself in an old well or a raccoon den.

Alarm fired along his spine at the thought that Levi might be in trouble.

Blake shouted for him again and traipsed through last year's dead leaves as they circled every tree and looked up into the overhanging branches. After half an hour Blake pulled out his phone. "I'd better call for help. Something's wrong."

Tears rushed to Paradise's eyes. "I'm going to keep looking while you make the call."

Blake placed the 911 call and reported his brother missing. His voice skipped when he had to say the word *missing*. He watched Paradise search, and some secret part of his soul knew Levi was in trouble. Had someone taken him? The thought nearly buckled his knees.

He ended the call so he could shout for his little brother. "Levi!" Panic edged closer as he joined Paradise, who was staring at something in her hand. "What do you have?"

"It's a note." She gulped and read it. "'You'll find Levi by the Knights in the Woods. The next time, you'll never find him. Vacate The Sanctuary.'" She stared up at him. "We were looking in the wrong direction."

He grabbed her hand, and they ran toward the marina.

⌣

Levi's face was muddy and tearstained when Paradise and Blake knelt beside him. Paradise gently pulled away the tape over his mouth while Blake worked at freeing his hands and feet. Tears spilled down his cheeks.

Paradise pulled him into her lap and rocked back and forth. "I've got you. You're okay."

"I want my mama," he wailed as Blake tore away the last of the duct tape on his ankles. "I'm never playing hide-and-seek again."

Blake balled up the tape and tossed it into a trash receptacle. "I'm with you, buddy." He held out his arms and Levi lunged into them.

"I'll call your mom." Paradise pulled out her phone and called Jenna, who sounded frantic as she promised to come right away. They'd taken a shortcut to the knights through the trees and Jenna hadn't heard everything yet. The note wasn't something they could talk about in front of the boys.

Blake's truck came fast up the road, the tires spitting gravel as it came to a hard stop. The door flew open, and Jenna leaped out with Isaac right behind her. "Levi!" She ran to them and fell to her knees to take him in her arms. "You scared us so much."

"There was a boogeyman." Levi's brown eyes were wide with fear, and he held out his hand for Isaac. "Stay close to me, bro. He might take you next."

"I'll punch him!" Isaac stood back, wide-eyed and with his fists clenched at his sides. "Did he hurt you? If he did, I'll beat him up." He took a fighter stance and flung his arms out in jerky moves.

"You can't beat him. He's the boogeyman." Levi buried his face in his mom's chest. "I want to sleep with you, Mommy."

Jenna smoothed the tufts of his dark brown hair that stuck up. "You sure can." She took his face in her palms and nudged him back from her so she could see his face. "What did he look like, Levi?"

"I don't want to think about it!" He buried his face against his mother again.

Paradise exchanged a glance with Blake. *Counselor,* she mouthed. He nodded. "You'd better let the police know we found him but he was abducted."

The police would have a child expert ask questions and try to get a detailed description of the abductor. Who would have been depraved enough to use a little boy? She needed to discuss all this with Blake and Jenna, but it would have to wait for now. Levi was much more important, and he needed a lot of comfort and reassurance. Tonight would probably be rough.

———

It was dark by the time the police cars left and the boys and Jenna were safely curled up on the sofa in her cottage. The food she had prepared had gone cold, and Paradise whipped up some grilled cheese sandwiches and chicken noodle soup. She made brownies while they gobbled up their meal, and the chocolaty aroma calmed the jitters she'd had since she first read the note.

Blake joined her in the kitchen. "He doesn't want Mom out of his sight. He'll probably have nightmares tonight."

"I thought so too. I think I'll stay. I can sleep with Isaac. He's probably going to need comfort too. He cries when he thinks no one is looking."

"I know. I can sleep in his room, but I'll feel better if you're here with us." Blake ran his hand through his thick dark hair.

"We all need each other tonight. I've never been so terrified in my life. Not even with artillery landing all around me in Afghanistan. Mom wants to move, like, right now. Turn the will over and get out of here. She's as traumatized as the boys."

"You think it was Dean?"

"I don't think so. The police sent me the composite sketch the artist drew. Take a look." He pulled up a picture on his phone and showed her.

She gasped. "It's Adams."

"I think so too. We know he's working on running us off. I don't know how he got hooked up with Dean, but I'm sure they're both involved. He's probably doing what he's told." Blake turned the phone's screen back around to face him and stared at it. "I emailed Jane and told her it looked like Adams. She's still got officers out on the hunt for him, but he must have a good hidey-hole to have evaded them all this time." His eyes narrowed and his mouth grew tight. "I'd better not run into him myself, because he wouldn't make it to jail."

"Do you really think Adams would hurt a child next time?"

"You're the best one to answer that—you know what he's capable of."

She tried to rid her memories of the man's soulless eyes. "I think it's all scare tactics. He's a weasel at heart. Stand up to him and he backs off. That's why I knew I could handle him when I was a teenager. He was never violent—and he didn't hurt Levi physically."

"Dean would have no compunction about hurting a kid, not when he seems to have killed his own uncle."

She pulled the brownies out of the oven and set them down to cool. "I haven't had a minute to tell you about talking to Elowen yesterday. I didn't want to bring it up in front of the boys with all of us riding to Bamahenge together. She said Dean told her he killed his uncle." She told him about the meth and the way Dean had rationalized his actions. "And Dean asked Elowen to forge Allen's signature on the will. That was a few weeks ago, which proves the will isn't an original, just like Hez's program showed."

"I'll tell Jane all about this. Maybe she'll talk to Dean and get to the truth."

Paradise listened to him tell Jane what they'd found out, but she didn't have his hope that this would end it.

CHAPTER 39

PARADISE SLIPPED ISAAC'S ARM off her neck and eased out of bed at ten thirty. He didn't move a muscle. He'd clutched her tightly until sleep finally loosened his grip. Tonight had badly frightened him.

She tiptoed out of the room and went to the kitchen to find her purse. It wasn't in the kitchen or the living room, and she got a clear memory of seeing it on the floor of Blake's truck. She'd probably left it in their haste to get the boys inside to some semblance of normalcy. She could wait until morning, but she wanted to check her phone for any emergency vet messages from Pawsome Pets.

Blake kept his keys on a hook in the kitchen, so she found them and unlocked the front door to head to the truck. She stood on the porch for a moment and listened to the familiar night sounds of the park. Even the tigers chuffing in the distance didn't make her heart seize in her chest, and she let herself hope the fear that had plagued her was finally easing.

Keys in hand, she went down the steps to the vague outline

of Blake's truck in the moonlight. She clicked the unlock button and quickly found her purse and withdrew her phone. No messages.

A movement came from the left, and she turned that direction. A figure bent over her back bumper. When he straightened, she saw the same dark hoodie they'd seen in Mason's videos.

Mr. Adams.

Without thinking, she dove her hand into her purse and extracted her small gun before marching to intercept him. For fifteen years she'd waited for this moment. There'd been no resolution to the anger and hatred she felt for this man.

She walked forward until she stood a foot away from his bent form. Was that a *tracker* under her bumper? Her fingers tightened on the gun's grip and she restrained a mad impulse to aim the barrel at him and pull the trigger.

He turned around, then froze when he saw her blocking his escape. "Paradise," he croaked.

Her tongue stuck to the roof of her mouth, and she swallowed, then licked her lips. Her pulse thumped in her ears, and nausea roiled in her belly. She could do this. "Mr. Adams." Her voice sounded creaky and weak to her ears, but her strength began to rise with the release of the first syllables.

He was trapped between her and the car. The only way to escape would be to brush her out of the way, but his gaze dropped to the gun in her hand and he didn't move. She was close enough to smell the overpowering stench of his Old Spice cologne. He used to practically bathe in the stuff, and he evidently hadn't changed that habit.

She swallowed the urge to gag. "Trying to frighten me again? You lost that power long ago. I'm not a kid anymore."

She saw him clearly for the first time—small, mean, weak of spirit, with the desire to make himself feel bigger by hurting others. With this realization strength flooded through her body along her muscles and tendons. She straightened to her full height, and he shrank back as if he sensed the power rising in her.

"You are despicable. It wasn't enough to try to terrorize me—you had to traumatize a little boy. But that's what you're good at, isn't it? What did you hope to gain here? Were you afraid if I stayed around, I'd tell more people what you did when I was a kid?"

"I didn't do anything to you. It's all lies."

"Gaslighting. You can't make me forget by denying it." She poked the gun toward him. "Leave this family alone. You can't break them no matter what you do." She studied his frightened expression. "You're not smart enough to be the mastermind. I want you to go back to your boss and tell him it didn't work, that it will never work. There's nothing you can do to drive me away. You've failed."

He wet his lips. "You need to leave town or things will get worse. I didn't hurt the kid, but I can't promise he won't."

Fear tried to grip her, but she pushed it away. She was done with that. "You've both lost. It's over. I won't be ruled by fear, and neither will the Lawsons."

His gaze darted from side to side, but he didn't look at her directly. "I didn't do anything really bad. The kid is fine. You're fine."

She glared at him. "You're small and cruel, but I want you to know you didn't break me. If you'd tried to enter my room again, I would have hit you with a chair or the lamp. I would have screamed and fought. You wouldn't have walked out unscathed. And that's why you're still trying to frighten me, isn't it? I didn't cave to fear, and you can't have that."

Intent didn't matter to him. Pity stirred for the first time. He was blind and weak and pathetic. She could talk about his misdeeds all day long and he'd never admit to anything. He'd never be able to process his wrongdoing to himself. Did that mean he was past help? Maybe. She could release the hatred that still muddied her heart, or she could be like him and hold tight to pride and self-righteousness.

She didn't need the gun when she had the ultimate weapon. "You can't scare me any longer, Lloyd." She said his first name deliberately rather than give him any status with the title *Mr.* "I've learned something important in the past few weeks—something that is stronger than you, stronger than anything. What you meant for evil, God worked for good. What I went through didn't break me. It made me stronger."

His hazel eyes widened, and he tried to step away but only succeeded in becoming more trapped between her and the car. "I don't even know what that means."

Or course he didn't—he was blind to anything but his own desires and what he thought the world owed him. She took a step back and dropped the gun into her purse. "I never thought I'd say this, but I forgive you. It probably means nothing to you, but it means everything to me. It destroys the last bit of power you might have had over me. I'm free from you, really free."

Her spirit soared and her steps were light as she turned and walked toward the house without looking back. She texted Jane as she walked toward the house. While Paradise had forgiven him, he still needed to answer for what he'd done here at the refuge. Maybe the police could catch him on the road.

———

Blake kicked the covers off his feet and glanced at the clock. Just after midnight. He'd wanted to sleep on the sofa downstairs, but Paradise had urged him to get some rest in his own bed. He swung his legs over the side and padded to his small kitchen to grab a bottle of water out of the fridge. When he glanced out the window, a light glowed from the cottage's back window. Someone was up.

He shoved his feet into Nike slides and went down the stairs to make sure the boys weren't upset and afraid after the traumatic evening. An owl hooted as he exited the garage, and a big cat chuffed in the distance. A wolf howled, and several more joined in. A male fox screamed out to warn off another male.

The normal night sounds here at the park wouldn't be found anywhere else. While they'd figured out the will situation, he had to do his best to uncover the source of the other attacks to ensure they never had to leave this place.

This sanctuary was in his soul.

He was halfway down the steps when his phone sounded with a text. He paused and glanced at it. If Jane was texting him at this hour, it must be important. *Call me when you get up.*

He sat on a step and placed the call. "What's up?"

"That was fast." Jane sounded tired. "We got Adams a few minutes ago. He'd been holed up in an apartment in Foley, and our officers nabbed him pulling into the driveway. And get this—we found a vial of Telazol in his bedroom."

All this time he'd been only fifteen minutes away. "He killed Ivy?"

"He admitted she was demanding money to keep quiet about who wanted to know more about Paradise, so we think that's what happened. He clammed up right after that and demanded an attorney, but he's sloppy. I think we'll find more evidence."

At least he was in custody and couldn't hurt Paradise. "Thanks for letting me know. Mom and Paradise will be relieved you got him."

"I hope to know more later today. Sorry to wake you up."

"I was up." He said goodbye and rose from the step to continue down. After unlocking the back door of the cottage, he slipped into the kitchen and found Paradise making a cup of hot cocoa. "Was Isaac sideways in the bed?"

She smiled. Something was different about her, lighter, happier. "I went outside to get my purse from your truck. Adams was putting a tracker on my car, and I confronted him."

Anger gripped him. "Jane has him in custody. She texted a few minutes ago."

She stirred the cocoa mix into the milk on the stove. "I don't think Adams is the kingpin. Number one, he's not smart enough to be orchestrating this—the attacks on the park, the ominous warnings, the Phantom music, the rattlesnake. That all took way too much planning. I think he's doing someone else's bidding. So I told him to tell his boss it's over. We won't be scared away and they've failed."

Blake processed the thought. She knew the man well, so he believed her. "Do you think the same person is behind trying to run you off and what's been happening at the park? I don't see how they're tied together."

"I think they're two prongs of the same fork. Driving me away from the park would leave you with no vet and no way to replace me with all of the criminal activity going on here. Destroying the park's reputation would leave you and your mom with no option but to sell out. Dean and Mary may even be in on it. Someone behind the scenes might have gone to them with an offer for a ridiculous amount of money, and they hatched the plan around the forged will. A major squeeze play to remove all avenues that would allow The Sanctuary to thrive. The kingpin would swoop in and buy up the land from either you guys or the Steerforths. End of story."

"I admit it makes sense, but we have no idea where to look."

She poured her hot chocolate into a mug. "So we dig harder. We know Adams was at Bea Davis's house and also at Mary's. Maybe I can get one of them to talk." She held his gaze. "Without you." He started to object, but she shook her head. "They're more likely to open up to me than to you. The Sanctuary is the main target. Bea seemed to like me, so I'll start there."

She was right, but he didn't like it. "I'll agree on one condition. Let's put a tracker on your phone. If you're stepping into the line of fire, I want to be able to find you."

Her eyes lit with enthusiasm. "That's a great idea. I'll get my phone."

She left her mug on the counter and went into the living room to grab it. When she handed it to him, he found a location app and installed it on her phone before connecting them together in the locater under *Lawson Family*. "I have this same app on my phone and so does Mom. So we're all together and can stalk each other." He handed it back.

She lifted a brow and smiled, then set her phone on the counter and stepped toward him. "So you'd better make sure you're not seeing an old girlfriend, or I'll find you out."

He pulled her into his arms. "There's never been anyone but you." Her arms came around his neck, and he pulled her in close for a kiss. "Promise me you won't do anything stupid like get yourself killed," he murmured against her lips.

She pulled away. "I'll do my best. I like being part of the Lawson family." Her smile widened. "There's something else I told Adams. I let go of my anger and hatred. I forgave him for what he did to me."

He caught his breath. "That was a hard thing to do. How do you feel now?"

"Like the sun is finally out after a long, dark storm."

He felt her joy and pulled her into his arms again. "I'm so proud of you." It would be a turning point for her, for them, and for the future.

CHAPTER 40

BEA HAD READILY INVITED her in, and Paradise settled on one of the two tan sofas facing each other. Bea took the other one once she'd brought in coffee. The pictures of her eight grandchildren on the wall had been updated with more recent ones since Paradise was last here.

"Looks like your granddaughter is quite the volleyball player."

Bea beamed and tucked a wayward curl of her salt-and-pepper hair behind one ear. "Oh, she is. She's a junior and is being recruited to USA." Her soft drawl was all sweet tea and black-eyed peas.

"The University of South Alabama is a Division I school. She must be really good."

"She's a center and has interest from all over the country, but she's set on USA. I'm happy about that since she can come home when she wants." Bea took a sip of her coffee and set it on the end table beside her. "What can I do for you, sweet girl?"

Sunlight slanted through the picture window and highlighted Bea's face. Her wary expression warned Paradise the older woman's smile was a front. Bea knew hard questions were coming.

"How do you know Lloyd Adams?"

A tiny gasp escaped Bea. "I—I don't know what you mean. He and his wife were friends a long time before they moved away."

"You haven't seen them recently?"

Bea reached for her coffee. "Why are you asking about him?"

"The police are questioning him in connection with Ivy Cook's murder."

"Murder? I thought a big cat killed her."

"Someone hit her with a tranquilizer dart and let the tiger into the outer perimeter so it appeared the tiger killed her. Someone is trying to destroy The Sanctuary. Adams took little Levi from our picnic last night, bound him with duct tape, and hid him for us to find. The little guy was traumatized. Is that the kind of person you want as a friend?"

"Oh my, that's terrible. You're sure it was Lloyd?"

"Positive. And I know his car was parked in your driveway recently." Paradise leaned forward. "Here's the thing—I don't believe he's acting alone. Someone else is telling him what to do, and I think you might know who's pulling the strings. Not much happens here in Pelican Harbor that you don't know."

The color washed out of Bea's cheeks. "I'll admit I realized Lloyd was involved in something when he stopped here recently. Weeks ago he'd stopped by to ask me questions about when your parents were murdered, about your life before that, anything I might know about toys and favorite movies, that kind of thing."

A sick feeling settled in the pit of Paradise's stomach. "You knew about the monkey music box and told him."

Bea clenched her hands together in her lap and stared down. "I'm so sorry. We were just chatting, and I thought he wanted to make amends for, you know, the difficulty. I thought maybe he wanted to get you a small gift to say he was sorry."

Difficulty? The word seemed so innocuous for something so awful. "When did you realize it wasn't a casual question?"

"I didn't. I mean, not until he said something about you ruining his life. I got rid of him right away, let me tell you." Her gaze lifted. "I'm sorry, Paradise."

Paradise realized her fists were clenched and forced herself to relax her fingers. "He's been terrorizing me with *Phantom of the Opera* lyrics, quotes, and memorabilia, so I'm sure he's not the least bit sorry for anything. And I ruined *his* life? I can't grasp how he could blame me for his disgusting actions." She gulped and swallowed hard. "Did he say anything about other people he's seen recently? Do you know who he was closest to when he lived here? Any family or in-laws still in the area?"

And had Paradise tried to remember any friends herself? She'd pushed so much about that time as far from her thoughts as possible. Maybe there were things from those two years in the Adams household that might surface if she let them.

Bea rubbed the furrow that formed between her eyes. "I think most of his family is gone. Well, other than his cousin Roger."

"Roger?"

"Your neighbor, Roger Dillard."

How had she never realized Adams was related to the Dillards? He'd never been at the ranch when she was there, and Abby had never mentioned it even when Paradise lived at the Adamses'. This new revelation sucked the oxygen from her lungs and made her pause. With Bea staring at her, she found it impossible to think through what the connection between the two men might mean—if anything.

She rose and slipped her purse strap over her shoulder. "Thanks so much, Mrs. Davis. I appreciate your help. If you think of anything else, give me a call. You have my number." As she rushed to the door, she had the sense she was fleeing some unseen evil. Was a scary memory pushing its way out of her subconscious?

She threw herself under the steering wheel and closed her eyes a moment. Her heart fluttered in her chest, and her lungs squeezed as panic swamped her. Whatever it was that was trying to emerge felt monumental and terrifying. The sensation ebbed, and she opened her eyes.

It would come when it was ready.

~

The otter's dark eyes stared at Paradise as if pleading for help. Roger moved out of the way to allow her to get closer. They stood behind Roger's biggest barn a couple hundred yards away from the pond where the otter had likely lived. A few curious cows stared their way before heading to the pond.

When Paradise got the call from Roger, she'd been on her way to Mary's from Bea's house, but she'd swung around and headed back. It wouldn't hurt to ask Roger about Lloyd Adams since they were related. Being with Roger might help her dig up that memory that refused to surface.

Paradise knelt on the muddy ground. The moisture soaked through the knees of her jeans. "Could you get her some water?"

Roger nodded before grabbing a bucket and heading to the hose spigot by the barn. The poor thing's leg was mangled by the trap, and Paradise's gaze moved from the injury to the animal's belly. The otter needed to be out of the sun more than anything right now.

She pulled on thick leather gloves to make sure the animal didn't try to bite in a frenzy of fear and pain. "I'll get her fixed up. I think she's pregnant."

Roger pushed his cowboy hat off his forehead. "Quinn found it before school, and I released it from the trap before calling you. I didn't want to move it in case I did more damage."

He grabbed a stainless-steel bowl and carried it back with the bucket of water. The breeze carried a whiff of his cologne, a masculine scent of leather and hints of tobacco and citrus. She'd usually seen him later in the day when the smell had worn off, and something about the leather and citrus combination brought familiarity that tugged at her memories. She struggled to grasp the shadowy thoughts as she wrapped the otter's leg and transferred her to a cage.

That whiff came again and this time brought an innate sense of revulsion. What was going on with her? Maybe the stress from yesterday and the lack of sleep were playing with her emotions. She put the crate containing the otter in the back seat of her Kia and turned to find Roger in her personal space. Her adrenaline surged, but she controlled her initial flight response and smiled at him.

"I heard something interesting today. I didn't realize you and Lloyd Adams were cousins."

The smile on Roger's face ebbed, and his gray eyes narrowed. "Who told you that?"

She didn't want to implicate Bea in whatever had caused his mood change. "Does it matter if it's true?"

He regarded her with a hard, appraising look, and in that instant she remembered. He'd been at the Adamses' house the night Lloyd had come into her bedroom. She'd run shouting and crying out into the yard where she'd stood hugging herself. A faint conversation from the side yard had filtered through her hysteria. It had been between Mrs. Adams and Roger, and it sounded like a lovers' quarrel.

While she stood absorbing the facts in the dark of a moonless night, he'd come around to the front yard, and Mrs. Adams had followed. They both saw her standing there, and Roger had come toward her with his fists clenched. "You saw nothing tonight."

"No," she agreed, because she hadn't. "Mr. Adams, h-he tried . . ."

His hard gaze took in her pajama top torn from one shoulder, and he cut her off. "Go back to your room and I'll handle it."

She'd done just that and had propped her desk chair under the doorknob to keep Adams from coming back in. There'd been no argument or shouting from the other side of the door, so she didn't know what he'd said. The next morning she wasn't sure he'd said anything at all. And maybe he hadn't, but at least Adams hadn't tried the door again.

The memory slammed into her. "You were having an affair with your cousin's wife. Is that why you and Abby never talk about him? Lloyd is trying to run us all off The Sanctuary."

"I don't intend to discuss it, not with you or anyone."

His back rigid, he stalked off without another word toward the barn, where he disappeared from view. His reaction astounded her since the affair had been fifteen years ago. Why would he be upset she remembered now?

She got behind the wheel and drove back to the park with the little otter. Once the animal was resting, she headed out Fort Morgan Road toward the Steerforth house. The storm gathering on the horizon matched Paradise's mood, and she dreaded the coming confrontation as she mentally rehearsed what she intended to say to Mary. It might get as turbulent as the clouds roiling over the water.

Mary was nowhere around when Paradise got out of the car. Lightning flickered overhead, and the faint odor of ozone wafted to her. She started to duck back into her car but spotted Mary under the house pilings. She lay unmoving on the concrete near the storage door. Lightning crackled as Paradise ran to kneel next to her on the cold concrete.

She touched Mary's arm, and the woman groaned and moved her head. A large gash ran from her forehead to her chin, and blood pooled under that side of her face. Her pulse was thready and fading. Paradise needed to stop the bleeding. She noticed an open trash bag with clothing spilling out the top and grabbed a tee. The material sopped up the blood as she pressed it against Mary's wound.

Mary moaned, and her lids fluttered open. "I hoped he'd get arrested for Allen's death, but it never happened. I'm sorry," she whispered. "All that money. And they had to have both properties."

Both properties? "I'm calling an ambulance, Mary. Hang tight." Paradise rose to run back for her phone.

The clouds opened up and dumped buckets of rain on her head as she thrust her phone into the pocket of her loose sweats. *The gun.* She pulled the little pistol out of her purse and tucked it into her other pocket, then ran through the deluge to rejoin Mary. Water dripped from her hair and ran down her face.

A furtive shuffle came from her left, and spinning on her heel, she started to turn to face whoever was there.

Something struck her on the head, and she crumpled into the darkness.

CHAPTER 41

WHEN HIS LAST TOUR disembarked and left, Blake decided to see how Paradise's talk with Mary had gone. He checked for her at the clinic and found Warren tending to a new otter. "Where'd the pregnant otter come from?"

"Roger found her injured on his ranch and called Doc this morning. She taped her up and brought her here. She's got a few more days before she gives birth."

"Paradise isn't here?"

"She got her settled and left. I don't know where she went."

"What time did she leave?"

"Before lunch."

Blake had expected her back by now, but maybe Mary was spilling everything she knew. "Thanks, I'll give her a call." He stepped outside the building and pulled out his phone. No one picked up on the other end, and he left a message. "Hey, babe, give me a call when you get a chance."

It was nearly dinnertime, so she'd been gone at least six hours. The first glimmer of concern came. He pulled up the tracker app and found her still at Mary's. Even if Mary was telling her everything, would it take this long? His jaw tight, he ran for his truck.

On the way out to the peninsula, he tried to call Paradise several more times but got only voice mail. With every failure to reach her, his anxiety increased. *Don't assume anything is wrong.* But his self-talk failed to reassure him. She always picked up, and she'd been out of touch with anyone for hours. It wasn't like her.

He turned off Highway 59 onto 180 and called his mom. "Hey, have you talked to Paradise today at all?"

"No, I haven't. I tried to call her twice but got voice mail. Is something wrong?"

"I hope not, but she's been out of touch for over six hours. She went to see Mary, and I'm on my way there now."

"Keep me posted."

He ended the call and increased his speed as fast as he dared. He passed the Kiva Dunes Golf Course and set his sights on Beach Estates, a few miles ahead on the left. It wasn't far now, but his sense of urgency escalated instead of dissipating. He tried her number one more time but still got routed to voice mail. He turned on Vacation Lane and spotted the house in the distance.

Squinting, he made out Paradise's green Soul parked by the back deck. The heavy weight should've lifted off his chest, so why did he feel worse instead of better?

He made the final turn and parked beside Paradise's car. His truck door was partially open by the time he turned off the key. He leaped out and ran up the steps to the door, then thumped his fist on it. "Paradise," he called.

When there was no answer, he tried the door and it opened. The house felt empty when he stepped into the living room still calling her name. There was no hint of her scent. The cat streaked past his feet and ran to hide under the sofa. He walked through the house and found no one. Retracing his steps, he went outside to Paradise's car. Her purse was inside, but her phone wasn't in it.

He got back out and went to the storage space under the house's pilings. What he took for a jumble of clothing became clearer. Someone was lying on the concrete.

He rushed to the figure and discovered Mary prone on her stomach with her face turned to one side. Blood pooled under her head. He checked her pulse and found nothing.

He pulled out his phone and reported it to 911. The dispatcher wanted him to stay on the line, but Blake told her he needed to find his girlfriend, who appeared to be missing.

He checked the locator app again and found Paradise's position had moved to somewhere offshore. It appeared to be heading west across Mobile Bay. Someone had taken her.

A loud whine penetrated the blackness. Paradise tried to move and found her hands tied together. The pounding in her head pulsated with another sound, an odd whooshing that amplified the pain. Other sensations began to penetrate—hard boards beneath her, the cries of seabirds, and the rhythmic lapping of water.

When she slitted her eyes, blue then green and gray flashed past her vision. Leaves interspersed with Spanish moss alternated with blue sky. A rotten egg odor mingled with salty air.

Swamp. I'm in an airboat navigating a swamp.

Angling her head, she found she was lying face down in the middle of the hull with her arms tucked under her body. Through slitted lids she saw water pooled in the hull and along one side of the craft. Someone coughed a few feet from her head, so he had to be on the elevated seat navigating. He'd be able to stare down at her, so she couldn't let him know she was awake.

She concentrated on managing her breathing and keeping her eyes closed for now until she figured out what to do. Infinitesimally she tested her limbs and found no pain. She felt the hard outline of her gun in her right pocket and her phone in the other, but she had to be free to use either one. And how could she manage that, knowing her captor could see her every move?

Little by little she tested the ropes at her wrists, trying to see if they would loosen. They didn't stretch, but she twisted her hands and tried to release one of them. The rope around her left hand felt slightly looser than the right, so she concentrated on pulling that one free in tiny movements.

The boat engine throttled back and the sound of the wind through the turbine lessened. It was dimmer now, cooler with patterned shadows on the hull that she could see through her barely cracked lids. Did he plan to throw her overboard to the gators? If so, she had to be ready to act. She kept her eyes closed when the engine stopped and someone shuffled alongside her toward the boat's bow.

It was hard to hear past the roaring of her pulse in her ears, and she prayed for strength and favor. She twisted her left wrist again and felt the rope slip, then loosen. Holding her breath, she maneuvered it and tried to slide her hand out of the loop. The left hand was free! She inched her right hand along the damp hull of the boat toward her pocket until it couldn't go any farther without her elbow's movement attracting attention. She'd wait for the right moment.

The tip of a shoe or boot nudged her. "I know you're awake."

Her labored breathing had given her away, and she knew that

voice—Dean Steerforth. Since it was useless to pretend she was still unconscious, she turned her head to face his foot. "Killing me will add to your time in prison. You already killed your aunt, but if you kill me, too, you'll face the death penalty."

He swore and kicked her with the hard toe of his boot. "Why'd you have to get involved? It was working great. Who knows about the will? I didn't want to kill Aunt Mary, but she wouldn't listen."

Would the truth deter him from killing her? "Too many people to mention, including the police."

"You've spoiled everything."

"You tried to steal what wasn't yours."

"The mining company had to have both properties, especially the park. The rare earth elements are richest in that bare field. The park isn't really using it, and it's crazy how much I can get for it."

Both properties. Paradise had a sudden flash of something Abby had said about being worried her dad was thinking about selling the ranch. Nausea roiled in her midsection. Dean didn't have to tell her—the truth had been waiting to erupt. "Roger Dillard owns the other property, doesn't he?"

"How'd you know?"

She wished she could see his face. "Abby said she thought he was thinking of selling the ranch, but that didn't make sense until now. How is he involved with taking The Sanctuary's property?"

"You remember that PI who pretended to be a TGU student? She was scouting for rare earth elements after some were found in an oil well Roger owns, so she expanded her search. Gas and oil deposits were found, but that's minor compared to the REE discovery."

Paradise frowned. "The park is small potatoes compared to the three thousand acres Roger owns."

"The best access is through the park's land. And like I said, that bare field is a gold mine of REE."

It would be useless to remind him he faced the death penalty. He'd already killed his aunt and one more wouldn't make a difference to his sentence. When he yanked her up, she had to grab her gun and end this.

"What are you going to do with me?"

"There's a gator family that lives through these cypress trees. They'll find you a tasty meal, and no one will find the body. Even if the law arrests me for forgery, that's not a big deal. There's nothing to connect me to your disappearance. With you dead, no one will know what happened to Aunt Mary. A robber could have attacked her."

She had to get that gun out somehow.

CHAPTER 42

BLAKE HAD CALLED ROGER and asked for help and his neighbor showed up with his airboat behind his truck. The locator app showed Paradise in the Mobile-Tensaw River Delta: 260,000 acres of wetlands and swamps to hide the body. He could only pray she was still alive. And that her phone stayed connected.

The sounds of birds and insects echoed from the cypress and tupelo trees as they navigated a tributary past blue herons and cranes. An Alabama red-bellied turtle snoozed in the sun on a rock as they passed, and frogs croaked from the seagrass as it brushed the sides of the boat. Blake moved restlessly, frustrated by the snail's pace at which they slid through the turgid water. The odor of mud and decaying vegetation mingled with that of salt and sulphur.

He waved away the gnats and mosquitoes buzzing around his head and studied the map on his phone. So many branches of waterways and creeks. Which way had they gone to get where the dot moved slowly along? The myriad possible paths were daunting.

They came to the end of the tributary with no clear path forward. Roger killed the fan. "We're at the end of the road."

"There was another creek that branched off about a quarter of a mile back. Let's try that one." He waited for Roger to start the motor again, but the boat drifted sluggishly in the muddy water. When he turned around to face Roger again, he found his neighbor studying him with hard gray eyes.

Blake's gaze dropped to the gun in Roger's hand and froze. "You see a gator?" Stupid question. The gun pointed unwaveringly at Blake, not at something in the water.

"I'm sorry about this," Roger said. "I've always liked you and appreciated having you as a neighbor, but I'm in a tight corner without any other way out." He gestured with the gun. "Drop your gun overboard. I don't have a lot of time, so don't make me tell you twice. Hold it upside down with your thumb and forefinger."

Blake saw Roger's finger twitch on the trigger. His neighbor was a crack shot. Blake pulled his SIG Sauer from the leather holster strapped to his waist. He slid toward the side of the boat with his hand extended and the gun dangling from it. Did he have time to get his fingers around the butt of the gun and aim it? Eyeing his neighbor, he didn't think so.

He let go of the gun and watched it splash into the black water. A gator, eyes just above the water, propelled itself in their direction at the sound. Was that the plan—shoot him and toss him overboard?

"Who has Paradise?"

"Dean. I regret her death even more than yours. Sweet kid I've known most of her life. Sometimes you have to do hard things."

"Is this about the rare earth elements? You don't have to do this if you think we're going to sell The Sanctuary. No amount of money would make us let go of it."

"I was sure your mom would refuse to sell, and when all the scare tactics didn't work, I realized the deal was in jeopardy. Then

Paradise discovered that Dean killed Mary, and I knew I had to make a move."

Out of the corner of his eye, Blake searched for a possible weapon. A red-and-white cooler held water and food Roger had brought. A black thermos rolling next to the hull on Blake's left would do if he could get to it in time. Roger would probably shoot the second he reached for it, but he could wait for a diversion or the right moment.

If he could keep Roger talking, maybe Blake could get him to reconsider, but every second that ticked by meant Paradise was out there somewhere facing Dean on her own. He didn't have much time to subdue Roger and try to find her.

He focused his gaze on something over Roger's shoulder and forced a smile. "I don't think what you want will matter much in a minute."

Roger wheeled his body in the direction of Blake's gaze, and Blake snatched up the thermos and threw it with all his might at Roger's head. It connected and Roger fell off his perch on the airboat's elevated seat.

Blake leaped onto the older man and grabbed his wrist holding the gun and slammed it back against the metal boat hull.

The gun flipped out of Roger's hand and slid to land three feet away. Blake let go of Roger and crawled toward the gun. He nearly had it in his hand when Roger grabbed his ankle and tried to haul him back.

Blake kicked out and his foot connected with Roger's chest. Roger let go of Blake's foot, and Blake lunged forward.

His fingers closed around the butt of the gun and he stood and turned toward Roger. "Stop!" His finger switched off the safety. "I won't hesitate to shoot you, Roger." He gestured with the gun. "Hands in the air."

Roger scowled but slowly raised his arms. "Let me go, Blake. I'll leave the country."

"You should have thought of that before you had Dean snatch Paradise." She was out there somewhere and needed him.

The drifting boat bumped against the shore, and he gestured with the gun again. "Get out."

Roger's eyes filled with hope until he surveyed the area. "Get out here? It's an island. I'll be trapped."

"That's the general idea. If you force me to shoot you, I will. Out."

Scowling, Roger swung his legs over the side of the boat and eased into the seagrass. Dark water stained his jeans up to his knees and he waded onto drier ground. Clouds of gnats and mosquitoes billowed around him. It wouldn't be pleasant waiting until the police came to get him.

Blake started the engine and moved away from the island with his phone in front of him. The dot was no longer moving and he had to find her. His inadequacy might result in her death. He groaned out a prayer for God to protect her, because all of this was beyond his ability.

Had Blake realized she was gone yet? Paradise didn't think Dean would wait much longer to make his move. Her senses sharpened as she stared at the boat's gray hull—the birds' chatter increased, and something splashed in the water on the port side. The hum of the insects intensified and she caught a whiff of wildflowers under the swamp's stench. She felt her lungs inhale and exhale as the boat swayed gently in the water.

Was this where her life ended? She wasn't afraid, but her heart squeezed at the thought of Blake's grief and how much her loss would affect him and the little boys. Jenna too. They'd all quickly become her true family.

It was do or die time. The tiny gun in her pocket was her only chance to spend more years with those she loved.

She infinitesimally lifted the left side of her body to give her a little more room on the right so she could get at her gun. "Lots of gators out here. Cottonmouths and copperheads too. Do you know it well?"

"Me and Uncle Allen used to fish for largemouth bass and catfish here. I'd thought about disposing of him in our favorite spot, but it needed to look like an accident."

Only a sociopath would consider killing his own uncle in such a gruesome way. "How could you attack Mary? She loves you."

"I had to stop her from calling Jane. With a crowbar."

Paradise shuddered at his matter-of-fact monotone that held not an ounce of remorse. "She's not dead. I'm sure she's at the hospital by now."

"Guess I'd better tend to business and get out of town."

If only Blake were here, he'd know what to do. But he'd taught her how to protect herself, and she had to gather the courage to do it. "I'd like to get up. I'm cold and my arms hurt from being under me."

"Probably a good idea to finish this. I have a date later and need to get back." For the first time he sounded animated and eager for the next few minutes to arrive.

She tensed as his hard hand grabbed her left shoulder and hauled her to her feet. In that same instant the ropes dropped to the hull. She worked on yanking her gun out of her right pocket, but it was resisting her. She bent over and plowed her head into his stomach.

An *oof* joined the chorus of frogs to their left, and she finally managed to pull her gun free from the pocket of her sweats.

Dean straightened and his gun came up. Paradise dove off to one side as he fired. She brought her gun up and took her firing stance as best as she could. "Drop it!"

"I should have frisked you." The arm holding his gun steady never wavered, and he kept it trained on her chest. "I bet I can shoot you before you shoot me. You can't quite bring yourself to shoot a man, can you? You're a healer, not a killer."

"And you're not a man—you're a monster. I'll have no problem putting you down." But despite her brave words, she wasn't sure he was wrong. She didn't want to pull the trigger, but she would have to. He wasn't letting her go without a fight.

A whooshing sound rose above the noise of the swamp. Another airboat coming this way? She smiled with more confidence than she felt. "Sounds like help is on the way. You're going to jail, Dean."

His mouth curled in a sneer, but his eyes filled with fear. "It's half a mile away. Nothing is going to save you."

Determination glowed on his face, and she made her decision in that instant. Her finger tightened on the trigger, and the gun's slight recoil confirmed she'd shot it. Dean reeled back, red blooming from his chest near his left arm. His gun clattered to the metal hull, and his right arm came up to clutch his wound.

His eyes widened, and the glee went out of them. He pitched over the side into the murky water.

Paradise rushed to the side and reached for his hand, but he was gone.

She sank to her knees and buried her face against her legs. Tears burned in her eyes and throat. She'd never killed someone before. And she never wanted to be put in such a position again.

The boat rocked, and she lifted her head. One wet, muddy hand clamped onto the port side of the boat, followed by another one. Dean was hoisting himself out of the water.

She stumbled to her feet and rushed to help him aboard. His face twisted in a snarl, he waved her away. Before she could take his hands, his eyes went blank and he fell back into the water. His body floated atop the water for several seconds before it sank again.

The noise of the airboat intensified, and she turned to face the craft that came her way. She blinked. Was that *Blake* on the navigator's seat? How had he found her?

Incredulous joy filled his face when he spotted her. "Paradise?"

As he neared her boat, tears glittered in his eyes. He tossed her a rope and she tied their boats together. The engine on his boat cut off, and he jumped onto her boat.

He took her in his arms and her embrace circled his waist. "You're alive." He kissed her with a desperation that matched her own.

CHAPTER 43

HER HEART WAS FULL. Paradise sat on the back deck and listened to the sounds of The Sanctuary—her sanctuary for now and always. The tigers chuffed in the distance, followed by lions roaring. Monkeys chattered in their habitat and the parrot squawked. Under those sounds she heard the distant clatter of Blake and Jenna cleaning up after dinner.

The door behind her slid open and closed, and two little boys ran to climb onto her lap. Levi wrapped his arms around her neck, and Isaac laid his head on her chest. They were both fresh smelling from their baths, with damp hair that smelled like Blake's cypress and eucalyptus soap.

Levi put his palms on her cheeks. "I'm glad you're ours, Paradise, and that no one hurt you today."

"Me too," Isaac chimed in. "You're our girl."

She pulled them both in for a tight hug. "I'll always be your girl."

The door opened again and Jenna called out for them to come to bed. "Aw, Mom," Levi said. "We want Paradise to read to us tonight."

"She's had a rough day, and I want her to rest." Jenna's firm voice held no room for disagreement.

"Okay." Both boys got off her lap. "See you in the morning," Levi said.

"I wouldn't be anywhere else." Smiling, she turned to watch them go. Jenna was right about her fatigue—the police had been here for several hours, and the day felt like it had been forty-eight hours long.

Blake exited after they filed into the house, and he shut the door after them. He settled on the glider beside her. The aroma of grilled burger still clung to his hair. "Mom says they were scared today. They overheard all of it as the search was going on. Jane and Rod had the Coast Guard out looking for both of us, and they kept checking in with Mom to see if she'd heard from us."

"Did they find Roger?" The Coast Guard had quickly located Dean's body, but Roger wasn't on the tiny island where Blake had left him.

He pulled her tight against him. "They found someone's foot, Paradise. They think he tried to swim across the waterway to the other side to escape and a gator got him. The boot matched what Roger was wearing."

She winced and tried to imagine the kind man from her childhood orchestrating all this. "Now Abby has to deal with what her dad has done in an even more horrible way."

She thought back to Abby's warning. "Though I think the plan she overheard was her dad's. I suspect she won't be surprised by this turn of events. She tried to warn me without implicating Roger. I assumed she'd overheard something at the bank, and that's why she wouldn't tell me all of it."

He nodded. "You're right. Abby told Jane what she knew when

Jane informed her about Roger's probable death. With all of it coming out, Lloyd agreed to a plea deal when they arrested him for Ivy's murder. He told them everything. Roger was determined not to let anything stand in the way of the fortune he'd get for the rare earth elements. He was dying, and he wanted to ensure his family would be taken care of."

Paradise pulled back. "Now I feel even worse for Abby."

"Adams blames you for the way his life turned out, so he was ready to do whatever Roger told him if it brought you trouble."

"Did he tell Adams about the *Phantom* connection and have him leave the music box for me?"

"Yeah. He already knew about that from you spending time at his ranch as a kid, and when Bea mentioned it to Adams, Roger dug the music box out of the basement."

She rubbed her stinging eyes. "I loved Roger, Blake. I still can't believe he'd do this to me. To all of us. What about the mining company's offer? Were they involved in the criminal activity?"

He shook his head. "Jane doesn't think so. She did some digging early on and it appeared to be Roger who was behind it all. He wanted that money. He hated what he had to do to you more than his plan to kill me."

She buried her face in his neck. "I killed a man, Blake. I keep reliving it over and over in my head. I can't seem to get past it."

His arms tightened around her. "I'm not gonna sugarcoat it. It will take time to deal with the guilt. Even when you know you acted in self-defense, the guilt comes. But, babe, you had no choice. If you hadn't acted, you'd be dead now."

"My head knows that, but my heart keeps seeing Dean fall into the water."

"Talk to God about it. That's where real healing is found."

"I know you're right." She leaned her head against him. "Drew texted me—he'd heard about what happened. He's taking some vacation days and is coming to see me next week."

"Maybe he'll help you get answers. You're starting to remember, and it might all come pouring out." He started the glider.

"I hope so." She enjoyed the companionable silence, and the rhythmic action of gliding back and forth soothed the last of her stress. "I think the park's future is finally secure. My social media posts will start to have an effect, and you'll be able to sleep at night knowing your family has a roof over their heads."

"It feels like it's been a long time coming. Frank brought Mom a check for another fifty thousand in donations. I think when word gets out about what happened here, the community will rally around us."

"And I'll see about planning some big event days. Maybe an Easter egg hunt on the grounds."

"And a predator feed at night, maybe during Halloween."

"We can expand the petting zoo too." So many plans raced through her head. With her brother arriving, she hoped to find who killed her parents. And the thought of getting to know Drew was like anticipating Christmas. She'd have the help of someone as determined to unravel the mystery as she was. Was the murder of his biological father related to the murders of her parents?

Blake pressed a kiss against the top of her head. "When I realized today how helpless I was to protect you, I finally understood what you've been trying to tell me. It's impossible to protect the ones you love from what happens in life. Life happens and we can't control it. All we can do is put it in God's hands."

Paradise squeezed his side. "And I realized that though I tried to summon as much courage as I could, I'm not brave at all. My strengths aren't the same as yours and never will be. There's no shame in leaning on each other to compensate where we need help. I'm going to try to remember how happy I was to see you coming toward me in that boat."

His head swooped down for a kiss that she felt all the way to her soul. It promised love and care, devotion and passion. When their lips parted, his breath was ragged and so was hers. This living apart wasn't what she wanted anymore, but she'd already asked him to marry her and he'd said no. Patience had never been something she aspired to, but it was something she'd have to learn.

In the meantime she'd work at making the clinic in town a success and keeping the animals here healthy and happy. She smiled up at him. "I'd take another kiss."

A NOTE FROM THE AUTHOR

Dear Reader,

What fun to be back in the Gulf Shores area again! It's become a favorite setting for novels for me, and every time I go back, I come up with new scenes and new ideas. I adore Paradise. She's so determined to stand on her own and make her own way. It's understandable given the trauma she experienced growing up.

This year has been challenging as we moved to a new state, discovered Dave's prostate cancer had returned, and lost Dave's brother Harvey and my agent of twenty-five years, Karen Solem. But through it all God has been faithful. And so have you, dear readers! You've sent me thoughtful messages of support and lifted me up in prayer. I can't thank you enough for your constant support.

I love hearing from readers, so drop me an email and let me know what you thought of *Prowl*. I hope you love it as much I loved writing it.

Love,
Colleen
https://colleencoble.com
colleen@colleencoble.com

ACKNOWLEDGMENTS

My HarperCollins family is the best! Always supportive, always encouraging, they make the writing journey so wonderful. I'm especially grateful to publisher, editor, and friend, Amanda Bostic, who has been such a huge cheerleader in my life.

A special thanks to my freelance editor Julee Schwarzburg, whose touch on my manuscript always makes it so much better. Thank you, Julee!

I have the best critique partner in Denise Hunter! We have critiqued each other's work for twenty-five years. Amazing! She knows what's missing before I do and offers the best support and help. Thank you, Denise!

My husband, Dave, and our kids, Dave and Kara, have always been the best support team at home for me, and my grandkids, Alexa, Elijah, and Silas, make the journey even sweeter. Thank you all!

DISCUSSION QUESTIONS

1. Clark is one of my favorite characters. I love the way he was willing to admit he was wrong about Blake. Have you ever had an enemy who became a friend? If so, how did that happen?

2. Have you had your genealogy done? Why or why not? Were there any surprises?

3. Paradise has a complicated family, and most of us do. How do you deal with family drama?

4. I admit I loved *The Phantom of the Opera*. Are there any TV shows or movies from your childhood that impacted you?

5. Why do you think Paradise disliked being taken care of? She called it "being smothered."

6. What was your favorite animal at the refuge?

7. My grandsons love kittens, and I had to write some in. Are you a cat person or a dog person and why?

8. Have you read any of the books that feature Jane, Hez, or Savannah? How do you feel when you unexpectedly encounter an old friend from another book?

ABOUT THE AUTHOR

COLLEEN COBLE is the *USA TODAY* bestselling author of more than seventy-five books and is best known for her coastal romantic suspense novels.

—

Connect with her online at colleencoble.com

@colleencoble

colleencoblebooks

@colleencoble

LOOKING FOR MORE GREAT READS? LOOK NO FURTHER!

THOMAS NELSON

Since 1798

Visit us online to learn more:
tnzfiction.com

Or scan the below code and sign up to receive email updates
on new releases, giveaways, book deals, and more:

@tnzfiction

THE SANCTUARY NOVELS

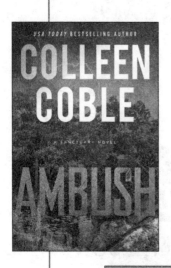

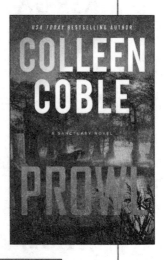

CONSPIRACY

Coming July 2026

Available in print, e-book, and audio

THOMAS NELSON
Since 1798

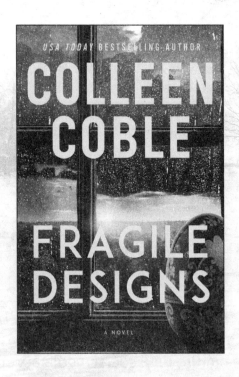

**DON'T MISS THE SECOND
TUPELO GROVE NOVEL FROM
COLLEEN COBLE AND RICK ACKER**

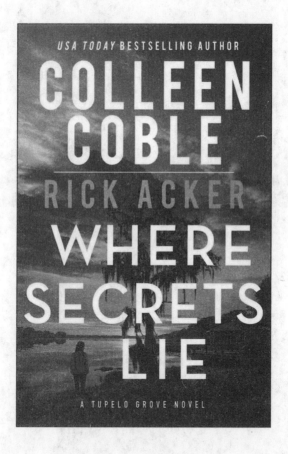

THE PELICAN HARBOR SERIES

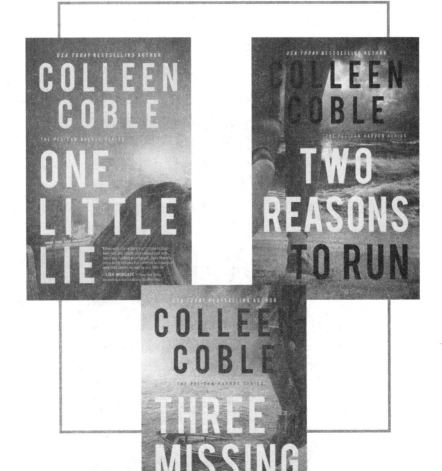

Available in print, e-book, and audio

THOMAS NELSON
Since 1798